Initiation

Part One of

Changels Genesis

By Peter King

Peter King Publishing
Wellington, New Zealand

MIHI (ACKNOWLEDGEMENT)

Because the theme of Changels Genesis is social responses to genetic inheritance this story is dedicated to my matrilineal great-great grandmother, Huihana Hopa te Arawaere of the Ngaiterangi iwi.

PERSONAL THANKS

To my friend Louise Wickham, for reading the first draft and despite its many failings encouraging me. And to my friend Sylvia Zlami (and her calibrated nose) for reporting the smells from the car park of Pacific Fair mall. I would also like to acknowledge the advice and support of the Wellington chapter of the Romance Writers of New Zealand, my father, John, for his practical help, my sons who inspired me to write, and my wife, Jenny, for her patience.

SPECIAL NOTE TO READERS

Initiation is part one of the six part story Changels Genesis. It is not a single complete story in its own right. To finish the story you will need all six books.

While Changels Genesis uses relatively simple English this is for the convenience of adult English as a Second Language (ESOL) readers. It is not appropriate for children under thirteen (13). As fact-based fiction it contains details about real war violence and crime not suitable for younger readers. Profanity has been included but with omitted letters. Where a sentence in the story is factual it is marked with a dagger symbol†.

The plot of Changels Genesis required supernatural abilities. As the author has no personal experience with supernatural phenomena all depictions are based on common elements in reports of supernatural experiences. The author has based the supernatural elements of the story on spiritualist lore common to many religious traditions and has no religious conviction or agenda. Readers are reminded this story is a work of fiction and makes no religious claims.

Because some Maori words and songs are referenced in the text these have been hyphenated to aid pronunciation and (parenthetically) translated. A non-standard accent acute has also been employed to aid pronunciation, e.g. Tané.

At some points the narrator is narrating events in the present (told in the present tense) and others in the past (told in the past tense). A boldface ellipsis seperates the narratives. e.g. ...

Much of the story is set in New Zealand which is an island nation in the South Pacific with a population of 4.5 million in a land area two-thirds that of Japan. The population is two thirds European and 15% indigenous Maori. Intermarriage is very common.

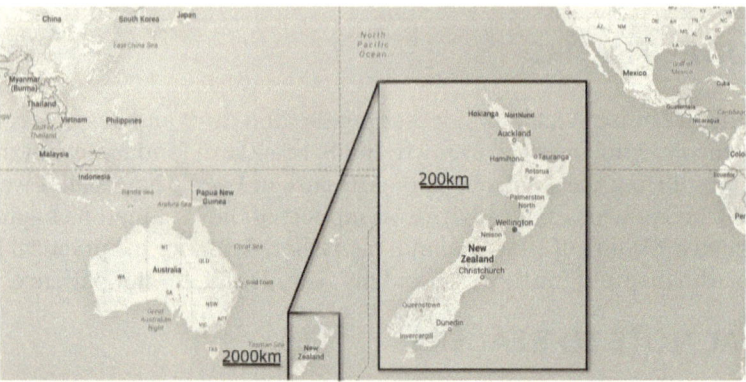

map data © Google 2016

Aotea Island (map p148) is fictional. For more information about the factual basis of this book please refer to the Fact and Fiction section on page 292.

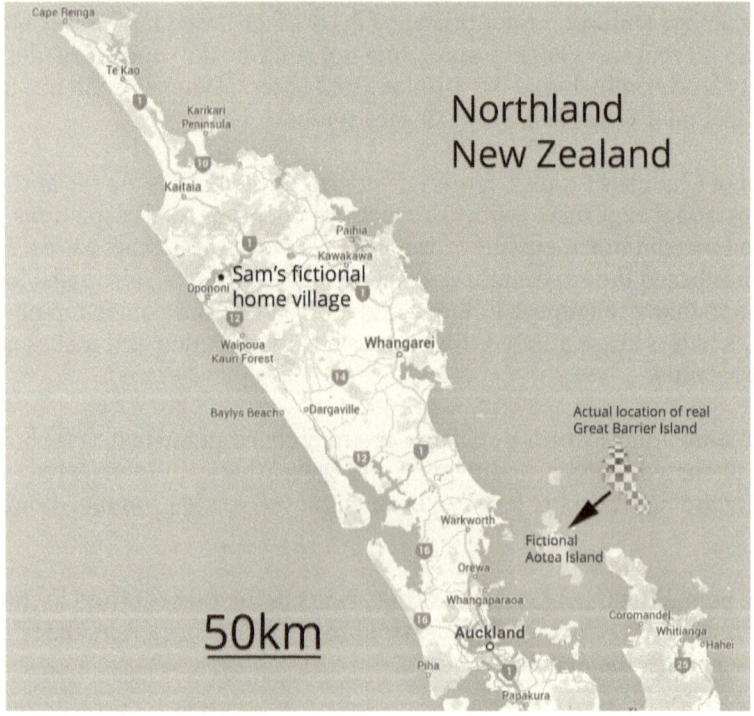

map data © Google 2016

Misery acquaints a man with strange bedfellows
- **The Tempest, Act 2, scene 2**

Sam, you aren't in trouble. We just need to ask you some questions about the fire."

It's two days later: Wednesday, 10:11 a.m on 11th March 2009, or that's what the worn out clock in interview room four at the central police station says.

Sixty seven hours ago, Sunday, about 3 p.m, the old mansion I was living in on remote A-o-te-a Island burned down and the twenty or so people living there vanished. It's been all over the news here in New Zealand, and even around the world. Mysterious deaths always make the news.

Some TV channels guessed it was some weird UFO suicide-murder cult like one in Switzerland before I was born. They called Dr Prosperov, the leader of our community, a "billionaire, Russian, UFO freak" who had been investigated in America, years ago, for insider trading.

Then, thirty seven hours ago, at 9:04 p.m on Monday night, I turn up at the local cop's house; the unexpected survivor. Sergeant Gavin Smith, the only cop on the island, zapped me a pizza and made up a bed in an unlocked cell at the station next door. He knew he shouldn't, but he only had a one bedroom house and there wasn't anywhere else to put me. Just for once I didn't mind him being a jerk. *They* wouldn't be looking for me in a police cell – not yet anyway.

Tuesday, I met the cops running the case and welfare took me off the island and into emergency foster care because they didn't have anywhere else for newly orphaned teens to go either.

Emergency foster care turned out to be Ruth and Dave Moore's halfway house in the eastern suburbs of Auckland, New Zealand's largest city. It was a place for teens in trouble and Ruth ran her home like a prison, but I can't blame her – at least they fed and housed me.

On the news this morning, while I ate my cornflakes, the cops announced they had found a fourteen-year-old survivor who they wouldn't name until they could contact his family. They said I was helping them with their inquiries.

Yeah well, actually, so far, that's just been so much dreaming. Here in cramped, neon lit, interview room four, the silence is dragging.

There's just two cops. Opposite me a cutie with short hair, blonde tips and a stud in her left ear, wearing a uniform. She's late twenties I'd guess. She introduced herself as Detective Constable Sue Williams. She's from Youth Aid. She's trying to look sweet and big sisterly, but she's just too staunch to be straight. The funny thing is I feel sure I know her already, and the last time that happened was with the others.

The other cop next to her is in charge. I met him yesterday. He's an old white guy, about forty, in a cheap gray suit with an ugly green tie. His name is Detective Sergeant Kevin Cooper. I think he's hoping this mystery will turn into something big that will help him make detective inspector.

Me? I'm Sam Kahu, Maori, and sitting here with my hood up. I'm saying nothing. I'm sweet coz I don't have to tell them anything.

"Sam, they are only trying to help you."

That's Geraldine Jones next to me. She's my social worker. I only met her about an hour ago. Mid-fifties, small and fat, with gray hair. The caring face of the system. I don't trust her. She suggested I live with my aunt and that is never going to happen.

"So Sam, where were you when you first realised your house was on fire?" Sue tries.

She's trying to be light but concerned.

The first mystery they want to solve is why *I'm* here, and the others have vanished. In fact, I was in a slum in the Philippines. But if I told them that they'd think I was crazy or just jerking them around, so I say nothing. I can see their eyes flicking around each other, trying to work out how to get this mistrustful, Maori teen to talk.

And to be honest, I really don't know what to tell them eh? My story is just way too huge, and plain weird to tell *anyone*.

"Sam?"

The woman cop still has her fake smile on. I look at her, trying to focus. I know at once she's all front. And behind it? Behind all this professional bullshit? Man! Her life is really this total mess. Fights at home with her girlfriend; her mum thinks she's a sicko; her dad's a drunk; endless crude jokes about lesbians from the lads in the station; sucking up to this guy next to her and hating it; years of swallowing bitterness. Readings are always like this. A jumble of impressions that flood over you.

"Rachel's moving out."

I don't say it very loud. I just sorta say it like you might if you noticed someone had a small spider on their collar. It just slipped out as I realised it. And the smile dies on her face – like the sun going down. In place of her fake smile is the face of an

3

angry woman who thinks she's being betrayed and embarrassed. I know she's gutted. And she knows what I've said is probably true – but she can't admit it. Not to herself. Not yet. And definitely not at work.

Here I am, a perfect stranger, another random file in a huge stack of cases she deals with, voicing her deepest, darkest fear in front of people she would never tell *anything* about her personal life. Saying *on tape*, that despite trying so hard for so long, Rachel, her partner of three or so years, has decided she's had enough and is off.

"Pardon?" she gasps, trying to pretend she hasn't heard me. Kevin, meanwhile, has written "Rachel" down on his notepad like it means something to *me*.

Sue's face is a mask of pleasantness covering anger and fear. I've said too much. I've crossed the line again. How often have I done that when I was younger? And still I keep doing it, like I can't control my dumb mouth. I silently curse my own stupidity. "Nothin'."

"Who's Rachel dear?" Geraldine asks loudly, like a deaf old grandma putting her foot in it. She thinks she's helping the cops. I've put a spear through Sue's heart. She's like a fish. She's stunned, gasping and bleeding in the water, and here's this silly cow twisting it because she can't see what I've done. My eyes flick off Sue who can't look me in the eye anymore anyway.

"Dunno. It... It was just somethin' I saw on that show *'Friends',*" I lie, lamely.

The silence drags again.

Kevin over there, he's losing patience. He's struggling to control his face. He knows I'm lying, but he hasn't the brains to look at Sue next to him. He thinks there was somebody at Renwick named Rachel who wanted to leave. It fits his easy little made-for-TV murder mystery. But there was nobody named Rachel at Renwick. I say nothin'.

The reading on Kevin sharpens. He's from down South and he's a racist. Thinks all Maoris are trouble. Two daughters, wife, church; very superior. Believes in living by setting an example to others, assuming if he can do it so can everyone else. He's got no idea.

Luckily he's going to do the big daddy thing to me coz he's read my file and he's heard of my dad – and anyone who's heard of my dad would pity his kids.

"Sam, we're trying to find your sister and your family. *Anything* you can remember might help find Rewa," he says quietly.

Because he's read my file he knows mentioning my sister is a red hot poker to me. My sister Rewa is the one person I've looked after all my life. He's using my uncertainty about how she is to wind me up. And he knows that he's doing it too! It pisses me off. He doesn't wait for a reply, but goes straight on, reading from his notebook.

"On Monday night you told Sergeant Smith that you went out fishing around the next bay at about two PM on Sunday afternoon. So where were you for the rest of Sunday and Monday? Did you go alone or did someone go with you? Did anyone know you were gone?"

Kevin's fishing himself. Fishing for lies. It's a trick. He winds me up by mentioning Rewa then goes straight into lie detector mode. It's what he's used to doing to crims. He thinks he's good at his job. Maybe he is. I don't care. I let the silence drag on while I stare at him from under my hood, my arms crossed. He's trying to stare me down like I'm a crim. I just stare back.

5

I'm simply not scared of him. He thinks he sees a cheeky kid of fourteen, but he has no idea what I've been through over the past two years. He's just some pudgy loser who gets off on bullying. I start back at him. I keep it calm but firm.

"I went fishing and when I came back Renwick was burning so I went to find help for myself. But you …". I sit back almost shaking my head, "you have the whole Auckland police force looking for twenty missing people, and after three days you haven't found any sign of them. They can't *all* have been in the fire. It was a big house! There were far too many exits! If you had to, you could even jump from the second floor. But you haven't found *anyone*. How could you lose track of twenty people like that?"

I glare at him from under my hood like he's unbelievably useless. Maybe if I were any other kid who'd lost his family I'd be upset. Hey, who wouldn't be? Your family and all your friends suddenly gone, and you left behind. But I can't think like that. Everyone's counting on me to cover them. Besides this isn't the first time I've lost my family. I am one survivor from a whole house full of survivors. The lone survivor. I'm the last one standing, so it's my job is to get back up and make things safe for when they come back.

Kevin's surprised. He's used to asking the questions not answering them. But he looks me in the eye and answers me straight.

"I don't know, Sam. But I promise you, we *will* find them, and we *will* get to the bottom of this … tragedy. But I think you could tell us more about what happened to you than you've told us so far," he says, trying to stare me down.

It's half hope, half threat. It's a hope because he doesn't know for sure there *is* a tragedy but it might help him if it was. But it's a threat too because survivors like me are always suspects to cops like him.

I may be a small fourteen-year-old, but he knows I've got big secrets, and to him big secrets mean lies, and lies mean guilt. He thinks something very bad has gone down and I know what it is. And he's right, I do. But I also know he couldn't imagine what it was in a million years and as far as he's concerned the others have disappeared into thin air, and he won't find any trace of them.

Maybe two years ago, when I was a bit more normal, an adult staring at me like that would have made me drop my eyes, and spill my guts. Not any more.

"Hang on, hang on! What *is* this?" I ask, as much for the video as those in the room. I keep it under control like I'm explaining something.

"All I know is that I went out fishing. When I come back the whole place was full of firefighters, and gawpers all watching my home burn down, with no sign of my friends or family anywhere. And now you're asking *me* where *I* went, like *I* had something to do with it? That's nuts! Think about it! Me murder twenty people including my own family, a dozen adults bigger than me, my best friends and two babies and then burn down the nicest house I've ever lived in? What for? Get real!" I show some frustration.

I take a deep breath as if controlling myself, then I start again. "Now I'll ask you yet again. Where is my sister? Where is my Aunt? Where is my Grandpop? And where the hell is everybody else? They can't have vanished into thin air! Why can't *you* find them?"

7

They shift uncomfortably in their seats. They know how this looks as well as I do. Questioning a fourteen-year-old who's lost his family as if he's a suspect instead of a witness looks bad no matter how you dress it up. But they are still frustrated with me. "Sam, we are trying to sort it out but it's complicated," Geraldine splutters. "We don't know anything about the people you lived with. And you refuse to talk to your father's family..." she starts on about that again.

That pisses me off.

"The Stephens's are *not* my damn family!" I explode with frustration and I don't care if they find it loud.

"I'm a Kahu! That bastard you call my father killed my mother! And you want me to live with that witch sister of his? When she isn't drunk, she's doing drugs! You know it's true! Her kids are in the gang. There's no way I'm going to live with them! I'd be safer living in the bush!"

There's a stunned silence.

Actually I *know* I wouldn't be better off in the bush. I'd tried that for two days, and I'd seen the lights in the sky at night, searching for me. I knew if I hid out there *they'd* soon find me, and probably Emma too. I had come in to avoid that, but right now nobody says anything as they check each other out. Finally Kevin takes charge.

"Sam, why won't you tell us where you went?" Kevin asks carefully.

I'm still angry, so I tell them where I stand.

"Because it's private, and it has nothing to do with finding my family, or anyone else, or finding out why Renwick House caught fire and burned to the ground. I wasn't there. I had nothing to do with it. But why can't *you*, with all your dogs, your scientists and shit, find even *one* of them on an island as small as Aotea?"

And now I stare *them* down.

This interview is not going the way that they had expected. They'd expected a scared victim or teenage Maori mumble. Instead they're getting a videotaped bollocking. They're shocked because I'm not acting like a vulnerable kid. But maybe that's because after two years of missions I'm not your average fourteen-year-old. When you've been hunted by drugged-out Congolese soldiers with AK-47s a few civilised police and a social worker in a room just aren't so scary.

Kevin's rubbing his chin. Sue glances uncertainly at him. Geraldine's biting her tongue in the corner.

"Sam, would you excuse me and Geraldine for a moment?" Kevin says.

They get up.

"Sure, don't mind me," I say sarkily.

Kevin glances at Sue and raises his eyebrows toward the video machine. Sue leans forward to the microphone.

"Interview suspended 10:32 a.m." and pushes the button, as the others leave the room.

Sue and I are left facing each other. She still doesn't want to look at me and reads her papers. The silence drags. I still feel I know her somehow and I wish I'd made a better first impression. I feel bad about Rachel.

"Sue?"

She doesn't look up.

"Constable Williams," I growl in the commanding voice Grandpop uses. She glances up at me, pulling that awful false smile, eyebrows raised questioningly.

"I'm sorry about what I said," I mutter, "I should have shut up."

"Sorry?" she shakes her head, confused.

"About Rachel."

She looks at me very directly – very pissed off. She thinks I'm trying to keep the prank going. It's like she morphs from an official policewoman into an angry lesbian. Her lips curl into an angry sneer.

"I don't know who told you anything about my private life but whoever it was is a piece of shit who should keep his nose out of other people's business," she hisses furiously, stares me down, and then goes back to her paperwork.

She thinks I'm just part of a cop's prank. I wait a moment.

"Nobody told me anything," I tell her quietly.

She ignores me. She's really angry.

"I'm psychic."

She keeps on ignoring me. So I do the full reading for about two minutes. Then I begin.

"Susan Ellen Williams, your dad's name is Evan Ross. Your mum's name is Karen Anne, previously Sharpe," I say gently.

She flinches a bit and although she's still pretending to read I know I have her attention.

"You have an older sister Josephine Alice. She's four years older and you never got on. Jo is married to Bruce Peterson. They have two kids, Joshua and Oliver. Your mum has never accepted the fact that you're a d ... that you aren't into men."

That brings her face up again.

"Shut up," she orders.

I shut up. She's mad-as.

"I don't know where you get off with all this crap and I don't care," she whispers angrily.

"I am here to do my job. This is about you, not me. Now if you were half as forthcoming with information about that group you were in as you have been about my private life we would be a helluva lot further along with this inquiry than we are now." She's glaring. I understand her hurt and look down.

"I was just trying to say 'sorry', that's all," I mumble.

She goes back to her papers. Nobody says anything for a while. You might wonder why I bother, but I have my reasons. The others have all gone, and I have no idea how long for. It could be days, weeks or even months. Impossible as it seems we must have been betrayed somehow. It must have been someone we knew, so it was safest to talk to someone who I don't know at all. Besides we have these funny feelings about people for good reasons, and when you are totally on your own, like me, you need *somebody* to be your friend.

Yeah, and I like her. She reminds me of a younger version of my Aunty Liz. Aunty Liz's a nurse and, like Sue, also "bats on the other team". Aunty Liz has looked after me for most of my life. Like her, Sue has obviously been through tough times but she's still there, still trying to be kind. I can relate to that.

But more important I can feel her vulnerability. When you see another's vulnerability, most people want to be kind, not cruel. It's the kindness of strangers and it is true. I've seen it all over the world. So I want her to understand that I never wanted to hurt her. Finally I speak again.

"Look, the only way you'll understand what was happening on Aotea, is by believing me, when I say I'm psychic," I tell her quietly, "If you can't believe that ..."

Kevin and Geraldine are coming back into the room,

"... you won't understand anything," I finish.

She looks up into my eyes. Hers are blue. She's still pissed off, but she's thinking about it. Kevin and Geraldine sit down again. "Anything for the record?" Kevin asks Sue.

"No, we were talking about me," Sue tells him, with a firm look that says "back off".

"OK?" Kevin agrees, thinking about it as a questioning technique. Then he leans over and presses the record button. "Interview resumes 10:36. Look, Sam, you've made your feelings pretty clear here," he begins, "and I hear where you're coming from. You're a bright kid and I won't patronise you. But no matter how you look at it until we find your family you're an orphan, in foster care. It's not the best place to be is it?"

I say nothing. He presses on, glancing at Geraldine for support. "So Sam, to be honest we really need your help. The house has been completely destroyed and everyone has vanished. We have no idea how, why, or even when exactly. My job is to find out what happened and if, as it seems, there has been a crime committed, by whom. To do that we need information. Anything, no matter how small or unimportant could help. Will you try to do that Sam?"

"Then you don't need to know where I went because it has nothing to do with everyone going missing," I tell him crossing my arms.

"For the moment let's say it's not relevant to our inquiry," Kevin nods.

"OK then, so what do you want to know?"

"OK, well, ah, let's start with the morning. What was the mood of everyone that day?"

"Sunday?"

"Yes."

It had been slack and happy. That's why I nipped off to visit
Eduardo and see how he'd been doing selling his balloons.
He's a sweet little guy and you can see why he'll be such a
great secretary-general when he grows up. Ashley had gone to
Washington to see Nathan – he'll be their president in forty
years or so. That's where someone must have put the trace on
her that set off the evacuation.

"It was good," I tell them confidently.

"Good?"

"Yeah, it was a good day, people were feeling relaxed."

"Nobody a bit upset?"

"Nobody I talked to."

"What about Dr Prosperov?"

"Dr P was busy. He'd done some deal with someone in Russia."
Kevin's taking a note, so I add, "And I don't know anything
about his deals. He tried to explain to us how they worked once
but he lost me after five minutes. He was full of deals. They were
very complicated."

"So as far as you were concerned, then, it was just another
Sunday before you left?"

"Yeah, pretty much," I shrug.

"Did Dr Prosperov ever talk about having enemies, particularly
back home in Russia?"

That would make a good cover story. I think about it. They
need something credible. Russian mafiya or something. And
Prosperov was visited by some pretty powerful oligarchs. I
answer slowly.

"Yeah, he had enemies. Not just in Russia either, otherwise he
wouldn't have come to a backwater like New Zealand."

"Any names?"

"He mentioned a few but *I* can't remember Russian names. They're *way* too long. Names like Corduroy-sky and Lemon-ov."

"Any Western names?"

"Nah, I don't really remember any."

Kevin's taking all this down in his notepad. The names I've given him were what he would expect me to mangle certain famous Russian oligarch's names into. I think he's starting to get the idea that the people Prosperov knows could not only be very, very rich, but could also be dangerous. That was true, but in reality had nothing to do with it.

"Was there any security at Renwick House?"

I can't help smiling. We were secure against threats that were literally out of this world. We could have won a war against half the U.N Security Council, but that wasn't our mission. Our security was defensive and it had mostly worked. That was why *they* hadn't caught anybody yet, even though the house itself had been lost.

"Nah. It was pretty casual really – though the ground floor windows were pretty solid," I say as if the idea of security was a bit odd.

"No cameras or security service?"

How cute.

"On Aotea? What could a security service do if we called them? It's an hour from Auckland by ferry when it runs. I mean twenty people in one big, old house on a small country island don't really need security."

"OK Sam, could we talk about the people at Renwick House?"

"Hmm, yeah sure, what do you want to know about them?"

"We aren't sure exactly who was there. The electoral register, the Immigration Service and the Health Department have no

14

records of *anyone* living at Renwick although Sergeant Smith also says there were about twenty people living there."

Then he pauses, and continues, eyes staring at me.

"And strangely enough someone stole the school's registers and erased all the records from their computers on Monday night."

I shake my head as if tut-tutting kids today.

"Who would do a thing like that?" I ask, as innocently as I can.

"We're finding out. They left hair clues."

Buullshit. He knows any hairs could have been there for weeks. My eyes give me away. There's a flash of suspicious annoyance from Kevin. He knows it was me eh? But he has to play it straight. That's the rules.

"So would you mind telling us the names of everyone who lived at your former home?"

"Sure," I begin seriously. "There was Deidre, Ken, Bernard, Zoe, Scotty, Patience, Soraya, Asal, Mitra, Tahira, Nguyen, Cam, Patricia, Ashley, Ali, Tarik, Elizabeth, Mike, Rewa, Gunter, Mariko, eKaterina or Katya, Irina and me," I tell him quickly.

Kevin isn't writing any of this down. He's pissed off.

"Their *full* names please, Sam," he says officially.

"Umm. Sorry Kevin but I'm not sure about them," I scratch my neck.

He looks at me, real irritated again, then picks up the look from Geraldine.

"As well as you can remember," he says putting pen to paper.

"Sure, well, umm eKaterina and Irina probably used Prosperov, though Dr P said it wasn't a real Russian name. Deirdre called herself 'Jones' but the name in her passport was Welsh with Cs, Ys and Ws everywhere and I couldn't say it. Ken is short for a longer Mongolian name but I'm not sure he even *had* a family name so I don't know. Zoe was born Apple-something but of course she married Scotty's father, and then Bernard so I don't know if she used her own name or a married name or if Scotty used his mother's, his father's or Bernard's last name. Patience probably had Bernard's name. Bernard's last name was African and long like 'Kilimanjaro' or something. Soraya, Mitra, Asal, and Tahira are Iranian but Soraya was Mitra's mother, and I'm not sure if they used her name or kept Mitra's husband's. I think it was 'Khanum' or something. Nguyen and Cam are Vietnamese. I think Nguyen's last name was 'Ba' but Vietnamese is very hard to follow. That's what Cam called him anyway. Ali and Tarik's last name was Arabic, like 'Akbar' or something. Mariko's name changed when she married Gunter and his last name was 'Grass' – I think. But I could be getting confused with someone else. I'm sorry Kevin, but we never used our last names because we couldn't all say them properly. The teachers were worse. They couldn't even pronounce Maori right."

I sit back and smile at everyone, trying to look like I'm so pleased with myself for helping so much and knowing it's all useless crap.

Kevin stares at me in silence. He wants to throttle me.

"Is that really the best you can do Sam?" he asks finally, knowing I'm messing with him, but also knowing Geraldine will jump down his throat if he said what he thought.

"Sorry Kev, but yeah. That's all I know," I grin, acting as dumb and happy as possible.

I feel a bit sorry for him, eh, but it's critical I make sure nobody gets named in the police files. *They* can hack the police easily and trace the relatives of anyone I identified. Any future we might have totally depends on nobody knowing who we are.

"Sam, if..." Kevin pauses thinking of a new angle, and then starts again.

"Well, if we *do* find some of these people and they have ...well...if they're deceased, we may need to ask *you* to identify the bodies." Geraldine gasps, but Kevin keeps talking.

"It's a very difficult and serious task to ask anyone, but this is serious Sam, and without any records there's no other way it can be done."

He lets that sink in for a moment. He's trying to threaten me into co-operating. He goes on quietly.

"When people die their families usually need the bodies. It's important for them. For a sense of closure. If we find bodies we will need to return them to their families and it's very important we don't get them mixed up. So any information that can identify anyone we might find would help everyone a lot Sam."

I stare at him, saying nothing for a long time. Everyone's wondering what I'll do. I reply just as serious-like.

"They aren't dead Kevin," I tell him. "They're just missing. If they were dead *I'd* know, but they aren't dead. *My* sister isn't dead." I let my voice shake a bit. I add that last bit to get Geraldine off the sidelines. She's sure I'm about to fall apart.

"Detective, I'm sorry but I don't think this line of questioning is going to do anyone much good. Sam's in no condition to deal with this sort of speculation right now. He's traumatised. I don't think he can help you the way you want him to. He needs time and proper counselling. Now I must insist you move on to another line of questioning."

Kevin takes a breath and stares at the ceiling. I try not to smile. He's not used to dealing with kids, and he wishes there were fewer rules and he was allowed to do more good, old fashioned, shouting. I'm taking up a lot of his patience. But he knows he's lost that one, so he starts a new line.

"OK Sam. That list of names. I didn't recognise many of them. So it's fair to say that most of the people who lived at Renwick House weren't born in New Zealand were they?"

"Nah, me and my family were the only ones."

"Did you ever feel that the others were all connected in some way that you didn't know about? That they had some kind of secret you weren't part of?"

We're connected in a way most people never dream of. And some, like Tahira, did have secrets, but not common ones.

"Nah. We were all very happy," I say, happily.

"How were you happy?" he asks, very seriously.

"Like happy" I shrug. He shrugs back to get me to explain.

" ... you know what that is, right?" I ask, like I'm worried he might be stunted.

"No, I mean what told you everyone was happy? How did it show itself?" he asks.

"Aww," I start, thinking this is easy, "well, we had great parties, and we swam, we had beach soccer, and barbecues and sang on the bus ..."

And suddenly I can't talk anymore! I can't speak! I can't breathe! As I reminded myself out loud how great it had been the reality that I am totally alone hit me like a brick. All my mates, all my family, my home, everything is gone and I don't know when, or even if, they're coming back! I turn away quickly because suddenly *my* eyes are streaming. Huge tears are rolling down my face which is screwed up with grief.

It was the best time of my life and it's *over*. The others are gone! I'm all alone, and all I know is if I fail *they* will get me!

Geraldine puts an arm around my shoulders and tries to comfort me. She means well but she's an annoying old cow. She rubs my back – which eases the stress a bit – but says stupid things like "you're a brave boy" which is just so dumb. She has no idea! She has just *no* idea what I'm dealing with. How huge everything's got. None of them have any idea how much I have to do now, and how small and alone I feel. I'd way prefer Sue hugged me, but she's on the other side of the small desk, I can't see and I don't know what she's doing.

"Kevin, I think we should stop there," Geraldine says quietly over the desk to the detective, her arm over my shoulder.

I hear him sigh a little and say, "Interview halted 11.07," in a quiet voice.

"Sam, what would you like us to do?" Kevin asks quietly.

He pisses me off so much with his big daddy thing. So I ask for what I want because I can't think of a cunning plan to get it.

"I'd like to talk to Sue for a while. Just me and her," I tell the wall. No one says anything so I check around quickly.

Kevin seems a bit surprised by that. So does Sue, who doesn't look so keen. Geraldine takes back her arm and goes back to looking grumpy. Kevin sighs.

"Do you mind Sue?" he asks her.

"No sir, of course not. That's why I'm here. I am the Youth Aid specialist after all," she reminds him.

"Should I stay too Sam?" Geraldine asks.

"No ... no ... it's OK. Thank you Geraldine," I say trying to be polite.

"OK, well Sue, if you could um ... see me when you're done here," says Kevin, "Geraldine I'll find a spot where you can wait for Sam."

And once again he shows Geraldine, who's thinking I'm the saddest case she's seen for a while, out of the interview room. It makes me angry with my own tears. Her pity I do not need. The door closes with a click. I look at Sue who's staring at me warily with both sympathy and some curiosity. Now, I find it hard to look *her* in the eye. I sit forward, elbows resting on my knees, head in my hands, hood still up. I'm trying to stop my breath from shuddering.

"So what is it Sam?" she asks me. She seems genuinely concerned now.

I look up at her, my eyes still wet, sitting back again, confused.

"What's what?" I ask, breathing out hard and looking around.

"What did you want to tell me?" she says sitting forward.

I feel defensive. I hadn't expected to crack like that. I feel battered. It must be stress from being hunted and on the run. Knowing what will happen if *they* catch me. It hasn't been that easy to sleep.

"Nuthin...I didn't want to tell ya anything, I just...I just wanted to talk to you."

"What about?" she asks, suspicious I want to go back to Rachel again.

I look around uncomfortably. I wanted to talk to her but now that I am, I feel kinda dumb. I dry my face on my sleeve.

"Nuthin...anything...I dunno...the weather and shit," I say confused.

"Why?" she wants to know.

I decide to fess up.

"Coz I haven't got anyone else to talk to!" I blurt out.

"That, and the other two get up my nose. I feel like I can talk to you coz you know what it's like."

"What do I know?" she asks sitting back suspiciously and folding her arms.

"To feel ... you know ... sorta ... on the outside," I say looking around for inspiration.

"I am still a police officer Sam," she reminds me.

"Yeah, I know, but at least you're not like Kevin," I tell her leaning forward.

"You don't like him?"

Her tone is neutral but it sounds like a trap. But hell, hung for a lion, as a lamb eh?

"Nah, he's *way* too straight for me eh?" I tell her playing with my fingers.

"You seem fairly straight yourself compared to most of the people I see."

"Yeah but ... I'm not ..." I can't think of the words. I'm trying to say I'm used to people who don't fit into the usual boxes but it gets all jumbled in my mind.

"You don't want to be straight? You want to be more like your cuzzies?" she guesses referring to the Stephenses.

"Oh, F____ no!" I say, without thinking.

"Sam, keep it seemly," she warns with a soft growl – a bit like a mother dog.

I smile a sorta gormless apology and try some of Ashley's southern manners.

"Yes May'am."

Sue actually smiles at that.

"So why don't you want to be like your cuzzies?" she asks leaning forward.

I play with my fingers some more while I talk.

"Coz they're dumb," I sigh.

"They're like my dad was. They think they outsmart the system but they're more scared of letting their guard down with each other, hiding behind booze or drugs, or being assholes, than admit to each other that they're scared. I *know*. I can read them."

"You don't think they had anything to do with this?"

"What?" I ask, wondering what she's talking about.

"The fire and everything."

"Who?" I ask, not seeing a connection.

"Your cuzzies."

Finally I make the connection.

"My *cuzzies* burn down *Renwick*? No way! They're *way* too small time," I laugh.

"You think this is big time?" she asks, trying to keep it casual.

Bigger than you can imagine, sister.

"It's gotta be eh?" I say quietly.

I think back to Kevin's Russian questions and decide to lead her down a garden path.

"Dr P ? He was dealing with some super heavy dudes back in Russia, eh? And they play rough over there, and I mean serious hard ball."

She nods. She's actually paying attention.

"That guy Corduroyov I told Kevin about? I mean he's got billions. Dr P never had billions. That's just crap! He's rich enough, but billions is *serious* big time. And Dr P says some mafiya oligarchs have soldiers in their pay because the government doesn't pay them. He told me one guy had 250 army paratroopers in his personal bodyguard! Just imagine what that could mean!"

"You think a Russian mafiya oligarch is involved with this Sam?"

22

she asks levelly. I get a hint that she thinks I've seen too many movies. But I don't care how dumb it sounds. It's a credible cover story.

"Well, one did visit Dr P a year or so back and I can't see who else would care about him enough to do anything about it. I mean making twenty people disappear if they don't *want* to go would be pretty hard. The teachers at our school couldn't get us to go anywhere we didn't want to go, and my Grandpop, he was in the SAS in Vietnam and I know how hard it is to sneak up on him."

"So what do you think mafiya oligarchs would want with Prosperov?"

"I dunno. Could be anything. He obviously wasn't expecting trouble. Maybe his business opposition figured it was easier to take *him* out here, than to get the others back in Russia. I dunno, I'm making this up, but it makes sense."

Sue isn't buying it but she'll humour me for the moment.

"Hmm ...well it's a possibility, Sam. But our job is to collect evidence. So far we haven't found much," Sue admits.

"Do you know how the fire started?" I ask, knowing the answer but wondering how far they'd got.

"Not yet, but the fire service investigators are pretty sure the gas supply by the kitchen exploded. We found steel bottles all torn open. They're very good those guys. They can often tell us where, when and how a fire started, how it spread and what was burned in it."

She's checking me for guilt, but there isn't anything I need to worry about.

"Did you check the beach?"

"What for?"

"Signs of boats."

"Yes, of course, there was nothing. No sign of boats or footprints anyway."

"*Before* the tide came in?" I check, knowing that was unlikely.

"Well no, it came in just as they were putting out the fire, but we did take dogs on Monday and there wasn't any sign of twenty people anywhere."

"None?" I ask, sounding surprised.

"Not from the beach. It's possible they went on boats from the rocks, but it seems unlikely."

"What about the helicopter?" I suggest.

Sue thinks I'm messing with her, but she wants to get my confidence.

"What helicopter?" she asks

"Dr P's helicopter. A Squirrel I think it was. Ken flew it."

"We didn't find any helicopter," she admits, "Do you remember the letters on its tail?"

"ZK something. I never paid much attention. It's not like we had to work out which helicopter was ours in the parking lot."

Sue actually smiles at that, but writes it down.

"I'll check if anyone saw the helicopter going anywhere. Civil Aviation will have the registration and may have flight plans. Of course a Squirrel isn't that big. It couldn't carry more than five at a time so I imagine you would have noticed it," she says, and then adds pointedly, "no matter where you were."

"No, I didn't see any," I admit, which was true enough.

There's a bit of a pause while I think about that.

"Sam?" she says gently.

"Yeah?"

"I think you have to consider the possibility that they haven't left. That they *are* still there."

She said it gently and quietly. She meant they might be dead in the fire. She was expecting more tears, I suppose. But that was one thing I knew she was wrong about.

"Nah, they *are* alive. I'd know if they weren't, Sue. Me, especially. Dead people are always finding *me*. I'm like a magnet to them. So they've gotta be somewhere."

Sue wants to say something but she thinks better of it.

"So Sam, where do you come from anyway?" she asks changing the subject, "and how did you end up on Aotea anyway?"

"Aw, that's a real long story, Sue."

"Well, you can tell me some of it. I'm booked with you 'til lunchtime anyway."

So I do. And this is what I tell her.

•••

CHAP+ER TW⊕: ⊕RIGINS

My families come from the Ho-ki-anga, the big bay way north of Auckland that's always warm, and which always seems to sound of cicadas. My tribes go back to the ancient canoes of Nga-toki-mata-whao-rua and Mata-atua who came here a thousand years ago.

I don't know if you know it, but the Hokianga is a strange kind of place because it's sorta rich and real poor at the same time. Everyone knows everyone else, so it's rich in history; it's warm, so it's rich in climate; and it's always rich in hope, but in terms of actual money? It hasn't got much.

The roads are bad and some of the people are too. People like my dad's family. People who live for drugs, hard out drinking and crime. It seems strange that a place that the sun makes so bright can have so many dark shadows as well.

I wasn't so happy as a little kid. Luckily I don't remember too much about it. My mum, Joy Kahu, was nineteen when she had me. My dad's court name was Alan Xavier Stephens but everyone just called him "Ax". He was twenty four when I was born. I mostly remember a lot shouting and hitting, either of my mum or me. I remember lots of huge men being very loud and scary. I remember loud music, the smell of beer, weed and stale cigarettes – they still make me freeze inside. I hate those smells.

I was four when my dad killed my mum. Rewa was two. I
remember it like a nightmare in black and white. My dad, huge
and smelling of beer, dragging her down the corridor by the hair
past our room, waking me up. Then throwing her on the bed
and hitting her again and again. She screamed and screamed
for him to stop. Her bloody face. I ran in and tried to stop him
and he threw me against the wall. She jumped up to defend me
and he smashed her down. And then he kicked her head again
and again shouting at her, over and over, where she was down
behind the bed and I couldn't see her. I was still stunned by the
wall. And when she was still, he stormed out and slammed the
door and it was quiet.

I crawled over to look at her bloody face and her eyes were
looking into mine but she wasn't there any more. How many
nights have I woken screaming with those eyes in my mind?

I slept with my sister in her cot that night with the body of my
mother still in the bedroom. In the morning we watched TV and
ate whatever we could find in the fridge. Me and Rewa? We've
never been apart for long ever since.

It was Grandpop that found us. I'll never forget his face. He's
dark for a Maori, but then so pale. His face hard with horror and
fury. He told me later he'd been worried about mum for weeks
and when nobody had answered his phone calls he'd come over
to find her dead, and me with her blood on me.

I remember lots of legs after that.

Police legs. Welfare legs. Doctor legs. Grandpop's legs. But the
face I remember was Aunty Liz. Elizabeth is Grandpop's oldest
daughter. Elizabeth wasn't married, nor did she seem to want to
be. But she took me and Rewa in with that sad and serious look
she has. And as far as we were concerned she became our mum

27

even though we always called her Aunty and our Grandpop
became our dad though we never called him that.

Ax was soon caught and sent to prison. He'd been there already.
He said he was drunk and couldn't remember any of it, but
admitted he was guilty of manslaughter. The judge sentenced
him to fourteen years. But after time off for "good" behaviour
he was only locked up for eight. It meant as we grew up our
dad was more of a distant threat. An echo of that evil night that
might come back one day and try to get us.

Grandpop already shared the old house over the road from
the sea with Aunty Liz. He and Nana had retired there after
Grandpop left the Army. Then Nana had got very sick for a long
time, with cancers popping up, then being beaten down, and
then popping up again. Aunty Liz had spent two years looking
after Nana before she died. Then she took on looking after us.
Nana had died the same year my mum was murdered. Aunty Liz
always worried that bad luck came in threes.

I was very scared for a while that welfare would take us away
from Aunty Liz and Grandpop but the judge was a kind old
white man and could see at once that the Kahu family had a
good record. Liz was a community nurse for the district and
Grandpop's war medals all helped. And so my mum simply
became a ghost who haunted us. Hanging around, with all the
others who could not, or would not, go to wherever it is they are
meant to go.

You see, for as long as I can remember I have been able to feel
dead people. It's not like in that movie, you know the one where
the kid whispers "I can see dead people" cos you don't really see
them. You sort of remember them there, even though you never
saw them before. It's kinda hard to explain to anyone who can't

sense them. A bit like explaining "blue" to someone who has
never been able to see, or the wash of the sea to someone who is
deaf. You think you can see or hear presences – sometimes very
clearly – but if you took a picture there would be nothing there. I
know, I tried when I was older and the best I ever got was blurs.
I s'pose in a way mum never left me, 'though for a long time I
wouldn't talk to her. I was angry with her because she had left
us. I was angry with her for not being there for us, the way other
kids' mums were.

Aunty Liz never wanted us to call *her* "mum". She was very
respectful of mum's memory and we kept a special picture of
mum in the passage. She missed her little sister.

Aunty Liz wasn't as pretty as our mum had been, nor was she
smiley like her. I think it had a lot to do with her job. She was
always visiting the sick, or the injured. There were some who
got better but there were a lot who never did. It always seemed
really depressing seeing all these sick, old people; guys who'd
been maimed in fights or driving, or at work; and women who
were always being beaten. She was always warm and calm,
Aunty Liz. She rarely got angry with us and if she did, we were
terrified.

But she looked after us, Aunty Liz did. She went part-time when
she and Grandpop took us in. The Health Board wanted her to
stay full-time but they couldn't find anyone else to do her job
so they had to put up with it. It was good because they gave her
a car and a big, old cellphone (that didn't work because there
wasn't coverage anyway) but now she could fit her rounds in
around looking after us.

Of course it wasn't too long after we came to live with them that
I started school. Both Rewa and me were scared sick about being

29

separated. We cried and screamed so they let Rewa play around
with us in the morning for the first few months. After that
Aunt Liz took Rewa everywhere with her and she became her
"assistant nurse" which the old people found very cute.

But at the end of the school day the only person I wanted to
see was my sister. To make sure she was OK. We would play
together, usually with Joey and his sister Annie, from next door
while Aunt Liz went back to work. Sometimes the Barrys would
keep an eye on us and sometimes, if he was back from a fishing
trip, Grandpop would. Aunt Liz would normally get home
around six.

Aunty Liz got me off to school, made my lunches, looked after
us when we were sick. She told us off when we were naughty
and played with us sometimes when she could. We never had
any money, see, so we had to make-do with whatever was
passed down or around. "Improvise" was Grandpop's word.
He said that was what they trained him to do in the army and
he could improvise a lot. He fixed mechanical things, electrical
things, or furniture. It wasn't pretty but he made stuff work;
working quickly and quietly with bits of wire, tape, plastic or old
cans. I was fascinated by the way he did things and often tried
to copy him with cardboard and Sellotape. I'd show him my
creations and he'd look them over carefully, sometimes making
suggestions on how to make them look better or hold together.
He never mocked me the way I saw so many other fathers mock
their kids.

Nobody mocked *him* either. Grandpop is a big man. A very, big
man, and very strong and quick too. The men who thought they
were tough never showed off when Grandpop was around. But
he's so quiet, just from habit, people often forget he's there.

30

There were a number of men around the village who were actually smaller than him but seemed bigger because they talked louder and had more parties. The Barry brothers Ed and Jack and their families were very large, very loud and everybody knew what they were doing because they talked so much about it. Same too with the Heki family which was really four families each with four or five kids. Old George Heki was the grandfather and the senior elder or Koh-ma-tua on the ma-rae or Maori meeting house. He was also one of the few World War Two vets left and was one of the senior members of the Returned Services Association.

My Grandpop wasn't a big talker. He had a boat and he fished and dove for pau-a, the big black abalone, that are everywhere. He'd often be away over night or for a few nights. Once he was away for a whole week. Sometimes in summer he chartered his boat out to tourists, which was better money than fishing. He drank a bit but he never got drunk, and he never completely relaxed either.

When I was young it seemed to me that he never slept. If I woke he'd be there. If Rewa cried, he'd be there. He'd doze in his rocking chair on the verandah but he'd never be asleep. If you tried to do something naughty, like tie his shoelaces, he'd tell you off from under his hat as if he'd been pretending to sleep the whole time.

My main playmates were Joey Barry, Tipene Baker, and my cousin Clive Stephens. Joey lived next door in the loud and busy Barry family home of Ed and Jacki. He liked coming to our place because it was quiet and I liked going to his place because it was noisy and there was always something happening. Tipene lived a bit further down the road. He was big on going into the bush.

He loved eeling, hunting and playing with his labrador, Jess.
His dad, Manu, took him hunting and I always wanted to go but
Grandpop was against it. He said kids and guns don't mix. He
hated us playing war and would tell us off angrily if he heard us
making shooting sounds.

Clive was a playmate, though to be honest I didn't like him
much. He's a year older than me. His mum was my dad's sister
and although she'd largely disowned my dad, family ties rarely
break completely with us Maori. Clive loved playing tricks on us.
He was pushy and in your face but he was also inventive so we
often tagged along because no-one else was going anywhere. He
was one of six children with: a sister, Moana, who lived at home
with her baby; two older brothers, Paul and Mark who were
regularly accused of stealing things; a younger sister, Amy, who
was scarily bossy and made Rewa's life hell whenever they met;
and a baby brother, Matthew, who was the cutest little guy and
seemed to be in for a life of disappointment.

Clive liked to wear shades at school and he was always in trouble
with the teachers and chatting up the girls. He wore a gray
leather jacket and if anyone tried to steal it he'd fight them. He
always fought dirty. If he lost, his brothers, Paul and Mark, were
big enough threats most kids would give it back claiming they
were "just kiddin". I never had anything worth stealing, though
everyone got smashed by a bigger kid some time. It didn't pay to
stand out and become a target.

Clive liked to make jokes of me and Joey, and then say "jus
kiddin cuz" and "turn that frown upside down Sam the man".
Some people thought he was clever. I wasn't one of them.

I hated schoolwork. I was no good at reading, and numbers
just confused me. I kept a low profile, mumbling along with

the others and trying not to get noticed. It wasn't that hard. My
teachers didn't notice anyway. I was just another kid in a class of
thirty or so. I played the games – although I was never that great
at sports. I sang and did Kapa Haka (Maori cultural stuff like
dances and songs) along with everyone else. But I didn't stand
out – except at swimming.

For some reason I've always been a natural in the water. I'm
small and skinny but I can hold my breath for half a minute
quite easily – even in cold water. I've always been able to dive,
and 'though I've never been taught properly, I'm easily the
fastest in my class over any distance in the pool.

But my biggest problem was constantly being haunted. For some
reason the spirits just wouldn't leave me alone. I didn't mind
Nana or mum, they were just part of the house, and I was used
to them being around, like old furniture.

Some visitors were very clear, almost like real people who came
to see me, but most were "fuzzy". A lot of them were scared or
ashamed.

There were the teens who had done something stupid and
couldn't believe they were dead. Some wanted me to take a last
message. Of course some were scary. Sometimes there were
little kids or women who'd been killed by bastards like my dad,
broken and covered in blood. I hated that. The worst was the
mum who died giving birth.

But the really scary ones were the very, very old Maori spirits.
Some might say they were A-tu-a – our old gods. They were
terrifying. They were huge, proud and strong, but utterly
ruthless like Tuma-tau-enga, god of war. Some, like Whiro, god
of evil, was so dark and so deep it felt like he scraped your soul
just when he noticed you. Tane was bright like sun through the

leaves. Mahuika goddess of fire, was the smell of smoke, and I could feel the heat from her. Then there was the breath stealing darkness of Hinenui Te Po; the great lady of the night or Death. I would wake up at night when a cloud was over the moon gasping for breath and know she was visiting because someone had died and I would meet a new spirit soon. I think the Atua thought I was a complete wuss because I cried and hid.

Some kids at school thought I was scary because I talked to people who weren't there, or carried messages for them to grown-ups. Some liked to smack me over for it too. They stopped when I learned to pretend to be able to put the makutu or curse on them.

The old women said I had the gift that my mother's grandmother, Tui Owen, had had. She could see spirits and foretell the future. Sometimes when Grandpop was away I had sleep-overs on the ma-rae with the old people. They would tell me stories about my old ancestor Papa-huri-hia who was an old Tohunga or wizard back when the whites first arrived in Hokianga. His father Te Wharete was another with powers. He could travel long distances instantly and Papa-huri-hia could make his allies invisible. That sounded pretty cool to me but I never seemed to get any magic powers. I just got nights full of scary dreams about old gods. I never slept well and hated them but the old people were very pleased when I told them about the dreams in the morning.

Grandpop was not so pleased. He called it "superstitious old crap". It didn't help that he and old George Heki didn't get on. The World War Two vets looked down on the Vietnam vets and Grandpop took it personally. He kept us away from a lot of Maori stuff on the marae because he hated them so much. I was half-pleased. The Maori spooky stuff scared me, but even I had to admit there were *some* advantages.

The big one was over Ax's sister, Aunty Rebecca. She was terrified of the idea of my mum's ghost. That amused both me and mum's ghost. Aunty Liz is pretty religious because her mother, Nana was a Catholic. She had no problem with the idea of spirits but she said I mustn't encourage them, so that they would go on their way. I knew mum wouldn't go. Grandpop just said he didn't believe in ghosts and was angry with me if I talked to any or told him about it. He was especially angry about me talking to Nana. He hated it when she told me to remind him of things.

At first I was sad that Grandpop wouldn't believe me and tried to prove it by taking pictures until Aunty Liz explained to me that Grandpop had too many of his own ghosts from the war and he couldn't help me with mine as well. It had never occurred to me that Grandpop had problems, and while I now knew *why* he wouldn't listen, it didn't make me feel any better.

My friend Joey was the only one at school who showed any real interest in the spirit world. Joey's world was always busy and crowded and the idea that I had a world of "invisibles" as we called them didn't seem to bother him at all. I think he liked being spooked and it made him excited if I said there was an "invisible" around. He had far more interest in them than I did and pestered me about them whenever we were alone. It took a while to make him understand I didn't *want* him to talk about it to anyone else. I didn't like the way everyone would fall quiet when Joey mentioned that I could talk to my mum or other dead people. I didn't want to be pitied.

I don't think I deserved pity either. My life between the ages of five and ten was not too bad really. Not compared to a lot of places. We weren't rich in terms of money but we could play anywhere we liked outside. There was miles of bush to explore and do stuff in. There were trees to climb, eels to hunt, the sea was warm enough to dive in. It was mostly warm, the air was clean, the water was safe and we didn't go hungry. How many kids in the world don't have that? Millions. I've seen them. So, we didn't have computers or game consoles? But neither did anyone else and with all that real world to enjoy it never occurred to us to miss them.

But when I was eleven things something began to change. At first I only noticed it when some families suddenly had a lot more money to spend. Clive suddenly got a brand new bike and his brothers got X-boxes each. They got a new car and new TVs. Clive started acting up, wearing more expensive sunnies and a red bandana like he had a chest full of treasure. At school he bought other kids ice creams all the time. Then Tipene got in on the act, getting a brand new BB rifle with a scope that he used to waste every bird he could get near.

There were more parties, and they went on for longer – sometimes all night. Clive sometimes fell asleep in class. Suddenly there were strangers wearing sunnies in new SUVs in the area. Not just during the day but at night as well. And trucks that would drive up our dead end road into the neighbouring bay in the middle of the night.

And now Grandpop and Aunty Liz seemed less relaxed. Grandpop used to drink his coffee on the veranda just enjoying the sounds of the sea and bird life. Now he was actually looking around, sometimes with binoculars, watching the boats and even the other houses. We started ignoring invitations from

Aunty Rebecca. Clive would tease me about it at school but
it didn't make any difference, the Kahu's were shunning the
Stephens's. Grandpop wasn't that keen on the Bakers either.
Fortunately Ed Barry next door remained in firm favour and
Joey and me lived in one another's homes.

I started to pick up hints of what was going on at school. It
started with the paua. Apparently, for some reason, the Chinese
think it has some sort of special powers and they buy the stuff
for good prices. But in return they send the ingredients to make
this drug called Ice or Meth, which we call "P" for Pure, and
selling that makes huge money. So I started to realise that all
of these toys everyone was getting came from the drugs and the
paua trade.

At first I had no idea what this was all about. But it seemed to
me that as we never had any money, and as these other people
were suddenly makin' heaps, that maybe we should too! So
one night at dinner I suggested it to Aunty Liz and Grandpop.
Boy, did they go off at me! They called the Stephens's all sorts
of names they usually threatened to scrub my mouth out for
using. They said the paua poachers were taking all the babies
so that all the paua would die out, and they said the drug was
driving people crazy, making them dangerous and wild. Aunty
Liz said that making "P" poisoned a person's house and that
taking it poisoned a person's brain. Grandpop said that when he
was a soldier they had been given something like it to cope with
the long dangerous night patrols. He said he'd rather face the
Vietcong in the jungle than be around some of his old friends
who couldn't stop taking those drugs.

When everyone had calmed down and Aunty Liz was putting
us to bed she explained that she and Grandpop had seen the

damage these drugs could do. But she said a lot of people couldn't learn from others and had to find out the hard way every time. She said lots of people hope there is a shortcut in life but there never is. The shortcut becomes the long cut, and while some people like to show off, eventually they come unstuck. And she asked me if having all of those things was really about me having them, or about proving that I was as good as Clive. I thought about that for a while, because it was true that Clive certainly got up my nose, but at the same time, even if Clive left town, I could see myself riding a new bike and that seemed a pretty good thing as well. So I was mostly convinced but, not entirely, by Aunty Liz and Grandpop.

I'd sort of hoped that this lesson in life would be over in half an hour, like a TV show, but that didn't happen. Instead it got worse. Clive got pushier, more and more people got involved and the whole community got crazier. Nobody seemed to want to listen to Aunty Liz or Grandpop. They said *we* were the party poopers, and to prove it they had all night parties all through the week.

The gang had always been around in our village. Young men joined it when they went down south to Auckland. Now the gang was in our face. Big guys in big cars who went around monstering people, putting the pressure on. People started to get angrier too. Angrier and more impatient. And while there had always been punch-ups now they were turning into severe beatings which Aunty Liz had to help with. It seemed the community I grew up in was unravelling like an old jersey. Grandpop's worst fears about the paua started to come true too. The boats were finding fewer and fewer of the shellfish but the pressure from the gangs, and the need for the drugs, drove the fishers to work harder and harder and cut more and more corners. The fisheries protection officers came around to look like they were doing something but everyone knew they had been paid to look the other way, so they did.

But as the pressure increased so did the bad feeling. This was the only time I met what Grandpop referred to as "my friend". I woke up late one night to go to the toilet and noticed a light on in the sitting room. Curiously I nosed through the door and saw my Grandpop drinking beer at the coffee table and cleaning a gun. It wasn't a hunting rifle either. I'd seen plenty of those. No, this was a soldier's gun with a long curved magazine like the ones I'd seen them shooting in wars on the news. I asked him about it but Grandpop quietly told me to go back to bed and mind my own beeswax. I never saw it again.

I don't know if he meant me to see it or not but I couldn't wait to tell Joey and by the end of the day the whole school knew – which meant that by that night everyone knew. I only realised later how crafty my Grandpop was. When Ed from next door asked him, in his usual big, friendly way, if Grandpop had a souvenir from the war hidden somewhere, he told them I must have dreamt it. Nobody believed I'd dreamt anything. But they had no proof, so they were left with this feeling that Grandpop had a Vietcong assault rifle hidden somewhere without having seen it themselves. It certainly stopped the drive-bys of the house, or the big men wearing sunnies from sitting on Grandpop's boat. They decided that old Kahu was too small and too dangerous to be bothered with – so they went for easier targets.

It was Ho-né Pou-kawa who they made the example of. Honé was pretty dumb anyway and he tried to cheat the gang. They

beat him so bad he was never the same. Aunty Liz had to visit
him every day after they finally let him out of hospital. She said,
he could barely cope on his own and wept a few tears for him
– which was pretty unusual for Aunty Liz who didn't usually
get upset about her patients. Grandpop told me a man's head
can't take much kicking without his brain being damaged. And
there is no doubt Honé's head had been kicked a lot. It was a
different shape and his face had been completely mangled by
gang boots. The police investigated but, of course, nobody had
seen anything. Anyone who knew anything was either tied up
with the gang themselves, or too scared to talk, and the rest
either didn't have anything useful to say or didn't want to mark
themselves out by being the only ones narking to the cops.
So Honé Poukawa's beating just hung over the community,
weighing down on everyone's minds like this big unspoken
cloud.

You'd have thought that at least Clive would have been enjoying
those days, riding around on his fancy bike, in his new threads
and talking on his cellphone. But even Clive seemed to have
something wrong with him. He seemed all nervous and twitchy.
He'd get real angry – I mean crazy angry – over nothing. And he
kept scratching himself. He looked thin and his face had sunken.
We never visited the Stephens's anymore and at school I kept
away from him because he wasn't nice to be around. He smelt of
glue.

But then something else happened that was even worse. My dad
remembered me.

I was eleven when Ax wrote his first letter to me. There was one
for Rewa as well but I never let her see it. I didn't want to read
it either but Grandpop took me aside and told me you should

always read the enemy's communications for clues about his intentions. What they say, and more importantly what don't say, give you useful clues about what they are thinking. So we read the letter together, stopping at the end of each sentence to talk about what Ax had written, and what he'd left out.

Mostly, the letter was asking for forgiveness. Grandpop said Ax had probably been told what to write, and he was doing it so he could get out of jail sooner. We read the letter to Rewa, which was full of lies and self-pity and made me angry, but Grandpop said this was probably what Ax really believed.

Grandpop said something which I've always remembered. He said *everyone*, even the worst of men, is a hero in their own minds. He said the lies Ax wanted to tell Rewa were probably the lies he told himself and to understand Ax, we had to study his lies. I really didn't want to. I said as far as I was concerned I had no father other than Grandpop and what Ax thought didn't matter to me. Grandpop didn't press it, but he put the letters into a shoebox and wrote "Enemy Intell" on it, which made me laugh.

But the letters didn't stop coming just because I didn't reply. For some reason Ax seemed to *like* writing letters to me, and we started getting them every month. Grandpop thought that must be when Ax was visited by the prison counsellor. The letters stopped asking for forgiveness and turned into a combination of diary and story of his life when he was my age. He talked about how he had become a Christian and wanted to be a better person. He always signed off "love, Dad", which always made me angry.

The letters had come for about a year, without us responding once, when a new idea seemed to have taken over. Now Ax had

41

decided he wanted to have his children around him. He kept talking about fathers and sons in the Bible uniting before the Lord. At first I thought it was just more raving from a nutjob but he kept going on about it. It started to make us nervous.

We got even more nervous as we began to realise that praying and writing letters weren't the only things Ax had been up to in prison. He'd been making friends. But his friends were not men of God. They were the high-up, city leaders of the gang that had taken over our village and Ax had apparently become quite senior among them. We began to realise he had a very good idea of what was going on in our neighbourhood and that his plans for his release were not those of a humble Christian seeking forgiveness but a very full-of-himself man who fully expected to inherit the whole place. What we didn't realise was the lengths he'd go to, to get what he wanted.

•••

CHAPTER THREE: BACKSTAB

Sue listened to my story closely without interrupting. I stop when the time reaches 12:17, partly because it's a good place to stop, but mostly because I'm hungry.

"By the way, Sue, is there any chance of getting some lunch here?" I ask.

"Pardon? Oh lunch! Yeah, sure Sam, I'll get you something." She gets up. Then stops.

"So, if you're psychic, then you would know if your family was dead wouldn't you?"

"Yep," I answer simply.

"And they're not?"

"No."

"But you don't know where they are."

"Not exactly, no."

"But you have some idea."

"Yep."

"Are they in hiding?"

"Yeah … you could say that."

"So why didn't you go to them? Why come to us?"

"Because I *can't* get there."

Sue stares at me for a moment and then it clicks.

"Oh, come on … you don't believe…" she begins.

"What?"

"That flying saucers came and took them all away?"

"Hell no!" I say, shocked by such a scary idea.

Sue looks relieved.

"They were *escaping* the flying saucers to get out of their reach,"
I explain.

She looks at me like I've grown an extra head. She was going to
say something and then stops herself.

"Let's get some lunch," she mumbles.

"Yeah!" I agree, enthusiastically.

We leave the interview room and walk along the corridors.
There's a lot of cops wandering about talking, joking and
carrying stuff. It's like the hospital Aunty Liz used to work in.
We go to the canteen, which is pretty full, and a bit like the one
in the hospital, and stand in a queue. I notice nobody talks much
to Sue although there were quite a few cops at the tables. Sue
gets herself a sandwich, some yoghurt, and a banana and I get
two pies. Call me a guts but I love pies and I'm damn hungry.
We then head to Kevin's office (which had "Detective Sergeant
Cooper" on the door) looking for Geraldine, but Kevin is on the
phone talking to someone, and he waves Sue back out of his
office, so we go to Sue's office to eat.

"So what are you going to do after you've ditched me?" I ask her
to make conversation.

"I'm not going to *ditch* you," she objects.

"Well, I mean after Geraldine's taken me back to the shelter or
whatever you call it."

"It's only temporary."

"I know, I know, but what will *you* do?"

"I have a few more interviews, and a family group conference."

"What did they do?"

"Who?"

"The bros?"

"I can't tell you. I'm not meant to talk about it."

"Oh," I pause for a moment. Reading Sue is surprisingly easy.
Some people, like Dr P, are real hard. Some are even dangerous.
"Green car. Real shiny. White doofus. Is one of them a racer?" I
ask.

She smiles, then peeled her banana.

"Can't tell you Sam," she says taking a bite. But she's looking at
me keenly.

We sit for a while eating our food.

"So Sam, this psychic thing you do, how does it work?"

"I dunno," I shrug, "It's multi-dimensional. Dr P's maths is full
of weird symbols. I don't pretend to understand it."

"No, I mean how does it work for you?"

"Oh, you mean how do I read?"

"Yeah, if that's what you call it."

"Oh well, it's a bit random. You get feelings, impressions, ideas."

"How do you know you aren't imagining them?"

"You just do. Everyone is different and has different strengths.
My speciality is dead people. I'm good with them. By the way
Detective Sergeant McLaren says 'hi'."

Sue freezes.

"What?" she says faintly.

"Woody," I reply, "he says 'hi' and he's right proud of you too."

I can almost see her skin crawl. Mine did it lots. I'm used to it.

"How did *you* know?"

"Well, it's not hard, he's right over there," I say, pointing to him
in the corner near the door.

45

She turns slowly. I don't think she can see him. She turns back. "He's right chuffed seeing you using his old office. Thinks you're doing a grand job," I tell her using McLaren's accent.

Sue gets up slowly. I'm quietly freaking her out. McLaren was a very cheery sort though. It even took Joey a while to get used to his invisibles and it was only Sue's first time.

"I'd better see if DS Cooper is free," she says, and goes off shivering.

Which was exactly what I was waiting for.

I jump on to her PC and shake the mouse. Sue's username "SE dot Williams" and password, "s+r4eva", I read an hour ago. McLaren's annoyed but I have things to do. I open the port on my watch and connect the USB to the sticky gel inside. It begins to glow green indicating a link. My watch is injecting a tiny program into the bios. Next I rip off my trainers and take the Omnicard from my sock. It's a credit-card-sized, plastic card about 2mm thick, but completely white. I press my thumb to the corner and it changes through various credit cards until my code comes up. The clunky old-style message program window from my watch comes up on the screen. I need to send two messages. The first is to the Para.no.ID dead letter drop with my eight character personal code, and the emergency "need assistance" code. That will go to Dr Morozov's friends in the ultra secret Para.no.ID hacker network. I didn't know them, but they were meant to be friendly. Then I exited the message program. I pressed a button on the watch and a small green hologram of Qi – the watch's user interface appeared.

"Qi send a webmail to Sir Michael. Tell him the New Zealand police are looking after me but I still don't have a contact address. Dr Prosperov sends his apologies and asks him to take care of me."

Qi pauses, then says, "done."

I push the button and Qi vanishes. I unpeel my watch and put it on. Then I stick the card back on my foot, and pull on my sock. I hear Sue and Kevin coming, get the screensaver to demo, then hop around to my seat and pull on my trainer. I'm doing up my laces when Kevin and Sue come back. From training I don't hurry but just tie the laces up slowly as if I'd just noticed they'd come undone.

"Hi Kev, where's my ride got to?" I ask cheerfully.

"Geraldine had to go. I'll take you myself," he says.

"Cool," I agree, noticing out of the corner of my eye that the screensaver had popped off. It prompts me to keep their attention.

"So what happens now?"

"You go back to the Moore's until the department finds a longer term arrangement. We continue our investigation, and if ... or when ... we find your family we notify you," he says.

"So you won't have any more questions for me?"

"Well, Geraldine thinks you should see a counsellor so she will organise one for you. We may have more questions later on but for the moment we will follow up the physical clues."

"But I'm not under arrest or anything?" I check.

"No, of course not."

"So they can't lock me up?"

"No, though you are temporarily under the guardianship of the department until a court gets to look at you, so until they find someone else to look after you, you are in their care."

"I can take care of myself."

"Not legally Sam. Legally, you're still a minor. Look, let's talk about this in the car."

"OK. Will I see you again Sue?" I ask her.

"Probably Sam, though I can't say when at this stage."

"OK, well see ya later then," I say and extend my hand.

She's surprised and shakes it awkwardly. She seems relieved as I leave her office with Kevin.

We follow the maze of narrow corridors to the lift. Something in Kevin's body language is closed up. He's thinking about what the Fire Service people have just told him about traces of Powergel, the explosives on the gas cylinders, and seems to be unwilling to chat. So we ride the lift down to the basement garage in silence. I tag along, following him to his car – a gray, late model Ford Mondeo. It still had that new car smell in the black vinyl.

Kevin reverses it out of its park, and noses up the ramp. The garage door opens automatically and the bright light of an Auckland day blazes in through the windshield.

For some reason after the gloom of the station it makes me feel quite hopeful again. What's really cheering me up, of course, is getting the messages away. We had drilled for this sort of situation and it was good to get the ball rolling. The news about me and Renwick had gone global and, although I knew we had been betrayed, I had to start reaching out for help. Given the news it wasn't like receiving those messages would surprise anyone. It also meant more practical help would soon be on its way. In the meantime I just had to sit tight. The world is a big place and New Zealand is out on its own when it comes to time zones. However if all went well I would soon have a lot of help. The silence between me and Kevin starts to drag. Traffic in central Auckland is as slow as ever. I size him up while we crawl along. Now he is thinking about police politics. Ambition, status.

Those were obviously his goals. For a moment I wondered what it must be like to be tied down to one place, one job, one future like that, but I couldn't face thinking about it. My mind drifted back to Sue, in her office.

"So who was Detective Sergeant McLaren anyway, Kevin?" I ask finally.

"Hmm?"

"Detective Sergeant McLaren, who was he?"

"He was a detective."

"Yes, I know *that*, but how did he die?"

"He was fatally shot on a drugs bust three years ago. He was a big loss."

"Oh ... he seemed like a nice guy. British?"

"Yes, 20 years there, seven here."

"Was he close to Detective Constable Williams?"

"He was her supervisor."

We pulled out onto the motorway for a brief run down to the next exit. Kevin accelerated away seeming to want to leave the conversation behind. I say nothing, I have nothing to say. It's Kevin who starts the conversation again.

"Did Dr Prosperov have any religious convictions that he spoke of?"

I try to think.

"Nah, I mean he grew up in the Soviet Union. All that was banned. His dad was a communist but his mother and grandfather were Jewish. I think he was still a bit of both but he talks about religion more as a bunch of theories."

"What about the flying saucers?"

"He investigated them for the Soviet airforce. I think you can find his report on the web."

"But he believed in them?"

"Sure. He still does."

"Do you believe in them?" Kevin askes, glancing at me.

"Sure," I say at once.

"Have you ever seen one?" he challenges.

"Yep. A few."

"Where?" he challenged me.

Greenland? Papua New Guinea? Yemen? The moon? I couldn't answer that one truthfully.

"Around. Few around Aotea." I didn't add "lately" and "looking for me."

"What did they look like?"

"Just lights in the sky. They just hang and then ... fiit ... they fly off so fast you can hardly follow it."

"And you don't think they were a satellite or a plane?"

"Nah. They move too fast and change direction, with no noise at all."

"I've seen one," he says suddenly. That's a surprise.

"Nah?" I josh him.

"Yeah. It was small though. Dull, very fast, low over the Gulf when I was on a mate's boat."

How embarrassing! It could have been me! I pretend to be interested.

"Did it spook you out?"

"No. That was the funny thing. It just zoomed by and I just thought it was a plane and then I realised it was far too low, far too fast and far too small. And of course, no noise. I was more surprised than anything else."

"So does that mean you don't think Dr Prosperov was a nutter?"

"It doesn't mean he *was* a nutter. It doesn't mean he *wasn't* a nutter."

"But you don't think seeing flying saucers makes you a nutter?"

"No Sam, and I've seen some spooky stuff like you did with Detective Sergeant McLaren before too. Sometimes *we* use psychics. But while there is spooky stuff in the world it's not reliable. You couldn't use it as evidence or policing would turn into witchhunts. It's just stuff that happens. The important things are the things you can rely on."

"Like what?"

"Logic. Reason and technology built using it. Like cars for instance. Cars, phones, maybe even computers sometimes. They make our world work. Spooky stuff is just spooky stuff. It happens but it doesn't go anywhere. Get hooked up on it and you end up waiting for things that never happen and making excuses when they don't."

"Yeah, I used to think that too."

I've noticed that adults don't like it when you hint you know better than they do. They obviously think: "hey I'm older than you, kid, I've seen some stuff, listen and learn". Grandpop always taught me to do that. He used to say, "shut up and listen. Not just hear, really listen. Listen hard to everything. Every sound, every voice has many messages. Those that listen, survive," he'd always said. When he talked like that I'd got readings of him in Vietnam where listening saved his life. And I tried sometimes to do it. Really listen hard. But I came to see that you can't hear everything coming and sometimes it's better just to keep moving to stay out of reach. So I talked into the silence.

"That's what Dr Prosperov was trying to do, make spooky stuff reliable."

"Did he?"

"It's how he made all his money."

We're getting near to Ruth and Dave Moore's. Kevin turns off the main road into the suburbs and we thread our way past the parked cars of the mostly empty streets to the emergency foster home.

We pull up outside and Kevin comes with me to the door. I'd only been here one night and I didn't like it much. I didn't like the smell and it didn't feel safe. We knock and after a bit of a wait Ruth answered.

"Geraldine had to go," Kevin explains.

"Sam's been helping us find out what happened out there."

Ruth's a white woman who's had four teenage sons and despite being small and gray, is very strict and bossy. She believes that boys should be treated like dogs: feed 'em, pat 'em, give 'em lots of exercise, and shout at them when they are naughty. She was good at shouting especially. She'd obviously been doing this for a long time so she had everything worked out, and it was up to us to fit in.

"Thank you Kevin, will you be needing to talk to him again tomorrow?" she asks.

"Probably not – unless we find something, of course."

"Good, well Sam, I need you to do some assessment worksheets for the department to find out what you've been learning at school all these years."

"Oh, great!" I groan.

"Well, we've all got things to do," Kevin says waving as he leaves."Thanks Ruth, bye Sam."

"Later Kevin," I say and get dragged inside by Ruth.

Ruth and Dave's house was once an ordinary home on the top level but now it has a dormitory, recreation room and bathroom on the bottom level. Ruth takes me downstairs to the Rec Room and puts a booklet and pen in front of me.

"You've got half an hour, try to do what you can," she says, not expecting much.

There are four bunks, so they can sleep eight but right now they only have three of us. They specialise in boys in trouble. The other two looked pretty big. Sailosi, is Samoan and the same age as me but he's way bigger – about six foot four. He's run away from home after a fight with his dad. I'd only talked to him for about an hour or two at most, but I liked him already. He was a cheerful sort of guy, although he was a bit down at the moment because of the problems with his folks.

The other kid I didn't like so much. He'd been pretty quiet while Sailosi was around so I'd talked with Sailosi instead. Jaden's a white kid of sixteen who's in care. He's scrawny, mean, and stupid, with blond hair, a fuzzy blond beard, and there's always a beanie on his head. I'd sensed bad things from him the minute I met him.

At the moment Sailosi is out, and Jaden's reading a comic on a bean bag in front of the blank TV set. Ruth won't let us watch daytime TV. Ruth goes back upstairs telling me she'll be back from time to time to see how I'm getting on. That was more of a warning to Jaden.

So I have a look at the booklet. I hate it already. I really do have trouble reading stuff like this. It makes me nervous. Ask me the questions and I'll give you the answers in a flash, coz I'm not dumb. I just hate reading and writing. I sigh and knuckle down to it though frankly I'd rather clean a septic tank.

"Too hard for you eh, nigger?" Jaden mutters, almost to himself while reading.

I'd expected that.

"Nah, nothin' harder'n me 'round here, eh?" I smile nicely at him, and go to work.

I smile to myself as he scowls trying to work out what I'd just said.

The first questions are actually easy. Simple arithmetic, fill in the blanks, complete the sequence. I have no problems with them.

"Cos he's too dumb, dumb, dumb, he's a dumb ass little nigger," Jaden sings quietly as he flips the page. Actually he's helping.

If he wasn't hazing me I might not feel like proving him wrong.

Ruth comes down again and Jaden shuts up. She looked over my shoulder.

"Good work Sam," she smiles, encouragingly.

She goes back upstairs.

Jaden starts making huge sucking noises like I'm sucking up.

"No thanks, Jaden," I say, not looking up, "I'm a bit busy now."

He takes a while to get that one too. Next they want you to use words in a sentence. The first ones are easy enough but I'd never seen the other ones. I couldn't make sense of them – and I never was a quick writer anyway. My letters look awful. I make a strategic decision and skip that bit. Jaden's pissed off now.

"Flip em all dumb c_____!" Jaden advises softly, not looking up from his comic.

"I was jus' looking for a page for you to colour in, while I was workin', Jaden," I reply, smiling.

"Oh you gonna be my bitch tonight, smart nigger," Jaden threatens softly reading his comic.

"You're full of shit, Jaden," I tell him calmly, working on.

Before Renwick he would have scared me. I would have

attacked, which is just what he wants. But I realised it wasn't personal. This guy would bully anyone. He just likes bringing everyone down to his slimy level.

Now the test had a map of the world and I had to match cities to letters. That was too easy – I'd been to all of them. Then there's some science. I knew the molecules, but I couldn't spell the seashore things, or I didn't know the names. I'm frustrated because some of the topics I know the stuff but not the right words. I find it hard to get the answers down.

Ruth comes down again. I realise she's coming down every ten minutes which means I have ten minutes left.

I skim through the rest looking for easy ones. There's one question on Maori history which is easy so I have to answer that. That leaves me with five minutes and only hard ones. I quickly decide to do the one on reading a story and answering questions. Meanwhile now that Ruth's gone Jaden's making horrible snotty throat clearing sounds to put me off.

Then a gob of spit hits me in the cheek followed by his bray of rattling laughter. Both of us are skinny and small, but I'm still a lot smaller than he is. Still, I'm not thinking clearly. All I know is he is going to get it now. I get up, wiping my face.

"Ooooooooo," Jaden jeers softly as if this means trouble. He's still sitting down, but he's tense now.

I walk around the table toward him.

"Sit down little c___!" he jeers.

Orders don't work on me now. I run at him. He stands quickly to meet my attack. My knee comes up. His hands go out to ward me off. My knee strikes his nuts with my weight behind it, we go over, the chair behind him with us. I land on top of him, my weight pressing him into the upturned chair. My knee has really hurt him. His hands go to my throat. Mine inside his arms go to his face. He tries to choke me as I begin to gouge him. He's losing, and screaming something, cursing me.

"SAM! JADEN!" I swear Ruth's voice sounds louder than a rifle shot.

Then she's on us pulling us apart, yelling at us while we're all yelling at one another. His face is bloody where I got him and he's doubled up from the knee shot.

"Jaden upstairs!" Ruth barks at him.

"You're dead meat, nigger!" Jaden snarls climbing the stairs.

"JADEN! SILENCE!" Ruth roars at him. For a small woman she can yell almost as loud as Grandpop doing his drill sergeant voice.

For a second I thought Jaden might get a knife from the kitchen. But I realise he's a coward so he will wait 'til he has me alone before having another go. Still, I made a mental note to be careful about knives.

Ruth's shouting at me. She shouts for quite a while about "in this house", the rules, and not taking a rise. I complain that he'd been hazing me and spat on me. Finally, when we'd shouted ourselves out, I give her the booklet.

I get sentenced to apologise to Jaden for losing my temper. He has to apologise to me too. We both lose access to the game machines for three days. As I never play them that doesn't bother me in the slightest, but I know Jaden loves his racer games and he's going to be highly pissed at me for this.

The apologies are about as unsorry as we can make them without Ruth making us repeat them. Then we get another stern lecture about "If I ever…" and, "in this house…", then we get separated. Jaden gets to do some chores with Ruth. I'm pretty sure that Ruth can see through Jaden and wants him under her thumb. This leaves me the rec room all to myself. Not there's that much in it. A TV with half a dozen channels; a Playstation 2 with a bunch of games mostly rated PG; a heap of graphic novels and comics, magazines; and a ping pong table. For someone like myself, more into doing things than reading or watching, it's pretty dull. I pick up some comics and start reading them half-heartedly.

At 4 p.m. Sailosi comes back from his family group conference. I can see he's pretty shaken up. I ask him if he wants a game of ping pong, so we play badly for about an hour. It helps him calm down anyway. Then Ruth rounds us up to make dinner.

I hadn't done much cooking before so I find it more interesting than reading comics or playing ping pong. Jaden doesn't say anything, so conversation is mostly between me and Sailosi with Ruth giving instructions or encouragement in the background. I don't see it happen but suddenly the whole pot of boiling potatoes is knocked off the stove top by Jaden onto Sailosi's arm. Sailosi screams.

"F____! sorry man," Jaden yells.

Ruth shoves me and Jaden aside and grabs Sailosi to put his arm under cold running water in the sink. Then Jaden winks evilly at me. Ruth yells at me to get the first aid box – which I don't understand because I'm finally realising what Jaden is doing, so Jaden gets it, pretending to be all sorry like he's worried for Sailosi.

Sailosi's brown skin is coming up in an ugly red burn, turning pale as it dies under the running water. Sailosi's weeping in pain in spite of himself. He's going into shock, shaking and looking pale, so I get him a blanket. Ruth gets on the phone and calls her husband Dave, telling him what's just happened, and that we have to go to hospital. Dave tells Ruth to call the ambulance because it's quicker and you get better attention in the emergency department. So Ruth calls an ambulance.

The ambulance must have either been waiting down the road or can fly because it arrives within ten minutes in the middle of the rush hour traffic.

This gives Ruth a problem. She can't go with Sailosi and mind us at the same time. Sailosi was already feeling bad before he was burned, and now he's looking pleadingly at Ruth to go with him.

"Don't worry Mrs Moore," Jaden assures her, "I'll take care of Sam."

He means it too – but not in a nice way. But I can see Sailosi needs her help more than I do so I don't say anything. Ruth calls Dave again who says he's still in heavy traffic about ten to fifteen minutes away. So recognising the ambulance can't wait forever and that technically she can leave us for the ten minutes it will take Dave to get home she gives us a stern lecture about fighting then goes in the ambulance with Sailosi.

I don't go back inside the house as the ambulance drives away. I'm far safer on the sidewalk. Jaden goes inside though and comes back looking pleased with himself.

"One nigger down, one to go," he says as he comes back onto the street, smirking to himself.

"Come inside. We can start now, save waiting til lights out," he adds grinning evilly.

So I turn and tell him what I think of him, none of which is polite, and he suddenly punches me in the nose. I go down on the ground. It hurts like hell but he isn't finished. I catch a glint of steel. I'm not going to wait and see what he's pulled out from his pants. I roll, scramble to my feet, and clutching my nose which is bleeding everywhere, barely able to see where I'm going, just run.

He chases me, and being bigger he can catch me too. I realise I need to trick him again so I let him get close, then drop suddenly so he trips over the top of me. I take his knees in my back but he goes right over onto the pavement. He lets out a gasp. The knife clatters.

I get up. He'd been holding the knife, handle forward, blade along his forearm, to make it less obvious. As he'd gone over he'd dropped it to break his fall but the knife landed handle down and he landed on it, stabbing himself in the right side. Now blood's quickly soaking his shirt on his side where the knife has stabbed him.

Now he's really scared, and swears at me, but his attention is on his wound and he turns back to the house, holding his side as the shirt becomes redder and wetter.

I've had enough. I've tried the system and it's too dangerous. Jaden's a poisonous snake and I'm not going to sleep anywhere near him if I can help it. I run off to a park and set off for the other side over the grass. Dave will seek me out with his car but if I use routes which are away from the road he won't be able to trace me.

As I walk I think about where I'm going to go.

I'd looked for police protection for good reason. I had tried camping on the island but I'd seen the lights at night and could see *they* were watching it very closely. By turning myself in and getting on the news I drew *them* away with me, away from Emma. With a case number and the cops watching me I had thought it would be harder for *them* to get me. Out of official

59

gaze *they* could find me and "remove" me without any problems so I wanted to stay close to the system. But that wasn't at any cost. I wasn't going to stay anywhere in a system that wasn't safe.

I'd been in much more immediate danger in other countries but then I'd had way more options. Now I was completely on my own with just my Omnicard and Qi. It was getting dark and I hadn't eaten since lunchtime.

I take stock like Grandpop taught us. Shoes? Good, nothing wrong there. Clothes? My clothes were a bit bloodstained from my nose, too thin if it got cold, but dry. There would be a dew with an overnight temperature in the range of five degrees. Sleeping in the open was out.

Situation? Jaden would probably tell Dave I'd attacked him. Dave would probably doubt that, given our relative sizes, but I wasn't there to defend myself. Jaden would need his wound looked at. They would have to take him to the emergency department too. So they'd probably notify the police I was missing. On the other hand there are loads of kids on the street in Auckland and the cops don't know where they are either so it would probably not get a very high priority.

So where could I go?

CHAPTER FOUR: SEEKING SUSAN

Sue Williams. Sue's name pops into my head – but I know it's
not for a good reason. I stop and sit down to read her and
staunch my nosebleed with my t-shirt. Then I remember I have
her card in my pocket. That will help. I take it out and look at it.
I feel sick. Sick as if my guts have been ripped out. Sick, scared
and numb. Something's wrong. Something's not good. She's
gone. Rachel has done it! She's gone! She's taken her stuff and
just left.

I'd been right, and now Sue is experiencing it as she arrives
home. I can feel her shock. Her sense of betrayal and bitter,
bitter loss. She feels stabbed right through the heart. She feels
weak, worthless and embarrassed at being so badly dumped as
she realises everyone else she knows probably knows already
that Rachel has left her.

She needs help. Hell! *I* need some help! So where would I find
her? Something turned me West to where the sun was about to
set behind the hills – but I would need a map to find her. A map,
and some food. And for that I need money.

My Omnicard was OK in an ATM but no good in a shop, where
it would look suspicious. My big fear is having a money machine
swallow it. Not that it had ever happened before, but there is
always a first time. I take off my shoes and socks and put the

Omnicard in my sleeve under my watch band. I have to keep it in contact with my skin or else it will self-destruct after ten minutes. So my next step is to find a money machine – which given I'm in the Eastern suburbs could take a while. I set off to find a shopping centre in the gathering dark.

The roads are busy. Adults walking alone are rare, teens walking at this time even rarer. I realise I will stick out and try to look purposeful while sticking to suburban back streets. Even so, this is a white or Asian area and Maori kids in hoodies walking alone here are sus'. Finally I make it to a shopping centre. It's a small cluster of grimy shops that look like their owners are struggling against the big malls. But there's a money machine and it appears to be working.

I stop for a moment, and then decide that if I'm going to lose the Omnicard, I would be better off losing it closer to the Moore's place than miles away. I select a Visa gift card profile that's still fresh and stick it into the machine. For a second the machine seems to hesitate, giving me a moment of panic, then the screen refreshes and I am challenged for my PIN. I enter the PIN for this card – once again it pauses for a worrying moment –and then presents me with my options. I ask for $50, cash. Then, to my relief, I get back both my card and $50.

I could have taken heaps of money of course, there's thousands on it, but it would look bad for a Maori teen in a hoodie to be running around the eastern suburbs with thousands in cash. That attracts attention and I didn't need that.

I head into the nearest corner store. An unfriendly Pakistani man looks at me suspiciously as I enter. He obviously mistrusts Maori teenagers. I knew he would expect me to sidle along the back rows so I put my hood down and walk straight up to him.

I ask for a couple of pies, a map, and where the buses go from. He doesn't know too much about buses, but he sells me a pair of lukewarm pies and an overpriced map. Naturally they didn't put anything as useful as bus routes on the map so I drift over towards the bus stop, looking at the maps and eating a not-quite-cold pie.

Fortunately the bus stop has an electronic sign on it telling me the next bus is ten minutes away. I'm keen to put as much distance between me and the money machine as I can. There's always a risk that my Visa gift card profile has been identified and *they* are tracing me. To avoid being spotted I put my hood back up, and stand looking at the map against the fence, so my back is to on-coming traffic. I'm trying to sense where Sue is from the map but aside from a definite feeling she lives in the western suburbs I'm too distracted by my surroundings to get any true feeling for it.

I decide to take the bus into the centre of town. There I can find somewhere quiet, get my bearings, and then either get a taxi or a bus to Sue's place. The countdown until the bus finally shows up seems to take forever. When it does the bus driver makes a big deal of having to make change. I don't care. At least I'm moving now. And it was extremely cheap. If I can work out where Sue is I might be able to avoid another money machine visit.

There are only three other people on this bus: two girls a bit older than me, and an old man, so I find a seat and settle down to study the map. I'm not the best in our team at doing this. Scotty's a natural but I'm pretty sure it's easier in the quiet of the African bush than the lurching noisiness of a bus. Even so, by concentrating on Sue I'm getting more and more certain of the area she lives in, even if I'm not exactly sure of which street.

The bus roars, shudders and swings its way into the centre of town, along the still-busy main roads with the light slowly fading from the sky. Streetlights are coming on, shops are closing, and people have their heads down rushing home. It's kind of enjoyable to be going in the opposite direction to everyone else. Finally we begin to navigate around the city centre. I want to get as close to the central bus stops as I can to find the bus I would need to take me to the west.

I get off in a rather grubby part of town full of backpackers' hostels, Asian takeaways, and sex bars, but I feel relaxed here because we'd done our earliest urban training in these very streets. Admittedly I was better equipped then, but I know this place well, and it makes me feel way more comfortable than walking in, say, Tondo, Manila.

There's still a lot of people about, and plenty of lights on, so I walk to Queen Street – the street running up the centre of Auckland's main business district – and head down to the Britomart rail terminal from which all the buses run.

I find a tourist information terminal on the street to help find the right bus route. I play with that for a while, and decide I need a no.72f. I look up the timetable and see that there's one leaving in about ten minutes. But where from? Finally I have to go into the railway station and ask the guy in the kiosk who directs me to a bus stop by a sex-bar.

I have about twenty bucks left. The bus should cost four. Should I get more? What I need is a bank card to copy. New Zealand uses EFT a lot more than other places and cash makes you stand out. If my Omnicard was pressed against a real mag-stripe or chip card it could match the design with undetectable precision. Only the name and account would be mine with my signature,

and or picture, still on it. I have a number of old profiles on it.
I've got an American Express standard, gold and platinum; a
couple of Visa cards from America, France and Belgium; a heap
of foreign access cards for all sorts of doors; but the one thing I
don't have is a regular EFT card I can use in a shop in my own
country! I've never needed one. We usually used gift cards and
my collection of those had burned to plastic ash.

I decide to risk it and not get any more out. If I have to use the
foreign cards I may as well get out a thousand and stay in a hotel
or something but for the moment I'll try to keep a low profile.
The bus in the dark – it's now 7:05 p.m. – is even emptier
than the one I'd ridden into town. There's just one older guy
in it who's reading a book. It's strange to be doing this without
backup and completely by senses. When we were operating we
had Control with loads of extra information to help us. But this?
This is operating almost naked. Once again I just clear my head
and let the feelings flow.

Sue's found a note. She's drunk and overcome by her own grief.
She's wallowing in it, and keeps reading and re-reading the note
and looking at old pictures of the two of them. She's going to be
a real mess. I can feel her incredibly strongly.

It surprises even me, when I get near enough to walk, how
strong the feeling is. I can feel her all fuzzy and weeping up
this street. The bus stop is past where I need to get off so I
have to walk five minutes to get back to the corner. I check
the map again. The street I'm following should take me into
the neighbourhood I had marked on the map. That was lucky
because I hadn't checked the map on the bus.

Lucky. Hmm. Perhaps it was Lucky, perhaps it was just me. I
must be on my guard against hope and fantasy. All I can respond

to is my inner sense of direction. I keep walking up a steep rise. A wicked part of my mind tries to convince me that my inner sense of direction could choose an easier path than this.

The closer I get, the more I start to doubt myself. Sue is confused, becoming addled. The drink is mixed with something else other than grief. It's hard to hold on to her. Plus what if I go to someone's door and it isn't her? Then I'd be alone in a strange part of town with no money and no clues. Well, that isn't strictly true, I had $16 and her cell phone number. It could be more hopeless than that. I decide I need to clear my head again so I sit down on the footpath by a wall and relax.

It's still warm. There's a little traffic about but I can see the flickering light of TV sets in the houses about me. The stars are drowned out by the sodium streetlights. Sue is huddled, retreating and weeping. I have to climb this rise, then go down into the valley on the other side for about four hundred meters. I get up and walk up the rise and there is the valley. I walk down the other side: one hundred meters, two hundred, three hundred. There is a side street, one way in and out. The neighbourhood was new once, but it's lost its shine. The houses are mostly smaller and cheaper. People here drive, they don't walk. Sue is so small now, almost not there.

I know I'm close though as I walk down the side street. I'm being pulled to the end; a house on the right side of the turning bay. I walk all the way down to the end of the street. It's a small townhouse, probably two bedrooms, a trellis with flowers growing up it and a carport with a compact Nissan car in it. There are a few lights but not many. This is the place! Sue is tiny, but still just there.

I hesitate. I know I'm right, but I can't believe it. The house

66

is just so normal and boring. It's so random! It could belong
to anyone. The rational part of my mind wants evidence. But
there's no mail in the mailbox and nothing visible in the car
suggesting it belongs to Sue. I just know that it does.

There's a movement at a window next door. I realise I can't lurk
in the shadows or someone will call the cops and I'll have to
answer questions about Jaden, so I have to put my conviction
to the test. I step up to the door and press the doorbell, noticing
the "Neighbourhood Watch" sticker on the door.

Nothing happens. Sue is almost gone. A thousand embarrassing
scenarios flood through my mind. Some old lady, or another
complete stranger answering. I ring again. Then I knock. Sue
revives. I hear quick footsteps. And then a small voice from a
heart in a million shattered splinters.

"Rachel?" It's almost too sad to bear.

"Sue, it's Sam. Are you OK?"

"Sam?" her addled mind is a million miles away.

"Sam Kahu."

"*Sam Kahu?*"

"The Maori psychic kid from this morning."

She's right behind the red wooden door.

"You! What are you doing here?"

"Open the door Sue."

Sue unlocks the door and falls into the opening, holding onto
the handle, barely managing to stand up. She looks terrible in an
ugly pink tracksuit. Her face is wrinkled with crying, but she's
also droopy, almost asleep.

"Why are you here? You should be at that home," she drawls.
Her lids are half closed. Her breath smells of alcohol, but there's
more than that.

"One of the kids tried to knife me. Sue? Sue, what have you done?"

She doesn't seem to understand the question. She can barely stand. And then her eyes close, she just gives up, and pitches forward. I catch her and lift her inside, but her knees have gone and she's too heavy so I have to lie her on the floor. She stinks of alcohol. I tap her collarbone, slap her face and call her name. She moans but isn't responding, I already know why.

I turn her on her left side, one knee bent: the recovery position. I know she's taken pills and that getting them out before they're fully digested is essential.

"Sorry about this Sue," I tell her.

I open her mouth and shove two fingers down her throat. She promptly vomits all over me. There are pills mixed with noodles and now *I* stink of booze. She starts coughing. I keep her on her side, making sure her airway is clear and she is in no danger of drowning in her own vomit. I stay with her while she relaxes but I know the pills are already working and she needs way more help than I can give her.

I run down the passage and find myself in a small kitchen. The place is a mess. Obviously Rachel left in a hurry and has taken everything she owns. On the table was the note from Rachel (very short I thought), photo album, a chemist's pill container popped open like bubblewrap, and a bottle of vodka. I read the pill container label "Imovane – for sleep". As I'd suspected, sleeping tablets. There's a cordless phone. I grab it and punch in the emergency number.

"Emergency services. What is the nature of your emergency? Fire, Police or Ambulance?"

"Ambulance. I need an ambulance."

"What address are you calling from?"

"I don't know. There's a woman here, she's taken a heap of sleeping pills. Trace me."

"Stay on the line please. Where is the lady?"

"In the house by the door."

"Is anyone with her."

"No, there's just me I'm going back to her now."

"Stay on the line please."

"Roger."

That might sound dumb but it's what we said and I was used to it.

"We have your address as twenty one Rosewood Avenue, Waitakere City."

"Great! I have no idea if that's right. But send someone asap."

"Stay on the line please."

I go back to Sue, lick the back of my hand and put it under her nose. I am real worried she will stop breathing. Fortunately she is breathing. I take her pulse. It's hard to find, and slow.

"Are you still there?"

"Yes. She's breathing but it's shallow. Pulse is regular but weak."

"What's your name please?"

"Sam. What's yours."

"Annie." She sounded Maori to me.

"How old are you Sam?"

"Fourteen."

"You're doing fine Sam."

"How long will they be?"

"About ten minutes."

Sue is lying there asleep. If it weren't for the mess around her you'd think she had just decided to have a nap. I stroke her hair idly, like I used to when I cuddled Rewa to sleep. I wondered if she'd dream of Rachel.

"How well do you know this lady?" Annie was asking to pass the time.

"Not very well. I only met her today."

We chat quietly. Annie's a quiet, calm woman very like my Aunt Liz. We're even from the same tribe. Finally I can see the flashing lights by the door.

I go get the pill container. The ambulance guys come to the open door and call out. I tell them she's taken too many pills and give the container to them. They know they don't have much time and work quickly putting Sue on a stretcher and into the ambulance. They ask if I'm coming to. I tell them I'm waiting for a friend who is on their way.

It's a lie, of course, but they don't have time. The neighbours have come out to see what's going on. They don't know me but then they don't know Sue and Rachel either so though they are suspicious of me I say I've called her Police friends and I'm waiting for them. I

get strange looks from the neighbours but nobody says anything so as the ambulance drives off, I go back inside.

Now I can call Kevin. I pull out his card, feeling a bit sad. Sue's tried so hard to be a good cop but this can't be good for her career. Still, there's no point putting it off. Tomorrow she would hardly be able to pretend she'd had food poisoning. I dial the number.

Kevin sounds very tired when he answers his cell at 8:30pm.

"Kevin, Sue's just been taken to hospital."

"Sue? Sue who? Who is this?"

"Sam Kahu. Constable Sue Williams, she's just been taken to

hospital."

"Sam! Where are you? What's happened to Sue?"

"I'm at Sue's place."

"Sue's place!"

"Yeah."

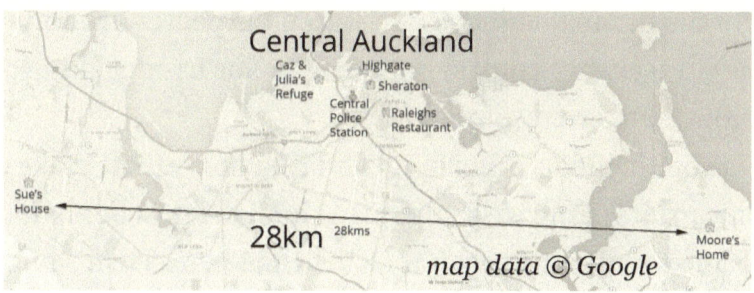

map data © Google

"Yeah, well there's a complaint we have to process in the morning, But what's happened to Sue? She didn't try to stab you too did she?"

I could hear the door of a car slam. He's on his way over and wants to keep me talking.

"No Kevin, her girlfriend, *Rachel,* left her today. She's taken too many pills."

There's a silence on the other end of the line.

"What did you say Sam? I'm not sure if I understood."

"Detective Constable Williams took too many sleeping tablets on top of about half a litre of Vodka. I got here just in time to make her spew them up and get an ambulance to her."

There was another long silence.

"Are you there, Kevin?"

"Yes. Sam, what's Sue's address?"

"Twenty one Rosewood Avenue, Waitakere City."

"Sam how did you get to Sue's house?"

"Bus and feet Kevin. How else could I get around the city?"

"Look OK, wait for me there will you Sam?"

"That was why I rang *you* Kevin. See you soon." I hung up.

I was now in Sue's bedroom. You could see where bits of furniture had been taken by Rachel. It was hard to know what was Sue's and what wasn't, but I guessed the drum kit and the posters of Sister Meg, Shiela E and Karen Carpenter drumming were Sue's. I feel a bit stink about being in Sue's room alone but I also know there are resources I need.

Her bag is on the floor. I pick it up and find her wallet. I take out my Omnicard from my wrist and press both sides to her bank card. I choose to use my account rather than hers. Then I find her cell. I open the back, take out the battery and find the Sim. I open the top of Qi, my watch, and put the Sim interface in the plastic putty which moulded itself to make contact. A second later it glows green to tell me it's copied the Simcard. I replace everything except her keys which I put in my pocket.

I find a small suitcase in the wardrobe and put it on the bed. I pack underwear (which makes me feel real creepy), loose clothes, and a jumper. Then I go into the bathroom. Rachel has ransacked it too. Sue doesn't have a lot of beauty stuff. Tahira had way more and she's fourteen. I grab a few things, which judging from where they are looks like she uses them most; plus her toothbrush – which looks very lonely all by itself. I put everything in the suitcase, close it and then put it by the door. Next I go back to the bathroom for a towel to wipe up the vomit. I wonder if the doctors might want a sample but decide they can get their own. I find the laundry and a carpet cleaner which looks useful and set to work. I'm making progress when Kevin drives up outside. I open the door and go back to work.

"I've made up her bag. It's by the door," I tell him while

scrubbing as he comes in.

He takes the bag and turns for the car. Then he comes back for me.

"Sam?"

"Hmmm?"

There's a pause. I'm still busy rinsing stink out of the carpet. I was thinking Sue would not need this smell to remind her what happened. It certainly isn't my favourite.

"Sam, why are you even here?"

"I couldn't stay at that place, Kevin, and I knew Sue was in trouble."

"So you crossed town by yourself and found Sue. Did you know where she lived?"

"Me? Nah."

"And now having called an ambulance you're cleaning up!"

"It's a bit disgusting."

"Sam you are amazing. I've never met a fourteen-year-old like you."

He means it too.

"I have," I smile, looking up at him, "there's five more of us where I come from."

He has nothing to say to that and puts Sue's bag in his car.

I finish up and put everything away again. Kevin comes back in looking awkward.

"Sam I ... I ... don't know what to do with you," he admits.

"What do you mean?"

"Well, I can't take you back to the Moore's tonight."

"No, you can't," I agree.

"But where else can I take you?"

"Well, I'm not under arrest am I?"

"You could be, but I'm not sure the cells in town are a great place for you either. I can't just turn you loose, you're a minor, you have to be in someone's care."

"Well, what about Sue's?"

"You can't stay here."

"No, I mean in Sue's care at the hospital."

"She can't care for you Sam."

"Kevin, I don't need care," I tell him looking him in the eye. "She does. I'll be in her care and she can be in mine."

Kevin looks doubtful. It's not so much about me, as about the rules.

"Just for tonight? We can sort something else tomorrow," I bargain.

"Oh, OK," he says turning to go. I follow him down the corridor. "At least I'll know where you are and if I take you anywhere else you'd probably just sneak off to the hospital anyway."

"That's probably true," I reply.

We get in the car.

"You smell pretty bad Sam."

"Yeah, she chucked all over me. I'm pretty damp as well."

"Have you eaten?"

"Not much."

"Tell you what, how about we go back to the station and I'll ask around to see if anyone's got some clothes your size then we'll get you fed and showered and then go to see Sue."

I'm surprised by this new goodwill. Kevin might have picked this up because he adds, "It's going to be a long wait at the hospital so you may as well be comfortable."

He's right so I agree. He calls up the station and there's a bit of a conversation about me in which he describes me.

"One hundred and fifty centimeters."

"One hundred and forty five," I correct him.

"One hundred and forty five centimeters."

"Fifty two kilos?" he guesses.

"Forty six."

"Forty six kilos."

"Waist is..." He asks questioningly

"Fifty six centimeters."

"Fifty six centimeters."

We always know exactly what size we are. None of us are large
– that's the point.

The station at night seems quite different to during the day.
More relaxed. More private too, in a way. They raided lost
property and found another hoodie, jeans and a t-shirt which
had the phrase: "Been nowhere, done nothing, stole the t-shirt",
on it. I like that because it's exactly the opposite of me. I have
a very quick shower because I don't want to be around any
beefy naked cops in case any come in. I get changed, put my old
clothes in a plastic bag, and get fed again at the canteen. I get
chicken and rice which is slightly better than boil-in-a-bag but
reminded me so much of Cam, whose dad had been the chef at
Renwick. I miss his cooking so much, it was so good.

True to his word Kevin gets me to the hospital by 10 p.m.
Kevin explains our deal to the nurse on the ward who says
it's impossible. Only adult relatives could be allowed to stay.
Children certainly not. We argue for about half an hour but it's
plain they don't want to know me. Finally Kevin says.

"Bugger this Sam, come back to my place, you can sleep on the
couch."

I agree. I'm really tired.

Kevin's house is about half an hour away. I doze in the car. When we get there Mrs Cooper – Diane – has already made up a bed for me on a convertible couch in the living room. I thank her and then we all go to bed.

For a moment I lie there in the dark in this strange new room trying to put together the day. Compared to many of the hard-out days I'd had over the past two years it was pretty tame. No one had been shooting at me and I wasn't seeing anyone bombed or shot, but in other ways it was challenging. I'd never been quite so alone as I felt now. At Renwick the challenges were greater but we faced them together. We were a team. Here, I have no back-up and no friendly advice in my head. There's just me, alone in a stranger's living room, with a motion detector on the ceiling with a tiny light that flashes every five seconds.

I thought about the messages and wondered how they would be received. One had gone to Britain so they probably only got it two hours ago. The other had gone to the network. They were spread around the globe so they never slept. They were Morozov's friends and called themselves Para.no.ID – and they were. I had no idea who they were. I wasn't meant to.

I drift. Everyone at Renwick has shrunk so that they could fit on a small glowing point of dust. I'm following this point of dust through Auckland calling out to them to take me with them and they're laughing and calling out, "not yet Sam, not yet", while I'm tripping and stumbling as they call out encouragements drifting ever higher out of reach.

Suddenly it's daylight and two little blonde girls in white woollen cardigans, blue velvet skirts with flowery embroidery and blue ribbons in their hair are standing staring at me with huge blue eyes. It's bizarre.

"He's awake!" they scream, and dash to their mum in the kitchen.

I don't want to be. But the morning cartoons, the radio, the noisy routine of a family getting ready for work and school isn't going to wait for a strange Maori boy asleep on a bed in the living room. Kevin comes over. He's in a suit looking fresh and ready for work.

"Don't you ever sleep?" I ask him crustily.

He smiles.

"Toast ? Milo ? Tea ? Coffee?"

I sigh and start to rouse myself.

"Toast and coffee – just black – please."

I find my jeans beside the bed and pull them on under the covers while the girls watch me curiously. Then I push aside the duvet and sit up. Kevin gives me a cup of coffee.

"Thanks."

I sit for a while on my bed sipping it, letting the coffee drift through my system. Tarik had taught me about coffee. He came from Turkey, though he was Kurdish.

I get up and start to fold up the duvet. We always made our beds at home. Grandpop had drilled that into me since I was five so it was almost automatic. Kevin's wife told me not too bother so I go into the kitchen to have some toast. Kevin drained his coffee, kisses his wife and kids, and we head out in the car.

"Now we have one little matter we have to deal with this morning," he says.

"What's that?"

"There's still you stabbing Jaden Smith to deal with."

"I didn't stab him. He was chasing me, I dropped, he fell over me and accidentally stabbed himself. It was all his own fault."

77

"Sure Sam, that's *your* story but we have to check out all sides.
Now, tell me what happened again, and leave out nothing."
So I do. He asks a lot of specific questions. I can see how he
would catch out anyone who lied. There's no lies in my story.
Finally he's satisfied. I was worried he was going to take me back
to the Moore's but instead we drove up to the hospital. He buys
a big bunch of flowers at the hospital shop and we then go up to
the ward. This time we're allowed in.

Sue looks embarrassed to see us. She's in bed wearing hospital
pyjamas. She looks strained and weak.

Kevin's surprisingly gentle with her. He doesn't talk about her
taking pills at all. He says a whole lot of stuff about stress which
seems to be aimed at reassuring her, and then says he needs to
go and run a few errands and that as she's the youth aid officer
she can interrogate me and still be on duty. Then he leaves us
alone. I'm liking Kevin a bit more. I sit opposite Sue in a big
armchair.

For a long time she says nothing and looks out the window.
Then the tears come to her eyes.

"You were right," she half gasps.

She sits there weeping. Then rubs her eyes, and blinks, putting
on that awful false smile.

"I was lucky you came along."

Her face folds and she looks down crying some more. I say
nothing. What do I know about why one adult can't face life
without another? It seems weird to me, but she's suffering, that's
clear to anyone. Finally my silence irritates her.

"Are you just going to sit there like a garden gnome? Say
something," she says angrily blowing her nose.

I laugh. That made her laugh too.

"I don't know what to say Sue," I tell her straight-up. "I've seen a lot of suffering. A real lot. But this is new to me."

It was the God's honest truth.

"It's love. A whole new form of suffering for you to look forward to when you're older," she says bitterly.

She looks at me again, thinking.

"You must be so tough," she says.

That surprises me.

"Me? I'm not tough."

"Your father kills your mother when you're a scrap, your childhood community ravaged by gangs and drugs, now you've lost everyone you care about to a crazy cult, and *I'm* the one in the psych ward, and *you're* here to comfort me. If that isn't tough what is?"

"It wasn't a cult," I say, annoyed.

"How do you do it?"

"What?"

"Keep going?"

I think about that for a moment. It doesn't occur to me not to. If I don't *they'll* get me and that, I didn't want to think about. Plus, the others will be trying to rescue me, so I just have to do my job.

"Hope, I guess." I reply, honestly enough. "Hope, and a bit of fear."

"Hope," Sue repeats. She's going to crumble again...

"You have to have hope to hope," and she bursts into tears.

Now I *do* know what to do and I go forward and put my arms around her. She holds onto me like she's holding on for dear life. She's crying uncontrollably. It's a strange feeling to be held by a grown woman who's falling apart. Her breasts are pressed against me which feels nice but I feel wrong about liking it. I wish I was older because I'm sure if I was, I'd know what I was meant to do. But slowly, as I hold her, I begin to realise that I'm not meant to *do* anything. I'm just meant to stand there, be held, and get my shoulder wet.

Finally she lets me go. She dries her eyes on the sheets and I go back to the chair.

"Thanks Sam, I really needed that," she gasps.

"S'Ok."

She sighs deeply.

"So how did you end up at my house?"

I tell her the whole story, except for the bits about the Omnicard and copying her sim. I just pretend I had a bankcard all along. She's shaking her head.

"You bussed clear across Auckland and found me by psychic powers alone?"

"It's not that special. Animals do it all the time. Cats and dogs can't *smell* their old families when they move hundreds of kilometers away, they just home. It's just knowing how to let it come to you. There are loads of powers we all have, but we don't listen to them. I just know how to listen."

"You didn't have my address?"

"No. You never gave it to me."

"That's still pretty special," she says appreciatively.

She smiles at me in silence for a while, and then a thought strikes her.

"Why did you bother?"

"What?"

"Not what Sam, 'pardon'."

"Pardon?"

"Why did you bother ?"

"What?" I'm totally confused.

"Why did you bother coming all the way to save me?"

"I didn't ... I was escaping that nutter Jaden."

"No, you realised I'd taken pills and you set about saving me straight away. Why?"

"I dunno," I say honestly, "I mean you can't let someone die ..."
I think about that." ... not if you can help it. And ... well ... I like you. You remind me a bit of my Aunt Liz and ... and..."

"Yes?"

Mum's there; a presence in the room.

"A bit of my mum."

We both sit there thinking about what I'd said. It's true. She's practical and gay like my Aunt, but pretty and fun like my mum. Like my mum she's suffered in a bad relationship – though obviously not as much.

Sue smiles.

"And you *could* save me," she adds quietly.

Ouch! She means when I was four I couldn't save my mum.

Now it's my turn to fight off the tears.

"Yes ... and I *could* save you."

There's a silence between us, but a smile spreads across her face like the sun coming out. She sighs.

"That's the first thing anyone's said to me so far that's made me want to be rescued. Thank you for saving me Sam."

I can tell my mum is proud of me too. I can feel a big smile on her face.

"Man, what a wreck I am," Sue reflects.

I say nothing.

"I feel like I'm in a helicopter and I've just been saved from this

yacht which was my life that's being destroyed by the ocean
and I'm looking down at it and thinking what did I think I was
doing?"

I smile, remembering.

"Dead people tell me the same sort of thing all the time."

For a second she looks shocked. And then thoughtful.

"Maybe death and losing love feel the same."

I leave that alone. What do I know?

She starts to tell me about Rachel: when, and where they met;
how she'd fallen in love with her. How they'd planned things
that never happened. The little betrayals. The social circles
they'd moved in. How she'd felt weird being a cop when so many
friends were hostile to the police. The gradual loss of love. The
fights.

To be honest she isn't talking to me, she's talking to herself. I'm
just an excuse. I shut up and let her go for it. It seems to help.
She isn't crying anymore, though sometimes she gets quite
emotional and angry with some memory or other. After an hour
and a half she sort of talks herself out.

"Do you think I'll see her again?" she asks. She means Rachel.

"Yip," I reply. I know it. It will be short, sharp and unpleasant.
Sue looks uncomfortable.

"You will," I predict, "but you won't take any more of her shit."
Sue sighs.

"I don't feel strong enough," she confesses.

"You'll surprise yourself."

"Will it be soon?" she asks. There's a hint of a hope that being in
hospital might bring Rachel back out of pity.

"Nope. A few weeks."

That makes her bitter and angry. Then she worries what her

parents will say. Once again she talks herself through it.

A ward psychologist pops in to say hello. The exchange doesn't last long. The doctor seems to realise I'm helping his patient more than he can so he leaves us alone.

We have lunch together and the conversation swings around to me. I still have no idea where I'll be sleeping that night. Then Sue asks me to pick up my story from where I'd left off last time. So I do.

•••

CHAPTER FIVE: LEAVING HOME

My dad's release was weighing on everyone's minds. It was the beginning of December 2007. The weather was getting hot and shiny with the first signs of summer. School was drifting towards the long holidays in a series of sports days that involved athletics and swimming. Everyone seemed more annoyed by Christmas than excited by it. Even the spray-on snow writing in the shop windows seemed dumber than ever. I was in the school swimming events for the two hundred meter freestyle and one hundred meter backstroke. By now I was at the end of junior school. Next year I'd have to go to Northland High. That seemed far off enough for me not to feel too worried. Right then I felt confident about my world. I knew the kids, the teachers and the way it all hung together. I was on road safety patrol before school and after. I knew my way around the area and all the shopkeepers. And I felt confident about my chances in the swimming – the one thing I knew I was good at.

But the parole board was meeting soon to decide whether my dad would be given parole before Christmas. They had met before and turned him down. He'd written letters dressing his rage in see-through Christian clichés: "judge not lest ye be judged," etc etc. It was obvious his interpretation of the Bible was all about his own righteousness. Christianity to him was all about "God's will" which he couldn't tell apart from his own. Forgiveness and love didn't really come into it.

But this time was going to be different, he said. Apparently he had this expensive lawyer the gang used representing him. Grandpop and Aunty Liz were worried that an expensive lawyer counted for more in the eyes of the parole board than the letters they had written asking the board to consider me and Rewa.

It felt like a summer thunderstorm: hot, sticky, and heavy. If they let him out over Grandpop and Aunty Liz's objections he would probably be back in town within a week. I wasn't sure what that would mean, but I was pretty sure I wouldn't like it. Not even Ax's allies seemed happy about the idea of him coming out. Clive tried to make a joke about it at school but it fell flat because nobody thought it funny. Some of the big men in, or near, the gang knew that Ax would mean less freedom from the gang's leaders in Auckland that Ax was tied up with. And although no one would admit it, I think a lot of people were scared of him.

There was a lot to be scared about. Apparently he was even bigger now than he was when he went in – and that was big enough. With nothing to do but work-out, take smuggled drugs, grease gang leaders and read the Bible, he was a dangerous combination of crazed, frustrated and very, very powerful. And yet for the parole board he would, "lie down with the lamb," in his own words. While at the same time he promised us he would "bring the sword" to the unrighteous in the community – by which he meant anyone who disagreed with him.

High on that list was almost certainly going to be Grandpop. Grandpop wasn't a big talker. I found him strangely hard to read. Most of the time you had no idea what he was thinking.

He had never talked to us about our mother when she was alive before, but now she seemed to be on his mind. He also seemed to be thinking about his life a lot. That night at dinner he even apologised to Aunty Liz for being "a useless father".

"Dad? What do you mean?" she asked, surprised at his talk.

Grandpop was bent over his food, his gray hair glinting in the light from the living room, deep shadows on his lined, brown face.

"I was never there. Your mum did all the work."

He paused to chew. Chew and reflect.

"I thought it was more important for me to be in the jungle fighting communists than looking after my little girls," he paused again.

"And the communists were going to win anyway. I knew that. The yanks didn't have a clue."

He rested his elbow on the table like he told us not to do, but he was distracted by talking to Aunty Liz.

"It was just vanity. I wanted see how good a soldier I could be. But who was I fighting for? It wasn't you, despite what I told myself at night in the jungle, it was me. I was as wrapped up in myself as that piece of shit (by which he meant Ax)."

Liz said something to calm his conscience but you could tell he didn't believe it.

When he wasn't fishing he started going out at night on "exercises".

I was only a kid really. I didn't realise that his midnight trips into the bush were a rehearsal for what Grandpop thought would be a final battle between himself and Ax. So one night when I saw him go out I slipped on my black tracksuit and followed him. I thought I was pretty cool at being a Ninja. I had no idea.

The bush at night is very, very dark. I walked in trying to be as
sneaky as possible because I thought I might find out where
Grandpop kept his gun. I'd seen him head along a path I knew
pretty well during daylight, and even twilight. But now with no
moon and the deep shadows of the trees it was hard to avoid
stumbling. Foolishly, I wanted to surprise Grandpop. I should
have known better.

Suddenly a shadow grabbed me in an iron grip, hand over
my mouth and I was off my feet and face down in the dark
being pinned by his weight. It all happened so fast I had no
time to make a sound. Then Grandpop whispered something
that terrified me. I didn't know what it was because it was in
Vietnamese. And I got a reading, a flash, that he had done this to
a kid in Vietnam before and that this memory was alive to him
right now as if the past forty years had vanished.

And that really scared me because suddenly he wasn't Grandpop
anymore but a foreign soldier; a soldier who might kill me in an
instant in a dozen different ways, and nobody would know 'til
they found my body, if indeed they ever did. And then he rolled
off me.

"What are you doing out here boy? You should be in bed," he
hissed.

The fact that he was still whispering showed that while he knew
it was me, his instincts were still locked in the war. I was still a
bit shocked.

"I ... I... wanted to see..." I began but trailed off, knowing he
wouldn't like my wanting to know where he kept his gun.

To my surprise Grandpop laughed for quite a while.

I was confused. Finally he stopped.

"You can't see – that's the whole point," he smiled.

He got up.

"Look, watch me."

And he slid off into the dark. I watched for a while. His shadow moved and then wasn't there. I listened hard. There were a few sounds but within half a minute I had completely lost track of him. Finally I couldn't stand it.

"Grandpop!" I whispered loudly.

"Behind you," he said, making me leap out of my skin.

I turned. He was smiling.

"You can't see Sam because there *is* no light in there. Even using a Starlite you'd never see anything. Now you try."

I tried to sneak off but I tripped, crunched something and while I was distracted Grandpop vanished. I snuck back to try and find him but I couldn't see any sign of him.

"Grandpop?" I hissed.

There was no answer.

"Grandpop?"

Still no answer.

I went back to where he'd been. He was gone. I looked around for him for a while but after calling a few times I gave up and went home. I kept a watch from my window but I fell asleep.

The day of the parole board hearing Grandpop was due to go fishing. I woke early. It was just starting to get light and the birds in the bush behind the house were singing their heads off. I lay in bed listening to them, and the sounds of Rewa breathing softly in her sleep, and Grandpop moving around in the kitchen. The air was still a bit chilly and while I wanted to see Grandpop off, I wanted to put off the moment when I actually got out of bed.

Finally, I reached the point where I knew it was now or never. I jumped out of bed, chose some clothes from the big old dresser with sticky drawers, pulled off my pyjamas, and shuddered into the fresh cold cloth, pulling on my hoodie. Then I went down the hall into the kitchen-dining room barefoot. The clock on the wall showed the time to be a little after six. Grandpop was listening to the news on the radio and finishing the last of his coffee and cigarette.

I knew better than to interrupt the news, so I went to the cupboard and made myself a huge plate of wheat brix with hot water and milk. Then I sat down opposite Grandpop and started eating. I have no idea what was in the news – in those days I didn't pay any attention to it – but the weather forecast said there would be fine weather for a few days until the tail end of a tropical cyclone (Murray, I think) would bring us a bit of a storm. Grandpop acknowledged this news with a bit of a grunt and a sigh.

"Have to make it quick I guess," he said, putting out the ciggy.

"When do you think they'll let us know about Ax?" I asked.

"Dunno ... committees like that take their time. I reckon the bush telegraph will tell us quicker," he said.

"If they let him out ..." I began.

"*If* ..." he said sternly.

"He won't ... well he won't be able to ..."

"What Sam?"

"Take us away?"

Grandpop looked at me seriously.

"Not while I'm alive, son," he said.

Then he smiled, a grim smile.

"And he may have paid his debt to society but as far as I'm

concerned he hasn't paid his debts to me."

I didn't quite know what that meant, so I said nothing,

"Don't worry Sam, you'll see," he said, "His bark is worse than his bite. He may pretend to be a mongrel but strip away all the talk, and he's still the sad little puppy, he always was."

I felt encouraged by Grandpop's toughness. It was just a shame he was completely wrong.

He stood up.

"Coming out to the boat?"

I came out and slipped my feet into my boots on the verandah by the front door. I strolled down the front steps with Grandpop, who lit another ciggy, and then down the road to the jetty. The jetty was only twenty five meters up the road – within view of the house. Grandpop's boat "Hua Kai" (named after a legendary fishing hook) was an eight meter aluminium cabin work-boat with two 500cc outboards and he wouldn't moor it anywhere he couldn't see it. Everyone knew better than to mess with it.

Today there was already other activity on the jetty. It was only about twelve meters long and could take four boats at most. Jack Barry had come back in and he and his brother, Ed, were unloading the catch into wheely-bins, and rolling them over the road to Ed's basement freezers next door.

The wheely-bins had been lifted from Whangarei early one morning before the rubbish contractor had made his rounds. The rubbish ended up on the mayor's lawn. Everyone thought that was very funny.

"Hey Mike," Ed called out cheerfully to Grandpop as he pushed his bin over the road.

Ed was one of those likeable guys who always seems to be smiling. Grandpop and Ed stopped to chat in the middle of the road – which was pretty normal around our place because there was no traffic – while I went on to join the other kids who were helping Jack on the boat. Among the kids was Joey so I joined him shifting gear onto the jetty. Then Grandpop came over and started talking to Jack about his catch and the weather while getting ready to cast off.

Suddenly this big new Land Cruiser came up the road heading towards town. This was strange because, as I say, there was never much traffic on the road. It slowed down and then crawled past the jetty. Normally drivers would find an excuse to stop and chat, but not these two. They cruised past, eyes hidden behind their shades, their faces unreadable through the open window. Then they roared off down the road.

Ed appeared with his wheely bin on the other side of the road and shouted after them.

"Don't be scared! We won't eat you!" Then he pulled a face and stuck out his tongue in a traditional challenge.

Everyone found that funny. Then he crossed the road to join us. The men were talking about the gang and the way they were encouraging everyone to take too many shellfish.

"Ay, but they're clever too," Jack said, "They get their fancy pants lawyers to buy fishing quota and all that eh?"

Not many people in the bay worried too much about official fishing quota much. Most relied on traditional Maori fisheries rights. There were numbers and sizes people stuck to because that was how it worked. They knew there was a special right for Maori because we were here first. The main thing was that the fishery was kept in balance and that was something we had done for hundreds of years without a whole bunch of forms and papers from the Government.

Everyone agreed the gang was a pain. Then the talk turned to the parole hearing. Ed and Jack weren't keen on Ax on the loose either and they ended up all agreeing that if anyone saw him on the road it wouldn't be a bad thing if they got distracted and ran over him. There were a lot of jokes about the stories they'd tell in court.

Eventually Grandpop cast off and the rest of us went back to Ed's place. I remember looking over my shoulder and seeing Grandpop powering away out into the bay, looking powerful and relaxed on his way back out to sea, and I knew I would never see him like that again.

I went back home and found Rewa having her breakfast with Aunty Liz. She was asking a lot of questions about Ax, who she couldn't remember, and was a bit scared of. Aunty Liz was trying to reassure her that everything would be OK and that he didn't want to hurt her.

Rewa looks a lot like Mum did at the same age. I've seen the old pictures. I knew that this reminder of her dead sister made Aunty Liz especially protective towards Rewa. At the same time I knew I looked a lot like Ax and it worried Grandpop, in particular, that this might attract my father's attention more than the little reminder of the woman he'd killed. So we set out for school with none of Rewa's questions answered. We were a thoughtful pair as we followed the familiar path to school.

"Why do they have to let him out of jail at all?" Rewa asked me. I had no idea. It didn't seem fair to me that Mum was dead and the man who killed her would be back walking around like nothing had happened.

"You know what I think," I told Rewa quietly.

"What?"

"I think Grandpop's planning to shoot him," I whispered.

"But then *he'll* go to jail," Rewa pointed out.

"Yeah," I replied defensively, "but at least we won't have to worry about Ax."

"I don't want Grandpop to go to jail and I don't want Ax to come out," she said.

She had a point. The only hope was the parole board would see it that way too. They didn't. Aunty Liz picked us up after a good day where I'd come second in the two hundred meters. It wasn't 'til dinner time that Rebecca called to say Ax had been granted parole and would be let out at the weekend. Then she dropped a bombshell.

"He says he wants visiting rights," she told Aunt Liz.

Aunty Liz couldn't believe her ears.

"What?"

"He says he's going to go the family court to get visiting rights, before going for joint custody."

"He's dreaming."

"That's what he says ... I thought you should know."

Aunty Liz kept this to herself, and pretended she was just worried about Ax's getting parole. She tried to shush us into bed early but I stayed up and listened in to her talking to her friends about it. That was how I found out. I guess like my Aunt I was hoping Grandpop's return in the morning would stop the rising sense of dread that was knotting my stomach. It didn't work out that way.

The next morning was a nervous sort of day. I didn't let on to Rewa or Aunty Liz what I'd heard. Aunty Liz was bustly. Grandpop would come back sometime today or tomorrow but we didn't know when. It depended on the fishing. On the way to school I reassured Rewa that Ax would probably bring her lots of toys to butter her up. But she could tell the difference between money and love.

Then, when we came back from school that afternoon there was more bad news. Two big utes were drawn up outside the Barry's house, but this time it wasn't the gang. One was the Police, and the other had Ministry of Fisheries written on it. Two blue uniformed men, one Maori, one white, in peaked caps were walking around the place while the local cop, Constable Rawhiri, watched on. I saw Ed following along after them and he was not his usual smiley self at all. He looked very worried and barely glanced at me as he opened the basement to the men. Joey came over and we went up into the bush to play for a bit.

Joey looked confused and hurt and talked bitterly about the men.

It turned out he was right to worry. Ed was taken away in the police car. We had tea with the Barry family that night. Aunty Liz and "Aunty" Jacky talked and we kids played for hours waiting for Ed to come back. But at ten o'clock when there was still no sign of him we all gave up and went to bed.

The next day on the playground we began to realise that the whole community was splitting into gang families and non-gang families. The Barry kids learned that the gang was behind the arrest of their father because they had fixed it with the Fisheries Inspectors. Worse was to come.

When we came home we found Aunty Liz weeping. I could see Huia Kai at its mooring so I asked the obvious question.

"Where's Grandpop?"

"They took him away," Aunty Liz told us.

There's an old Maori poem about death that goes that when a

great tree falls another takes its place. But right now it felt like a great tree had gone and left us completely exposed. That night Ed came back but he was still not smiling and worse he couldn't look any of us in the eye. He cuddled his own kids and wife a lot and told them they would be OK. He was nothing like so reassuring to Aunty Liz though. He tried to nervously reassure her it was just a bunch of questions about catch figures.

The week was running out. Soon Ax would be released and Grandpop was locked up! We were a very quiet trio at tea that night.

Then in the middle of the night I awoke to wild cheering. There was a flickering light on my windowsill. I ran down the hall to the living room to find Aunty Liz in the dark, staring out the window, with tears running down her cheeks. Over by the jetty there were two SUVs silhouetted by the blazing fire on Huia Kai.

"They're burning Grandpop's boat," I yelled and ran to the front door.

Aunty Liz chased me and caught me before I could open it. I always thought I was pretty strong but Aunty Liz was that much stronger. She stopped me.

"You are not going out there! You saw what they did to Honé Poukawa and don't think they wouldn't give it to you too!"

"But we can't just watch!" I shouted.

"We can, and we will," Aunty Liz said.

Woken by our shouting Rewa came out sleepily with her teddy-rabbit, Mr Nibbles, in her arms and we all hugged together and watched Grandpop's boat burn.

Of course we called the cops and Constable Rawhiri came out in the morning. But as Aunty Liz explained, old Wiremu Rawhiri wasn't going to come out and risk being killed for a boat. Ed didn't come over to show solidarity, but at least Jacki did. You could tell she was angry, even though she also knew her husband had ratted us out.

School that day was awful. Rewa was worried about Grandpop, and Ax. And now, to make matters worse, the gang-related kids picked on us too. I was glad Clive was at High now. Rewa was crying on the way home, and I admit, I was close to tears myself. When we got there we found Grandpop was home. He gave Rewa a huge hug and me one too. He seemed strangely calm. He told us to go and tidy our room while Aunty Liz made dinner. He sat at the table with the Auckland Star open and his reading glasses on. Then at dinner, looking over his half-moon glasses, he made his announcement.

"Liz, I want you and the kids to move out tomorrow."

"What? Are you crazy dad? This is our home. I've got a job, I can't just walk off!"

"As of last night Elizabeth, this isn't a place for children."

"But dad..."

"No, Elizabeth! I don't want you or the kids around. I want you to go to Auckland, find a place to stay and make a new life. This life is over! Now, I've got a few thousand put aside. It will be enough to live on while you get yourself sorted. There's a lot of demand for experienced nurses so you won't have any problem finding work."

"And what are you going to do?"

"Don't worry about me."

"No, I do worry about you. What are you going to do?"

"I'm going to finish what they started," Grandpop said grimly.

"Dad, don't be a fool!" Aunty Liz cried

"I'm not a fool. I'm a soldier," he replied matter-of-factly.

"So you want to fight them," Aunty Liz asked, as mockingly as she dared.

"Elizabeth I'm not a silly old man with a fantasy of being young again. I know what I'm talking about. *I* know what's at stake. I don't want to fight them, but they've declared war on me and given me no choice. I don't fight because I want some fun, I fight to win. 'To put the enemy out of action and eliminate his ability for attack as quickly and efficiently as I can'. Like the book says. But to win I have to have full latitude of action. I can't win if I'm outnumbered and forced to defend you and the kids," he explained patiently.

There was a pause as we digested what he'd said. To me it made sense.

"So," he continued, "the solution is simple. I must get you out of harms way. You have to be hidden and safe and I must have no idea where you are until it's safe for you to return."

Aunty Liz was still looking unhappy.

"But the kids' school is here," Aunty Liz objected.

"The year's nearly over. Kids shift schools all the time."

"But their friends..."

"It doesn't feel like we have a lot of friends at school, mum... Aunty Liz," I said.

She looked at me struggling with emotion. We always were careful to acknowledge my mother, but Aunty Liz was the only mum I could really remember and now, as the pressure was going on it seemed natural to call her 'mum'.

"What about my job?"

"Take leave, you've got months, then give notice."

"What about the car? I can't take the car it's hospital property."

"Take mine, I've still got the bike and that'll be more useful to me anyway."

"Dad..." Aunty Liz began, but Grandpop interrupted.

"Kids go to your room and pack everything you need. Pack your favourite toys, your favourite clothes. If it's not your favourite leave it behind. OK, off you go. Aunty Liz and I need to talk."

So Rewa and I went off to pack, feeling like something huge was about to happen and not having much idea what it would be like. Finally, Aunty Liz came in to see us.

"Well, I've talked to Grandpop and we've agreed that we'll go away for a few weeks. Work owes me months and months of holidays anyway. If we find something we like, we stay, but if we don't, we can come back. So it's a kind of holiday eh?"

Rewa is always quick to spot a chance. She came up and sat on Aunty Liz's lap.

"Aunty Liz, if we're going to have a holiday in Auckland can we go to Rainbows End?"

The idea of visiting the kid's amusement park made Aunty Liz smile for a short moment.

"Maybe we can Rewa," she said, "maybe we can."

...

"And that's how we came to leave my home village," I told Sue.

CHAPTER SIX: REPRIEVE

By the time I finish telling my story it's starting to get dark. A nurse had interrupted to tell Sue she would be moved to the psych' ward tomorrow for assessment and, all going well, she'd be back home by tomorrow afternoon.

I'm getting edgy. The day's nearly up and I have no idea where I will be sleeping tonight. On one level that's good. If *I* don't know, *they* can't know either! Then just as the 6 o'clock news is starting on TV, Kevin comes in. After talking to Sue and being told I'm providing a lot of useful background information, he turns to me.

"Sam, there's been a bit of a development in the case involving you."

I look surprised. Sue looks interested too.

"You have a lawyer. Actually a Queens Counsel, which is the most senior kind there is."

"Michael!" I reply happily. The message *had* got through.

"You *know* him?" Kevin asks, surprised.

"He's Dr Prosperov's English immigration lawyer. He has others."

He had also helped our family, and very well too.

"Well, because your Aunt signed a document making him your legal representative in her absence, he is temporarily also your

99

legal guardian."

"But he's in London," I point out.

"No, he's on his way here," Kevin tells me.

That is not a total surprise. Michael loves to fly – he has a large historical aircraft collection as well as his Dassault Falcon business jet.

"Anyway it means that your accommodation's organised. Apparently he's hired someone to ... um ... well ... mind you ... until he gets there."

"Who?"

"I don't know. So long as you are safe, and in the custody of a legal adult, it doesn't actually matter for the moment."

That set off a silent alarm in my head. Someone *did* know where I was sleeping tonight and I *didn't* know them. Maybe I had been too relaxed about my uncertainty. But I didn't want to make a fuss just yet.

"Oh. What about Jaden?"

"Hmm? Oh him! He withdrew his complaint. His story was hopeless. Um ... now could I have a quick word with Sue in private Sam?"

I wander off to the ward reception. I wonder where Michael, Sir Michael actually, had put me up. I also wonder who my minder would be. I imagine some sort of heavy movie dude in a suit, with a fast car. On the other hand it's a risk, because we'd been betrayed by someone we knew. If the minder was one of *them* I'd have to escape. I didn't have any of our normal weapons. I feel nervous. I also wonder if I could get some new clothes. I feel a bit cruddy wearing the lost property bin stuff.

Kevin joins me and we make our way to his car. He manoeuvres through the hospital driveways, which is slow because it's drive-time, and we get out into the heavily congested evening traffic.

"Sue says you are really helping her," he tells me.

"I'm just listening."

"And talking," he adds, "she says listening to your story makes her feel better."

"That's good."

"Would you mind talking to her tomorrow Sam?"

"No problem. Though she has to see the psychologist tomorrow. Is that to make sure she won't do it again?"

"Yeah."

"Kevin?"

"Yeah?"

"Is Sue going to lose her job?"

Kevin won't say anything for a moment. He's not sure.

"It's complicated Sam. I hope not."

The traffic crawls slowly on. I notice we are driving back into town.

"How's the case coming along?" I ask eventually, more for something to say than anything, as I know he hasn't a chance of getting far.

"Well, your friend Sir Michael Hamilton-Smythe Q.C is going to hold it up a lot."

"Why's that?"

"He's insisting that Renwick House is a private home which may have burned down by accident rather than because of any criminal act. He says it's quite reasonable to presume that your friends and family are somewhere else so while we can investigate the cause of the fire until there is actually evidence it is a crime scene, we have no right to treat it as one."

Kevin is wondering if Sir Michael is already in contact with Dr

Prosperov. I knew that was not very likely because he didn't know much about us, really. Nothing secret anyway, but I wondered why he wanted access to the house.

"You mean never?" I check, surprised.

"Well, that depends on what the judge says."

"When will that happen?"

"After the weekend probably."

"Oh."

"So how do you know this Sir Michael?" Kevin wants to know.

"He visited Renwick a few times."

"What's he like?"

"Umm, well, he's nuts about flying. He gave us a trip in his business jet once and he loves air shows. There's an old Russian plane at that air show they have down south that gets him excited. Wanted to buy one I think."

"So he's rich?"

"Not as rich as Dr Prosperov, but yeah, he's pretty rich. He helps very rich Arabs or Russians move to other countries or buy islands and stuff."

"And English?"

"Yeess, but he's not old and crusty."

I think a bit more about him.

"... Speaks Russian and Arabic, and, oh yeah, he likes rugby. He went to school there."

"Tall? Short? Dark? Blond?"

"Tall and blond. Good looking. Blue eyes, very blue eyes."

"How old? Wife? Kids?"

"Oh, he's pretty old, about same as you."

Kevin chuckles.

"What?" I ask.

"I'm only forty four."

"Yeah."

Kevin sighs, "so family?" he asks.

"He has a daughter, but he's not married now. She died I think. The daughter's a bit older than us, about seventeen or eighteen. I think she goes to school in Switzerland or something. Anyway, I've never seen her around, or met her. He has a picture of her on his desk though."

"I thought he was based in London. How do *you* know?" Kevin asks me suddenly.

Whoops! I am going to have to watch this guy. I was getting sucked in there! I'd only seen the picture when I was bugging him one night for Dr P.

"On his plane," I lie quickly.

"Why were you on his plane?"

Man, this guy is seriously on my case!

"He flew us to Northland for the non-mol ... you know, where the judge says my father can't come around," I say.

"So Sir Michael knows *you*? You're not just one of the crowd to him?"

"Yes. He actually helped us Kahus out with some legal problems we had with my father."

"For free?"

"To us," I shrug. "Dr P probably paid him heaps. We couldn't, we never had any money. I mean it probably cost more for him to fly us to court than my Grandpop ever made in his life."

"Hmmm ... interesting man," Kevin remarks.

I could have said that compared to most of the people at Renwick Sir Michael is a rich playboy who knows nothing. But looking at Kevin I realise he still has a simple awe of people so much richer than himself.

"*You* could say that," I agree.

Town comes gradually closer. We pass under the high rises, negotiate the busy motorways and drive down the narrow streets until we come to ...

"The Highgate," says Kevin.

We get out and a young man in a dark green uniform with a dumb hat comes up and drives Kevin's car off to park it. I'm not much into international hotels. They seem like embassies of the rich and the greedy to me. We go through the foyer to the lifts.

"Officially, of course, you aren't a guest of the hotel. You're the guest of your minder, who is the guest of the hotel. My instructions are to take you to room 527 and so long as I'm comfortable that he checks out, and you're OK, to leave you in his care."

We get into the lift. I'm getting really nervous now. There's something here that isn't right. Something's wrong. Not close by, but somewhere. It's just an instinct, but I take my instincts very seriously. They've saved me quite a few times. If this guy is an infiltrator I have to act immediately. Their mind control powers are way more powerful than mine.

"Kevin?"

"Hmm?"

"It's really good of you to look after me."

"That's OK, Sam."

I can't think of anything much, but I don't want to have to track Kevin's place down the same way I had Sue's if it everything turns to crap.

"Kevin?" I ask again as we get out of the lift into the hushed hallway.

"Yeah?"

"Could I have your home address and phone number?"

He looks a bit questioning.

"Just in case."

"Sure Sam."

I take his rather crumpled card out of my pocket. He writes his number and address on the back, against the wall and hands it to me. As Grandpop had always told us, *always* have a back-up. We knock at the door. To our surprise a woman's voice answers it.

"Come in, it's open."

Kevin opens the door. It's quite a spacious room with a lounge, and dining area with a huge flat-screen TV, all in brown, white and gray. The last light of the day is streaming in the window, standing next to which is a tallish woman about the same age as Kevin, wearing a crisp, white suit with a purple, silk blouse, drinking a cup of something, still looking out the window. She has long, dark wavy hair and now turns her sparkling brown eyes on us.

"Hi, I'm Leonora," she says in a casually English accent, nose in the air.

I don't like her already.

"Detective?" she says, coming forward and shaking Kevin's hand.

"Detective Sergeant Cooper," he replies "Kevin."

And then the big glow for the cameras as her face breaks into a huge smile and she falls on me in a way which told me she'd never had anything to do with teens in her life.

"And you must be Samuel," she says pretending delight.

"Sam," I correct her quietly.

"Sam. Well you and I are going to have a jolly nice time together until Michael arrives. He's told me I have to spoil you rotten. Sounds like fun doesn't it."

"Yes," I admit smiling. It jolly well does.

Best of all she's human, and, as far as I can tell, exactly what she says she is.

"Good ... so Detective?"

"Ma'am?"

"Do I have to sign anything?"

"No, but if you have a card I'd appreciate one. Sam is technically still a witness in our inquiry."

She gives him one of those huge fake smiles she specialises in. She's way better at it than Sue. I wonder if she's an actress.

"But of course," she replies and goes to her bag.

She *is* a private detective. Her reading is quite clear. She is safe. Nothing to do with *them*. Sir Michael has sent her ahead. Her accent is fake, she originally came from Liverpool and her name had been Debbie. She'd been in the Police briefly, then moved to London and joined a private detective agency. After a while she had started her own company. She likes deceptions and is naturally nosey. She gives Kevin her card.

"I'm afraid it's not much use to you Mr Cooper. As you can see I work from London but my 'phone works here just as well."

Kevin's wondering whether Leonora is her real name, and what sort of other things she hires herself out for, but he remains friendly.

"Well, thanks very much. I suppose you'll be here and contactable on your cell?"

"Of course."

"Sam, I know Leonora wants to spoil you rotten and after the past few days I'm sure you're up for that, but I'd just ask you to remember Sue tomorrow afternoon."

He's really interested in seeing if he can get me to tell Sue everything he hadn't got out of me back in interview room four.

"I won't forget Sue, Kevin," I assure him.

"Thanks," he straightens up. "Well, I'll leave you to your spoiling. Have a good time."

He turns and leaves. I feel vaguely abandoned.

"Well Sam, I imagine you're hungry," Leonora says picking up her bag. "What would you like to eat?"

She ushers me back out the door.

I almost say "McDonald's" just to confirm her expectations, but I want to enjoy a good meal again after a week of grabbed pies and rubbish. So, what with Cam's dad being the chef at Renwick, and because I'd learned a lot about different foods from around the world over the past two years, I decide to tell her what I really want.

"Vietnamese, but Thai's good too," I add, trying not to be too difficult.

"Oh!" Leonora exclaimed, "And here was me thinking you'd want McDonald's!"

"There's plenty of Thai places in Auckland. Vietnamese too if you know where to look," I tell her.

We walk to the lift.

"I just ask the concierge, they usually have a worthwhile suggestion," she says, letting me in first.

And Leonora is right. The concierge has a suggestion not five minutes walk away. He calls for us, and reserves the table in the name of Cartwright.

"So why do you like Vietnamese food, Sam?" she asks as we walk along the pavement. It's still sunny and quite warm.

"Because of Cam, my friend at Renwick and her dad who was the cook there."

"Oh I see. I thought you might have been there."

"I have, several times."

"Several times?" she asks in a half mocking sort of voice suggesting I'm making it up but that she likes me anyway.

"Yes, but only once just for the food. Do you like it Leonora?"

"Me? Ah, well I don't really know. Is it like Thai or Chinese? I like them."

"You'll like it then, trust me."

We find the restaurant without too much difficulty. The best sign is most of the people eating there are Vietnamese. We're shown to a table by a pleasant waitress named Aimee who speaks English with an Auckland accent. I know she's a student studying medicine. It's her parents' place.

Aimee asks if we want to order drinks. I ask for a sugar cane juice, and Leonora asks for some kind of French wine. We also get a plate of rice-paper wraps, spring rolls and prawn crunchies with sauces while we explore the menu.

Leonora is feeling chatty.

"So, Sam have they been treating you alright?"

"Yeah, it's not been too bad. I mean I knew it would be tough but the way I see it I have to just sit tight and wait it out."

"So, you're sure that Dr Prosperov's 'disappearance' is ... um how can I say this delicately ... not ... permanent?"

"Very."

"I think Michael's just a bit put out. Nobody let *him* in on the plan."

"How do you think *I* feel?" I say, with a bit more feeling than I'd meant.

"Yes ... well, you have a point," she admits.

I was not going to say this to *her* but I'm beginning to suspect that the community would not return until it understood what went wrong. Somewhere, there had been a security breach.

And that meant that I had to regard everything and everyone as potentially suspect.

"Well, I suppose in the meantime we can probably have some fun with all the money," she says.

"What money?" I ask, busy with a crunchy and pretending not to know.

"The money Dr Prosperov left in case this happened."

"Oh, I didn't know there was any," I lie.

"Thousands," she says eyes flashing for emphasis.

I smile. She's lying again. There are millions, but it doesn't matter to me, I don't need millions. But just to wind her up I put something new under her greedy, artificial nose.

"Is that the gold from all the treasure we collected?"

"I don't know," she admits, "what treasure?"

"There was a lot of treasure. Spanish, mostly."

"Really? Oh, I don't think Michael knows anything about that. I'm just talking about Dr Prosperov's British bank accounts."

"Well, I guess he has even more money tucked away then," I shrug.

I knew this would drive her nuts. People who care a lot about money are easily distracted by it.

"So when you say you collected treasure. What do you mean by that?"

"We went to some very out of the way places, picked it up and took it home. It was fun."

"How?" she asks doubtfully.

"If you don't know I can't tell you," I smile.

"Why not," she asks. She's enjoying this game.

"It's a secret," I tell her.

"If it's a secret why are you telling me about it," she asks.

"Because it's fun," I smile.

"But you might be just making it all up," she accuses good naturedly.

"I might," I agree in a way she knows means I'm not.

"Have you told the police this secret," she tries.

"Hell no!" I laugh.

"Why not?" she fakes surprise.

"Because in the first place they wouldn't believe it. And secondly because it's not going to help them."

"But if they wouldn't believe it, why should I?" she asks sulkily.

"Different motives," I smile.

"What do you mean?" she asks, ready to be offended.

"A cop's job, as Kevin said, is to find out if a law has been broken and bring those who broke it to court."

"And my job?" she prompts.

"Is to spoil me rotten," I smile.

She holds up her glass and we clink them. She wrinkles her nose up at me.

"You're pretty clever really, aren't you Sam?"

Damn straight.

"So what should we order? I don't know anything about this."

"Well do you want a soup or dry food? The soups are full of stuff like noodles, meat and veg, plus broth, while the dry food is rice based with salads."

"Hmmm those soups look a bit risky to me."

"Well, they can be pretty hot, but the dry ones can be too," I warn, trying to be helpful.

"No, I mean risky for a woman wearing a white suit. It would be very easy to end up walking through Auckland with a big yellow stain on my jacket and everyone would wonder where you'd picked up that grubby woman."

I laugh. She seems to enjoy the effect. She closes her menu.

"So what have you chosen?"

"No idea, I'll get her to choose a salad for me."

It seemed to be my turn to ask a question.

"How long have you worked with Sir Michael?"

"Oh, we go back a very long way. He was the one who encouraged me to set up on my own."

"What's it like being a private detective?" I ask, wondering if it was a job I might like.

"Well, you know the TV shows?" she says, as if sharing a secret.

"Yeah."

"Well, it's sort of like that but in very, very, very slow motion. So sometimes it's exciting and you're following someone or staking a place out, but most of the time it's rather dull really: going through computer files, accounts, all that sort of thing."

"Do you ever carry a gun?" I ask playing up to her image of me.

"No, of course not dear, for a start it's illegal in Britain to carry a handgun and second I'm a terrible shot. No, if you want people who carry guns I am definitely not your girl."

"Good!" I say.

"You approve?" she asks, surprised that I wasn't disappointed.

"Yes, I don't like guns. They hurt people," I say, remembering.

Aimee comes up to our table with a nervous smile. I order a chicken Pho with pickles in my best imitation Saigon

Vietnamese which makes her laugh, and Leonora asks her to pick a salad that isn't too spicy.

"So tell me more about Dr Prosperov," Leonora demands playfully.

"Oh, he's a genius. He studied Electrical Engineering at Leningrad University. Then he worked for the KGB."

"So he was a *spy*!"

"Yes, he was a spy when my Grandpop was a soldier."

"Then what happened?"

"He found a way using his spying techniques to make truckloads of money during the 80s in London."

"There were a lot of people doing that then," Leonora agrees.

"But it got him in trouble with his Government so they put him in Siberia. It's incredibly cold in Siberia in winter you know."

"I've heard."

"Anyway then there was a change of Government and they let him out."

"Perestroika," she guesses.

"Yeah, that's it."

"But Dr Prosperov went to America and made a number of new discoveries which astonished even him."

"What were they?"

"Secret. But they made him heaps more money. Then got in trouble with something called the S.E.C which polices money over there. He often complained about them. Then he went to Switzerland, made even more money, and travelled a lot in disguise in Africa, the Middle East, India and Asia. Finally he came here and decided he wanted to set up a community here."

"Why here of all places?"

"He wanted to disappear and, as he said, New Zealand is a place the rest of the world forgets about because it's small, reasonably well off, and tucked down at the bottom of the Pacific where most people can't be bothered going."

"Can't argue with that. But what sort of community was he trying to establish?"

"A ... a different community."

"How was it different? ... Oh, I know, it's secret!"

"Yeah, I'm afraid it is."

"So was it a bit strange, this community?"

"Yes, we were all a bit strange."

Now it was her turn to laugh.

"Well, I suppose its true," she says, "you *are* a bit unusual for a ... how old are you exactly Sam?"

"Fourteen."

"Really? You're rather small for your age. But much cleverer than I expected."

"Yeah, I know. We're all small ... *and* clever."

Our meals arrive. For a while we eat in silence. It's great to taste the South Vietnamese flavours again. It brought back a lot of happy memories of Cam and her dad. But the problem with memories is that you can't live on them. And the reminder only makes me think more about my situation.

It's been ninety three hours since the evacuation. How long would this last? Were the others OK? When would they be able to come back? I knew they were safe from all the dangers I knew about, but what if there were dangers I didn't know about?

All we knew was that when the alarm went we had twenty minutes to destroy Renwick House and get into the emergency transporter, but where that went, we had no idea.

Also, off and on, I had been thinking about Ashley. The fact that she had been tagged was central to the whole situation. It meant that she had been expected in Washington D.C. It meant *they knew*. For, of all the poor black teens in the U.S capital, *they* too must be watching Nathaniel Robinson.

That was a huge worry in itself. If *they* were expecting one of us, it might mean that *they* had a clue as to our mission. It didn't seem possible that anyone at Renwick had ratted us out because the only people who knew anything had the most to lose. The only other possibility was that *they* had linked us to Nathan somehow themselves because *they* were watching him for the same reason that we are: Nathan has a strong chance of making President in forty years time.

The other possibility was that it wasn't *them* but the infiltrators. The infiltrators might be able to manipulate *them* and were certainly annoyed enough with us. Perhaps this was their revenge.

I knew ever since the police had announced finding me, *they* would have been working on a plan to catch me. *They* have artificial agents everywhere who look like ordinary people but luckily, to a psychic, are completely obvious. *They* also have to play by the rules, first and foremost of which is to remain hidden so that our planet develops naturally. The infiltrators are different. They aren't artificial and they've been here for centuries, but they are way more dangerous to humans, psychic or not.

This was the unsaid part of my chat with Leonora. She wasn't either one of *them* or an infiltrator, but was she working for either of them indirectly? That's what I wanted to know before I ended up going to sleep in the same hotel suite as her. The only way I could find out was go along with her, and give her enough temptation to make her show her hand before anything that I couldn't undo happened. That was why I'd flashed money under her nose. *They* don't care about money and the infiltrators have heaps. Leonora had shown a normal interest in money. That was good. It confirmed her readings. She was as simple as she seemed.

"So Sam, what do you want to do tomorrow?" she asks conversationally

That's an easy one.

"Go shopping," I answer.

"Excellent idea," she enthuses taking a mouthful of salad. And then after she swallowed that.

"What do you want to shop for?"

"Clothes. These are from the police lost property bin."

"Yes, they do seem a little … used. Anyway that definitely sounds like fun."

"And I want to get a phone."

"That's another idea I approve of."

"And in the afternoon I want to visit my friend Sue."

"Is she your girlfriend?"

I thought at once of Emma. I hadn't called her in days. As soon as I got a phone I'd be able to do that.

"No, Sue's a policewoman I'm helping. She's on the investigation with Kevin."

"And she's your *friend*?" she asks, surprised.

"Well, she is now."

"That doesn't sound nearly as much fun."

"Well no, it isn't really, and it's actually a bit … well, it's just between her and me really."

"So you're saying you don't want me hanging around?" Leonora

115

pretends to pout.

"If that's OK?"

She looks at me thoughtfully.

"Is she your plan B if your family are never are found?"

I'm surprised to find that, at the back of my mind, that had been my half-formed plan, and that someone as simple as her had just guessed.

"Well, no, I mean …"

"Go on, you can tell me. I won't blab," she blabs.

"They will show up …"

"But you don't know when, so in the meantime you'll need some adult to take care of you and …"

"Look, it's a long way from that, we're …"

"It's OK Sam, I'm not jealous! Really! Michael just sent me here to make some inquiries and when he heard from you he thought he'd better do what he promised for Dr Prosperov. In the long term he isn't planning to adopt you. We're just looking out for you as arranged."

"Did Dr Prosperov make any other arrangements if he didn't come back?"

"None that I am privy to, Sam."

I must have looked a bit down.

"Cheer up Sam, Just think of me as your fairy godmother, with a very large expense account, here in your time of need."

She so surprises me I decide to use the challenge codes "blue" and "maroon". That will tell me if she's actually an ally, rather than a threat. It takes me a little while to think up a sentence so I pretend to think about my feelings.

"I guess I just feel a bit blue about being marooned."

"Well, there are worse places to be marooned."

Nope! A pity. I'd hoped she might be a contact who can help but she definitely doesn't know the response words.

"That's true."

We order dessert which involves chocolate for her and Chua for me. Then we wander back to the hotel. I'm pretty sure Leonora is not an agent of *theirs* anyway. The more I think about it, the real question is, why is a man like Sir Michael so interested in a single survivor from Dr Prosperov's community? If I were just a case of welfare he could hire a legal dream team of locals to represent me. Instead he's taking time from his business, which is not small; to fly his own personal jet at who knows what expense; just to see an orphan on the other side of the world. Why? It's definitely sus'.

It seems Leonora's job is just to get me comfy and receptive to whatever he's coming for. I doubt if she knows anything at all. If *they* were fishing for me, and I was the fish, Leonora was the bucket of chum to get the water all bloody and me snapping at things. The hook would be hidden in something else later on. When we get back to the hotel it's about eight. I feel like an early night, so I'm in bed with lights out by nine. It feels strange to be so comfortable. If you get used to grabbing sleep in barns, police cells, foster care dorms and detective's sofas having a king-size single bed in a hotel room feels *too* comfy. So when Leonora checks on me at nine thirty I pretend to be asleep. Then she makes an interesting phone call.

She's quite quiet so it's hard to catch what she says, but Michael seems to want to know if I have anything with me. She says I don't even have a case. I could have read her more, but there's no threat and by now I just feel so sleepy.

It all starts to jumble in my head and I find myself in an

underground tunnel with the others, being chased by a huge silver skull. There's this strange singing in my ears. The skull wants our blood. I make a turn and lose the others, to find myself following all these copper pipes of different sizes. There are hundreds of them and I somehow know I'm in the basement of an airport ... Then it begins to get cold and I know a ghost is coming, but I take a side door out of a cleaning cupboard into the airport. A plane's landing with someone on it which I have to meet but I don't know which gate, or the flight number.

Then I wake up.

It's nice to wake up somewhere comfortable for a change. From my bed I can see out the window over the harbour. Today it looks a bit gray but it's nice to know that at least I'm not under a bridge in Lima or living in a cardboard box in London. I'm one of the lucky ones who is relatively warm, secure, and likely to have a good breakfast. I lie back and doze.

The room is still and quiet, with Auckland harbour still spread out before me, out the window. There are bright points of violet light like dust catching in the sunlight. I sit up and look at the tiny dancing lights. Maybe the others can see me!

I'm a bit grumpy they haven't tried to contact me yet, and then I realise with a shock, I'm also suspect. Someone's betrayed us and everyone has to be checked out – even me. And here I am in a fancy hotel! The lights stop dancing, like tiny fireworks that just fizzle out.

I feel restless so I decide to get up. I slip out of bed and pull my clothes on. I'm just doing up my laces when the suite door opens. I go to my own door to investigate.

It's Leonora in a tracksuit with a towel around her shoulders. "Hello sleepyhead. Ready for some breakfast?"

"Yeah ... Thanks," I say – a bit confused.

"Just been down at the gym. Give me a few minutes for a shower and we'll go down to the café. Check out the TV, they've got channels for nearly everything."

I sit down on the couch and pick up the remote. The news doesn't interest me (I learned long ago the most important things aren't usually on it), nor did the brain numbing cartoons, but there is a show on orcas which I find interesting so I settle down to see what National Geographic has to say about them. It must be interesting because I don't even notice how long Leonora takes to get ready – she just suddenly is.

I confess I pig out a bit at breakfast but there is so much that I like and Leonora encourages me to go for it. There's fruit, yoghurt, cereals, bread, pastries, eggs just about every way, bacon, hash browns, ham, pancakes, sausages. I guess I hadn't eaten much for the past few days and I feel like making up for lost calories.

"Well, at least when we buy your clothes they'll have to fit you with your tummy full," Leonora observes, drily.

So then we go shopping.

Now I'm not big on shopping for clothes. But I guess that was because we never had any money and shopping on the cheap is depressing. But this is different. For once there is no shortage of money and unlike Aunty Liz, Leonora doesn't care what I buy so long as it looks good and is fun.

And it is. I get a whole gangsta outfit because Leonora thinks it suits me. But I'm not into being a gangsta. I just like the black hoodie and the shades. She's surprised I want to keep my cheap looking watch and drags me into a jewellery store just to have a look.

Realising I might not get another chance I'm bigger on the outdoors clothes. And if you want to spend big money on clothes? Man, can you go mad on outdoors gear!

Leonora has no idea about outdoors clothes but approves of me being fussy and spending heaps. I get a very cool rain jacket, a well designed and tough backpack, and some amazingly tough and comfortable hiking boots.

The next step is to Vodafone to get a cell. I make sure it's a prepay. Leonora wants to get me an account but I know that's so she can check who I call, so I make a fuss and because she doesn't want to upset me she gives in. I come out with a phone with user removable dual Sim card, dual SD cards, weather proof, drop-proof, and all the usual trimmings.

By lunchtime we have about fifty kilos worth of shopping bags, and we've spent about ten K – which is more money than I've ever had spent on me in my life. At my suggestion we then get me a Gift Visa card with $1,000 loaded on it (which I then copy with the Omnicard when Leonora goes to the bathroom).

We take a cab back to the hotel and have a quick lunch in the café. I'm still digesting breakfast so I'm not all that hungry at lunchtime. Then Leonora wants a fashion show so we do that for about half an hour. I end up in my high tech rain jacket, styley jeans, ultra-comfortable boots and a cool wool top, I like.

"So what do you want to do now?" she asks.

"Well, I should go visit Sue," I say checking my watch.

"You don't have to."

"I want to."

"Well OK, but Michael wants to catch up with us at dinner so be back by six."

"OK."

Leonora walks me to the lobby where there are taxis waiting. It's strange to suddenly have some control back again. Strange too because I'm not doing anything so out of the ordinary for many rich kids all over the world – and yet it was all completely new to me. It made me suddenly realise how easy it is to live on the same planet with people and have no idea how they live their lives.

The taxi driver is Persian so we chat about places in Iran we both know, which surprises him a lot. When we get to the hospital I arrange for him to pick me up at 5:30 for the return home. It takes a while to find Sue. The psych ward is painted the kind of pink Rewa likes but which I can take or leave. I find Sue sitting in the canteen eating her lunch off a plastic tray and reading the paper. She's dressed but looks a bit down, like a balloon left over from a kid's party. I instantly feel bad I've forgotten to bring her anything. Still, she cheers up a bit at the sight of me.

"Sam!" she smiles. "I barely recognised you. You look ... well ... you look so respectable! What's happened?"

It bothers me that being poor didn't look respectable but I let it slide. I tell her all about Leonora and my shopping trip. I ask for her phone number – even though I have it already – and show off my new phone.

"Wow rags to riches in five days!" Sue smiles, obviously happy for me.

"It's only money Sue," I tell her, "Prosperov has heaps. He's just looking after me until he gets back."

"Might this lawyer know where he is?" she asks. That was a question for Kevin.

"I doubt it," I say, doubting it a lot.

We look at each other for a moment in silence. I feel a bit awkward standing there.

"What will happen with you now Sam?" she asks.

"I dunno, I guess they'll try and put me in some fancy boarding school or something."

"Well, you do need to get back to school," she tells me.

"How are you?" I ask her to change the subject, and sitting down.

"I'm OK," she says, remembering a little too late to give me that fake smile.

"What's the matter?" I ask at once.

She looks a little vulnerable for a moment and then does the smile again.

"They say I can go home."

"OK," I say doubtfully. You didn't have to be psychic to see she was dreading facing her empty house.

She says nothing.

"Has Kevin been in?" I ask, wondering how her work was with her being in a psych ward.

"Yeah, he came in."

"Is he OK with you going back to work?"

"Well, he's sort of got me on light duties," she looks at me. "I'm looking after your case. He's got to do something else this week."

"Great!" I say enthusiastically.

"Well, it is different to my normal job, I guess," she concedes unenthusiastically.

"Ooh yeah," I agree.

She says nothing.

"When are you allowed to go?"

"Any time really ..."

She pauses, and now she's close to tears, "… actually I've been discharged since ten o'clock."

I wasn't sure what to do. I wondered what would cheer her up. My first thought was shopping because it had cheered me, but she had a houseful of stuff and more crap wouldn't help. So I suggest something which seems like a great way to stop her thinking about her loss.

"Great! Why don't you come with me to Rainbow's End."

"What!? Sam, I don't…" she says, being all grown up.

"Come on Sue, we'll ride the terror tower and eat hotdogs and be idiots. It'll be great!"

"I've got to …"

"C'mon, you can be monitoring your witness or something."

She's hesitating.

"I'll pay."

"Sam you don't …"

"Come on!" I say and grab her hand, tugging her. "Beats moping around the Psych ward doesn't it," I tease.

She smiles.

"Oh all right," she gets up, then stops.

"How do we get there?"

"I'll call Hussein."

"Who's Hussein."

"The cab driver."

Hussein turns out to be busy so the cab company sends a Sikh dude named Maresh62 instead. He thinks Sue's a truancy officer and I'm a naughty school kid so he has a lot to say about the education system which Sue is very polite to put up with. We drop off her bag at her Auckland Central Police station and then go to Rainbow's End, much to Maresh62's annoyance. He's even

123

more annoyed when I pay the cab fare but his opinions don't stop him taking my money.

Rainbow's End isn't exactly busy at 2 p.m. on a damp Friday afternoon so we get most of the rides to ourselves. We have a great time bashing each other on the Dodgems; I make her get on the rollercoaster; but she refuses the terror tower. Then we buy hotdogs and play mini golf where she completely wastes me. But about three the clouds roll in, the rain comes down, and Rainbow's End isn't any fun anymore.

I call a cab.

"Where do you want to go?" I ask.

"I guess I'd better get it over with and go home," she says.

But the mindless fun has worked and she looks happier than I'd seen her. The next cab driver is very into his new satnav and keeps pushing buttons on it as we go. Finally we get to Sue's suburb, her street and her house. She looks nervous.

"Sam, could you come with me?" It's a request, not an order, or a plea. Of course I say "yes".

The place smells a bit when we open the door. I obviously hadn't managed to scrub out the smell of sick as well as I had thought, but Sue doesn't seem to mind. She opens the windows and walks through the place inspecting it like a crime scene. Then she sighs and leads me to the kitchen and looks in the fridge. She pulls out a carton of milk, gingerly sniffs it and then pours it out into the sink.

"Would you like a drink Sam? I've got coke or coffee or tea but no milk."

"Coke would be great, thanks."

She pours me an almost flat coke and puts the kettle on for herself. I sit at the table and watch her. She seems to be thinking a lot to herself and I let her collect her thoughts.

"You know Sam," she says, "I was really lucky to meet you."

I chuckle to myself.

"What?" she asks.

"Lucky," I reply smiling.

"Yeah lucky. I mean I would ... I'd be ... and you, you're somehow just what I need now. If I was alone I know I'd be a mess. Seeing all the things she's taken with her, like I don't mean shit. But somehow having you here ... I mean you make me feel ... different," she pauses, knowing she sounds kinda weird, even though I know what she means.

"You make me feel like there's hope. That's what it is. It's not just what you do and stuff, it's ... well, it's who you are as well." she stops.

Deep down I know what she's saying. My situation was (if anything) worse than hers but I keep going. That's inspired her. But there was more. She did youth aid, not just because she liked kids, but because deep down she wanted kids of her own. With a difficult partner like Rachel that had been buried and forgotten. But now, with her gone, and me around, she was starting to get in touch with it again.

"Do I sound like a raving loon?" she asks.

"Straight out of the psych ward," I reply, smiling.

We laugh. She makes some coffee and sits down opposite me. She says nothing for a while, and then I decide to confide in her.

"You know how I was telling you about how I came to be at Renwick?"

"Uh-huh."

"Well Lucky was involved in that too."

"Lot of luck Sam," she corrects.

"No, I mean Lucky."

"What, like a name? Who was Lucky?"

"Well, we didn't understand it at the time either."

"Understand what?"

"The relationship between Dr Prosperov and Lucky."

"Sam, you aren't making a whole lot of sense."

"Maybe if I pick up where I left off."

"Sure."

•••

CHAP+ER SEVEN: DR PR⊕SPER⊕V'S ISLAND

It was Friday after school that we loaded up Grandpop's old Toyota stationwagon and left the only home I'd ever known. All we had was a full tank of gas, an old AA accommodation guide, a couple of suitcases and a few of our most precious possessions. The whole thing had a kind of strange unreality about it. I kept thinking at any moment I'd wake up, or we'd get a call to tell us Ax wasn't really being released and Grandpop's boat hadn't really been burned to the waterline. But the kilometers between where I was and everything I knew just kept mounting up.

The highway south seemed to be full of busy people and us escaping our home was just one story of many on that road that day. At about five we stopped at Wellsford for some pies and chips for tea. Aunty Liz didn't want to eat on the roadside because just about everyone in the entire region seemed to be driving past, and sitting on a park bench there would be very obvious to anyone who might recognise us.

Aunty Liz was very nervous and she was clearly in two minds about going at all. Rewa and me played "I spy" and "Horse" until it got too boring. It was about six when we began to come into the outskirts of Auckland and the biggest traffic jam I had *ever* seen. There were cars *everywhere*. For Aunty Liz who was used to quiet country roads the huge jams just made her even more stressed-out than she already was. After about half an hour she was freaking out. I spotted a motel near an off-ramp. Aunty Liz got us out of that traffic and up to that motel in no time.

There was nothing nice about the "Hibiscus Motor Lodge" at all. The rooms were gathered in two stories around a car park and the view was of the motorway. The place was painted a pink even Rewa found ugly, and everything was worn out and run-down. We got a two room unit with a room for us and a living area and kitchenette with a bed Aunty Liz would sleep in. The bathroom was tiny with a pink washstand and ugly tiles in the shower.

"Are we going to live here Aunty Liz?" Rewa wanted to know. At the price the owner wanted Aunty Liz was very clear – the answer was no. We hunkered down in our room and watched TV that night and went to bed early. Unfortunately we were woken up by this woman in the next unit screaming. I asked Aunty Liz if we should call the police but she said "no" and it wasn't long afterwards that the woman was giggling, and then stomping out the door in her high heel shoes. There were a few presences about the place but even they seemed to be no more than passing through.

I woke up early on Saturday morning with this strange feeling about the day. It was cool, but sunny, with a sense of promise about it which seemed completely wrong given our horrible unit. Maybe it was a premonition, or maybe it was just that I thought things couldn't get any worse, but for some reason I felt sure that our luck was about to change.

We checked out early, loaded up the stationwagon and headed into the city. Even on Saturday morning the motorway was busy.

We drove without knowing where we were going. Aunty Liz just kept following the motorway. The motorway kept heading south and before we knew it, we were crossing the Auckland Harbour Bridge for the first time in our lives. It felt kind of strange to come to the city and Rewa and I were looking around at all the tall buildings and the gray concrete. I didn't know then, that as cities go, Auckland is quite small, with only a million or so people. It seemed enormous to a twelve-year-old country kid from the sticks.

When we got to the middle of town Aunty Liz took an off-ramp and we ended up driving around, looking about like visitors from Mars, or something. Finally we found a car park and then, more importantly, we found a McDonald's where we could have breakfast.

We had probably had McDonald's about twice in our lives before, so this was a real treat. Rewa got some little toy pony or something and I got stuck into a quarter pounder. Aunty Liz had bought the newspaper which was very thick on Saturday. She started looking through the jobs section. Rewa did the puzzles in the kids section while I looked through the houses section for something to do.

It was completely weird the way the ad jumped out at me. It was quite large and it said, "Wanted: Nurses, Baker-Chef, Groundsman-Gardener, Receptionist (multi lingual), Electrical Engineer. Free accommodation and meals provided. Families welcome. Immigration assistance available." Then it gave a whole lot of detail about Renwick House on Aotea Island. I showed Aunty Liz who was not having as much luck with the jobs section. Then she noticed something.

"Please apply in person at Meeting Room 5, Sheraton Hotel,

Auckland at 11 a.m. Children most welcome."

She checked her watch. It was 10:30! Where was the Sheraton? She asked "Mandy" and "Steve" at the McDonald's counter but they had no idea. So we borrowed the telephone book and got the address. Then we ran up the road to the big book shop on the corner and bought ourselves a map of Auckland.

It turned out the address we were looking for was just up the road from where we had parked. So we dragged Aunty Liz up the hill again to the hotel and got there, gasping for breath, at five minutes to eleven. We felt pretty out of place in such a fancy hotel but the meeting board showed us where to go and we soon found ourselves in a room with a lot of seats facing a front desk. To our disappointment there were quite a few people already there. Everyone was sitting down quietly, wondering what would happen. There was mix of people in the audience with Asians, black people and a few Middle Easterners. To our surprise we were not the only kids. Obviously the promise to help with immigration had attracted many of them.

Then two men came into the room. One was old, small and slightly balding with messy fine gray-white hair, and a fine gray goatee. He was thin and wore a dark gray suit and tightly knotted blue silk tie and carried an odd walking stick that was full of carvings in its twisting dark wood. He had big, deep brown eyes, set in wrinkled lids that looked like everything seemed funny to him. I remember trying to read him and got nothing but complexities I couldn't understand.

The man next to him was bigger, and far stronger. He seemed to ripple like a tiger when he moved. Although he wore a suit too, the shirt had a button instead of a tie. He was Asian with very high cheekbones, very pronounced eyelids and black eyes. He seemed a bit scary because he didn't say anything. Unlike the old guy he was easy to read, but he didn't really know what his boss was doing.

At eleven o'clock the old man checked an old-fashioned pocket watch and stood up lazily leaning with both arms on the tables. His voice was strong but had a heavy accent.

"Is too many people here. Simplest to say all those without children please stand up."

A number of people stood up uncertainly.

"Thanking you for coming but first priority is for greatest need."

One man wanted to argue

"I've got kids, I just didn't bring them," he called out as he stood.

"Then you have somewhere else they can be," the old man said lazily.

"This is totally unfair," he said as he filed out.

The old man made no comment but his eyes held no mercy. I thought "he is one hard dude".

There was a fair degree of grumpy muttering about this but the heavy Asian dude opened the door and stood next to it with his hands clasped in front of him. The old man remained where he stood, eyeing people with a look that told you he was not the kind of person you mess with. It looked like a pretty firm hint and it emptied out the room quickly.

"Now raising hands please. Who has nowhere to live?"

We put our hands up, like everyone else.

"Others, thank you for coming but clearly need not so bad. Leaving now please."

Once again there were more complaints but the Russian just stared and the people left.

"Please to lower hands," he instructed. Now he walked out in

front of the table. I had thought that he had propped himself up
on the table out of weakness but no, he was light on his feet. He
pointed to a woman in the audience.

"Where are children?"

"I ... I left them at my sisters ... we've got to move out ..."

But the same merciless stare was directed at her and she finally
got up and left crying.

The heavy dude moved back behind the table. The old guy
walked up the aisle in the middle.

I caught his eye for a moment and for a split second there was
a slight smile, almost of recognition. And the feeling of good
fortune just swelled in me. I knew then we would be chosen.

He came back to the front and lightly half sat on the table.

"OK, so how many nurses?"

Aunty Liz and two others put their hands up.

"State last hospital, nursing type and city," then he pointed at a
black woman with a daughter next to her.

"Martin Luther King Jr, Urgent Care, Los Angeles and a'fore
that Lindy Boggs Medical Center, New Orlins."

We all remembered Hurricane Katrina had struck New Orleans
just over a year ago.

Everyone turned to look at her. She seemed very different to
everyone else but she sat calmly, her eyes on the man, who
turned now to a younger white woman with a small boy.

"Te Aroha Community Hospital, elder care department."

And finally Aunty Liz

"Whangarei Base Hospital, Community care, Whangarei."

He nodded.

"Is no requirement for geriatric nurse," he said looking up.

The woman looking very disappointed started to get up.

"Is to advantage to please wait outside," he told her with a slight smile. Uncertainly, she got up and left, closing the door quietly behind her.

"OK, you two are nurses," the old man resumed.

We were in! Although, I wasn't yet sure if we wanted to be.

"Requirement is for Baker Chef. Applicants please raise hands." And he went through all of them. He took no arguments and picked quickly just as he had chosen us. But he told a number of people to wait outside. Others he did not. Finally we had been whittled down to six families. We started to check each other out. We certainly were a different bunch. There was us three Maoris, two black Americans, two Asians, two Arabs, Four Iranians, and one black and one white Zimbabwean. Five women, two men, five girls and three boys.

"Excellent!" the old guy said. "Is time for self-introduction. My name is Dr Gennady Achillovich Prosperov, and you probably tell I am Russian. My offer to you is simple. You work for me and live free at my house on Aotea island. Meals will be prepared by chef except on day off. All staff work six days on, one day off. Job description is simple: everyone helps everyone, to Housekeepers direction. Pay is same for all, that is double average local income. Paid annual leave is three weeks. If you want to quit please to give one month's warning. Immediate start. Any questions?"

The black Zimbabwean man had one.

"Yes?" Dr Prosperov asked.

"Am I to understand that you are employing us as servants?" his voice sounded warm and strong.

"Yes and no. Yes under law. No, because purpose of my clinic is not my comfort."

Now the black American lady had a question.

"Sir, what sort of clinic do you intend to establish?"

He studied her for a moment as if assessing what her reaction might me.

"Parapsychology clinic."

I had no idea what that meant but it seemed to surprise the American who looked at her daughter. It seemed I wasn't the only one who looked blank so Dr Prosperov filled us in.

"Parapychology is study of psychic phenomena. Includes mind reading, remote seeing, fortune telling, ghosts etc. I am already expert, hence fortune. Where other research centres in Germany, Scotland, California study by experimental research[+] I am interested in therapeutic research. My plan is for free Parapsychology Therapy Clinic for advanced psychics. Fortunately Government here, like most governments, does not regulate parapsychology because is not classed as medicine. Thus I am free because house is not hotel or hospital. It is just large house. Your job to provide assistance to myself and guests. So to question, 'are you to be servants?' Answer: technically yes; functionally no."

There was a kind of pause where everyone wants to say something but nobody knows what to say. Prosperov smiled. I liked his smile. It mixed cunning, caring and fun in one expression.

"Now time is," he looked at his pocket watch, "... twelve twenty three. Lunch is in meeting room four in seven minutes. Please to excuse for brief moment."

He went to join the Asian man who handed him a briefcase. Then they went outside.

Almost at once everyone started talking. The main themes

were: Is this guy crazy? Who is this guy anyway? Will he really do what he says? Where is Aotea Island and what is it like? When do we start? What is his house like? Can we trust him? Aunty Liz is usually quiet at times like this but she found the outgoing Iranian lady who was to be the receptionist, and the Zimbabwean man in particular agreed with her concerns. Most of us kids let the adults speak for us except the Arab-looking kid who seemed a bit full of himself and who kept saying we needed everything in writing. His father, who was the engineer, was a more patient man and kept telling Tarik to quiet down and listen. The black American girl who was called Ashley summed it up for me when she said to her mother that they were not in a position to inspect a gift horse's dental work. The feeling was one of excitement from the kids, and caution from the parents. The Asian man came back into the room and opened the door, waving for us to follow him. We started to come out as a group, with every one chatting excitedly. I noticed the nurse and the small boy who had been sent out of the room were parting from Dr Prosperov. The nurse had tears in her eyes but looked very happy and was clutching a large brown envelope. The little guy looked confused while Prosperov had that smile on his face again. I thought to myself immediately, "this guy is alright". As we came in we wrote our names on peel-off name badges with "Introducing" already printed on them and stuck them on our chests. It seemed to change the crowd from a collection of unknown bodies into a group of people. The lunch for the adults was on plates along the back wall of the meeting room where they could mingle and chat. The lunch for us kids was at a table, on top of which was also placed a laptop computer and a projector that was showing a slide show of Renwick House and

Aotea Island. The funny thing I noticed at once was that, while there was a large stack of plates at the adults table, there was exactly the right number of kid's places.

The food was pretty much the same as the adults were having. Everyone had an orange juice. Sausage rolls, filled rolls, Asian things I didn't know then were Vietnamese, pizzas, slices and cakes. We sort of filled our plates from whatever was nearest. Even though I'd just had a big feed of McDonald's I wasn't going to pass up a chance to eat this lot.

Now I could read the names of all the other kids. All the bigger kids were about twelve, the same age as me. Ashley Robinson was the black American girl. She was about the same size as me, which was small for my age, thin, round faced, with glasses, a kindly expression, shoulder length hair in braids and her clothes were girly. Cam Trân was Vietnamese, even smaller, with sharp eyes, a cute snub nose and short straight black hair. She was dressed like a tomboy in a black denim jacket but very pretty despite that. Tahira Khadem was the Iranian girl. She was drop-dead gorgeous with shiny brown eyes, light brown skin, curly brown hair and a pink polo neck. Her sister Asal, who was about ten, and if anything even prettier, sat next to her. She was the same age as Rewa and they looked like sisters. Both were light brown, with shoulder length black curly hair, pretty eyes and dressed in pink. Scotty Khumalo was from Zimbabwe. He was small, blond with brilliant blue eyes and slight freckles on his white skin. He seemed to fill a very small space and not say much, but when he looked around he seemed to be both out of place, patient and very determined to be here. Much bigger and louder was Tarik Gursoy. He was taller than most of us, but very skinny. He had short curly black hair, brown lively eyes, and a long, thin nose. He wore a silver bling necklace and a t-shirt. He seemed to be permanently twitchy and could hardly sit still but he was also the most outgoing and seemed to delight in talking to people just to see what they'd do.

"Hey Sam! Wotcha know 'bout this island,mate?" he asked me. He had a strange accent. Half English like someone on TV, and half something else.

I said I'd never been there.

"Whatcha think about this guy, Prosperov, Sam? 'E on the level?"

He had the annoying habit of asking a question and not looking as if he actually cared what you said in reply.

"I think he's cool."

"Ya fink he's cool dyah mate? Anyone else 'ere fink e's cool?"

He was trying to get Tahira's attention but she was talking to Ashley about their flight out to New Zealand from Paris. Cam was more interested in the girl's conversation too.

"Hey Sco'y, mate! You agree with Sam, yeah? This guy alright?" Tarik asked turning to him.

Scotty shot me a look of bright blue. I was surprised how penetrating his glance was but then he went back to looking at the table.

"He's OK," he said quietly.

"OK ? OK? What's thaat? OK, good ? OK, so-so? OK, doesn't mean much, init?"

"He's good," Scotty said even quieter than he did before.

Tarik looked around at Prosperov then drooped down and put his hands out.

"Yeah, but isn 'e talkin bollocks about psychic 'ospital?"

Then he sniffed and cleared his throat.

Scotty checked me out and for an instant we realised we
were both reading each other. We both stopped, shocked and
surprised. Tarik had put his finger on it. Dr Prosperov was a very
strange man and we were a strange group of people.

Renwick house came up on the screen again. It was a big place,
made of brick and wood. The slides said it had started out as
an invalid's hospital for soldiers coming back from the First
World War. It had been built set in bush overlooking a beach
on secluded, beautiful Aotea Island, a one hour ferry ride from
Auckland City because it was thought the quiet would help
soldiers recover. After the war it had become a quarantine
hospital, then a mental hospital which was closed in the 30s.
Since then it had been used as a storehouse by various farmers
and finally by the Department of Conservation, but they had
leased it to Dr Prosperov who had promised to restore it. The
restoration was still in progress but most of it had been done up.
It looked very grand. More like a museum than a house and it
was hard to imagine anyone really lived there.

I didn't know anything about how adults got their jobs but I
could tell from the way they had reacted that Dr Prosperov's
method was far from normal. And how come he had known
exactly how many places to set at the kid's table but not how
many adults?

I didn't know the answer to Tarik's question but it bothered me
and I could tell it bothered Scotty too.

Aunty Liz came over and knelt down by us.

"Well kids, what do you think? Shall we give it a go?"

She looked stressed, but we could tell she was sold.

I nodded. "Couldn't be worse than the Hibiscus Lodge could it?"

"I don't know, but so far he's answered all my questions. He

seems straight-up and it's not like he owns the whole island. If
we want to we can simply go again."

"Well, I'm up for it," I replied.

"Rewa?"

"I think it's cool," she said.

"Right, well, I'll go sign up then," Aunty Liz decided.

Everyone did.

There was a queue of them: Patricia Robinson the black
American lady, a little fat, but tall, well dressed with short hair;
Neat and tidy Mitra Khadem and her stern looking mother
Soraya; Fit and intelligent looking Bernard Khumalo with very
short black curly hair in a loose shirt and cargo pants; Timid,
thin and graying Mr Nguyen Trân in his dark blue jeans; and
thin Dr Ali Gursoy, with gold wire-rim glasses, slightly balding,
with a brainiac look, in a gray suit. They seemed an odd
collection of people.

There was a brief pause as everyone sorted out how we would
get to the ferry. Aunty Liz offered to take Ashley and her mum
Patricia in our car because she wanted to get to know the other
nurse. Finally we all broke up into smaller groups, with Dr
Prosperov being driven off in a shark-like, shiny black Mercedes
by the Asian dude.

As we went to the car the first thing we noticed was that Patricia
and Ashley had no luggage. The second thing I noticed was a
presence attached to Ashley that followed her like a shadow.

"So how long have you been in New Zealand Patricia?" Aunty Liz
asked, as we walked to our car.

"Waall, to be honest wid you 'lizabeth, we only been here since
six this morning!" she said. Man, she was loud.

"Oh! So you came to that meeting almost straight off the plane?"

"Yeah! Crazy ain't it?"

Aunty Liz was too polite to agree out loud. We came up to our old car. It looked like the biggest heap of crap in Auckland. I imagined their gleaming American car back home.

"Sorry about the car, it's a bit of a mess," Aunty Liz muttered.

"Don't sweat it 'lizabeth. We down't care jus so long as we don't hav-ta walk."

We got in. Patricia sat in the front with Aunty Liz. I sat behind Aunty Liz, Ashley sat behind her mum and Rewa sat in the middle.

"Da only thing I cayan't git used to is dis driving on da left, it jus feels *all* wrong," she laughed.

"I suppose it would," Aunty Liz agreed.

"So how long have you been thinking about settling in New Zealand Patricia."

"'bout four hours."

Aunty Liz said nothing. It was obvious she didn't want to pry but the answers she was getting, had us all fascinated.

"Daddy cayme here one time," Ashley volunteered.

"Oh ..." Aunty Liz was just about to say something when it became embarrassingly obvious that daddy wasn't there. I knew at once who the shadow was.

"When did he die?" I asked, wanting to know.

"Sam!" Aunty Liz started.

"S'awl right Elizabeth. My husband died two years back on active duty in I-raq."

Ashley was looking at me with interest.

"When d'your momma pass away?" she asked.

"Ashley where are your manners child!?" Patricia laughed, embarrassed. "She obviously ain't dead is she?"

"Actually I'm their Aunt, my sister died eight years ago," Aunty Liz told Patricia.

"My father killed her," I added in case they wondered where he was.

"Oh my god!" Patricia said. "How awful!"

"Yes ... yes, it was," Liz agreed and she began to tell Patricia our story, more or less as I've told it to you.

But that was background to me and Ashley staring at each other, because we both realised we could both do the same thing, and until I'd met Scotty and Ashley I had never met another one. I don't think she had either. It was something we knew we really, really wanted to talk about, but away from adults who might tell us off for talking about it, or try to keep us quiet.

The ferry was already busy for the weekend and it was only two o'clock. We had to get out and go with Patricia while Aunty Liz parked the car on the deck. The others had made their way by minivan shuttle and had formed a small group at the worn out waiting lounge. The Iranian family had the most luggage, while Tarik and his dad also had a couple of large suitcases. I could not but wonder at how little Ashley and Patricia had, nor Cam and her dad, or Scotty and the black man with him. Eventually they let us onto the ferry and we pushed through to claim a seat. It was too busy in the lounge so we went onto the deck on the roof.

The ferry to Aotea has an open car deck on the bottom, a lounge over that and an outdoor deck above that. It carries about twenty cars at a time and it was completely full as we put to sea. It wasn't warm, but it wasn't especially cold either, so we all gathered around to watch the land slip away behind us in a trail of pale, bubbly seawater. I was surprised how fast the ferry

moved and we kids started a watch for dolphins, which often
hitch a lift on the wake, according to the video in the lounge.
In fact it was great to have a bunch of kids my own age to play
with. Tarik was tearing around like a mad thing pretending all
the small boats around us were pirates we had to escape from
and Cam seemed to find that attractive for some reason. Scotty,
Ashley and me were half playing along at repelling the pirates
and half looking for dolphins. For a while Tahira tried to sit with
the adults and look pretty, but she got sick of being the only one
listening to their boring talking and joined us. Rewa and Asal
were looking for mermaids and dolphins on the other side too.
When the ferry hit open water it started to get a bit rougher and
colder and the adults went down inside. But that left us with
the whole deck to play on. We were having a great time with the
waves bucking us about and it never occurred to me that anyone
wouldn't. But down below it was a different story and Aunty Liz
ended up spewing in a bag and looking very unwell. Aunty Liz
came upstairs to get some fresh air again with Patricia, who also
looked uncomfortable, keeping her company.
The whole trip took something over an hour and although it
seemed to pass in no time to me, Aunty Liz complained it took
forever. As we began to approach the island our games were
forgotten and we became interested in looking at the place we
had agreed to call home.

The island was quite large with hills at each end and a ridge
down the middle that dipped like a horse's back. The highest
parts were in bush but there was also grass paddocks as well. As
we got closer to the harbour at Port Carlyle we could see more
and more houses. The village seemed to be about the same size

as the one I'd known back home.

The ferry approached the dock with the kind of casualness which showed the driver did this all the time – which he probably did. It seemed too fast but it turned out to be perfectly timed and the front ramp of the ferry was lowered onto the dock in no time. Everything felt as if time seemed to be going too fast for me. I hadn't got used to the idea of leaving Grandpop yet and here we were arriving somewhere new to live. I guess I wasn't the only one feeling that way. Everyone was looking a bit uncomfortable and grumpy – and it wasn't just from feeling seasick. We trooped off the ferry, down a gangway and found ourselves in a pretty empty parking lot. Most other people were getting into their cars and driving off. Aunty Liz would meet us once she'd driven off the ferry but after that we had no idea what was going to happen.

Just as we were wondering what we would do a big yellow American style school bus drove up into the carpark at some speed and braked noisily just short of where we were all gathered. The doors opened and a very small Asian woman with bright pink strands in her hair, bead wristlets, a silver nose stud, wearing a Bob Marley t-shirt leant out the door and casually shouted:

"Awwrr aboard for Rlenwick House!" and disappeared back into the bus.

Everyone starting filing up the steep stairs past the driver who seemed far too small to be allowed to drive, but who seemed very pleased to see everyone. Aunty Liz finally drove up into the car park and, spotting us, drove over to where we were all boarding the bus. I stood with Rewa at the bottom of the stairs unsure what we should do.

"Hey kids, you coming to Rlenwick?" the driver asked.

"Ah yeah, but our Aunt's coming in the car." I told her.

She made a noise of understanding and with surprising speed leapt down the stairs, past us, to where Aunty Liz was getting out of the car. I was amazed to notice that although she was an adult she wasn't bigger than I was. Still, she moved with speed and determination as though the rest of the world was stuck in slow motion.

"You want to follow to Rlenwick?" she asked Aunty Liz.

Aunty Liz seemed a bit surprised by this lady's appearance but replied that she did.

"Cool. It's narrow gravel road and Betty," she nodded at the bus "kick up rots of dust, so you hold back out of cloud and keep lights on. You OK on gravel?"

"Yeah," said Aunty Liz who only drove on gravel back home.

"OK kids, who ya wanna go with, mum or me?"

"Aunty Liz, can we go on the bus?" Rewa pleaded. Like me she already thought this tiny lady was the coolest adult she'd ever met.

"OK," she agreed

"Cool! Ret's go!" the woman yelled punching the air.

We ran up the stairs

The bus's engine roared to life and a split second later the bus was filled with this disco song about being excited. "Yeeehah!" yelled the driver who had a microphone plugged into the PA and took off at surprising speed.

The upbeat happiness of both the driver and the music was catching. People who had seemed a bit down a few minutes ago suddenly had smiles on their faces.

"Hi new pepul. My name is Mariko and I'rl be your driver and d.j for this trip to Rlenwick House."

She paused for the beat of the music.

"The shit tip we're driving through is Port Carlyle. Velly small brains!" she held her finger and thumb up about an inch apart above her head. Everyone laughed. She paused again.

"Journey take 20 minutes. Average speed 20."

She paused for the music again.

"That's kay not miles. Road? Hah!"

The bus roared up the hill through Port Carlyle music blaring. We crossed the ridge and then down the other side through a series of bays filled with houses, shops and cafes.

"This tourist beaches for surfers," Mariko said.

The brief bit of speed did not last long. We started to climb a big hill, the bus roaring up the narrow road. At the top of the hill the seal turned to gravel and the bus swung along the twisty, potholed road. The ride was exciting, scary, fun and interesting. We were all looking out over the island taking in the scenery. There was a lot of grass but there were also hillsides covered in gorse and ferns. In some places there were forests. You could always see the sea which looked big, blue and wild, and there was the odd hint of fantastic beaches. You couldn't see a thing out of the back of the bus. It was just a huge cloud of dust. I hoped Aunty Liz wouldn't have too much of a problem following us.

We took a fork in a road and began following *another* ridge which branched right, off the main ridge of the island. We were still in sheep country but as we got closer to the sea we came up to a small church that overlooked the sea and then down into a pine forest as we zigzagged down the side of the hill.

Suddenly we pulled out of the pine forest and drove into a

145

sheltered bay and there, right next to us, was Renwick House, against the pine trees, looking out over the shingle, and white sands of the beach, to the sea. To me it was gi-normous.

Mariko drove the bus right up to the front steps and killed the engine and the music. The sudden quiet caught up with us like the dust cloud that had been following us. It was almost alarming. Now all you heard was the breakers roaring up the sand. Everyone was looking around with butterflies in their tummies.

"Home sweet home!" Mariko yelled and threw herself down the stairs. Outside she yelled again.

"Gunter! Gunter ? Where are you baby?"

I felt disorientated getting out of the bus. I think we all did. I looked around at the bay. It was quite deep and sheltered but we were still getting warm orange afternoon sun. In front of Renwick House, which was big and made of brick and looked all old and pointy with fake turrets and things, was a lawn. The lawn ran to the shingle which blocked the view of the beach. To the left (facing the sea) was a stream, which cut through the middle of the bay. The left arm of the bay was marked by an old lighthouse on a slight hill. Around the right arm of the enclosing bay (behind the house) were a lot of rocks and the bay ended in a small cliff at the top of which a track seemed to lead to old forts from the war that looked out to sea.

Just as Aunty Liz drove up, out of the front door came a biggish man with thinning blond hair, a goatee, round pebble glasses, wearing a purple polarfleece, a carpentry belt, olive green board shorts, and sandals. This was obviously Gunter, and he introduced himself to all the others, shaking their hands and smiling a lot.

Then an old woman appeared at the doorway and came out to join us. She said her name was Deirdre Jones. She had pale white skin that showed blue veins, with messy gray hair and dressed in a gray cardigan, and pleated gray skirt with a big pearl necklace. She had a black shawl and a plain face and looked very frumpy but she spoke with a musical accent. I liked hearing her and Bernard, who was Scotty's black guardian, talk together because they both had nice accents.

I was listening in to the adults talk, when Ashley tugged my arm and pointed quickly up at the house. I followed her gaze up to the gallery of windows that looked out over the beach. Looking out of the windows at us, I could see the face of a man sneering out at us. I looked along the gallery and then I saw something that chilled me. It was another face – or should I say, half a face. The mouth was twisted, the nose smashed and one eye had completely gone. It was all an awful red suggesting it had been burned. Then it noticed me and simply vanished. I looked for the other face but that had gone too.

Ashley slipped close to me. She looked worried.

"You see 'em too?"

I nodded.

So now we knew what was wrong with the deal. Renwick House was seriously haunted.

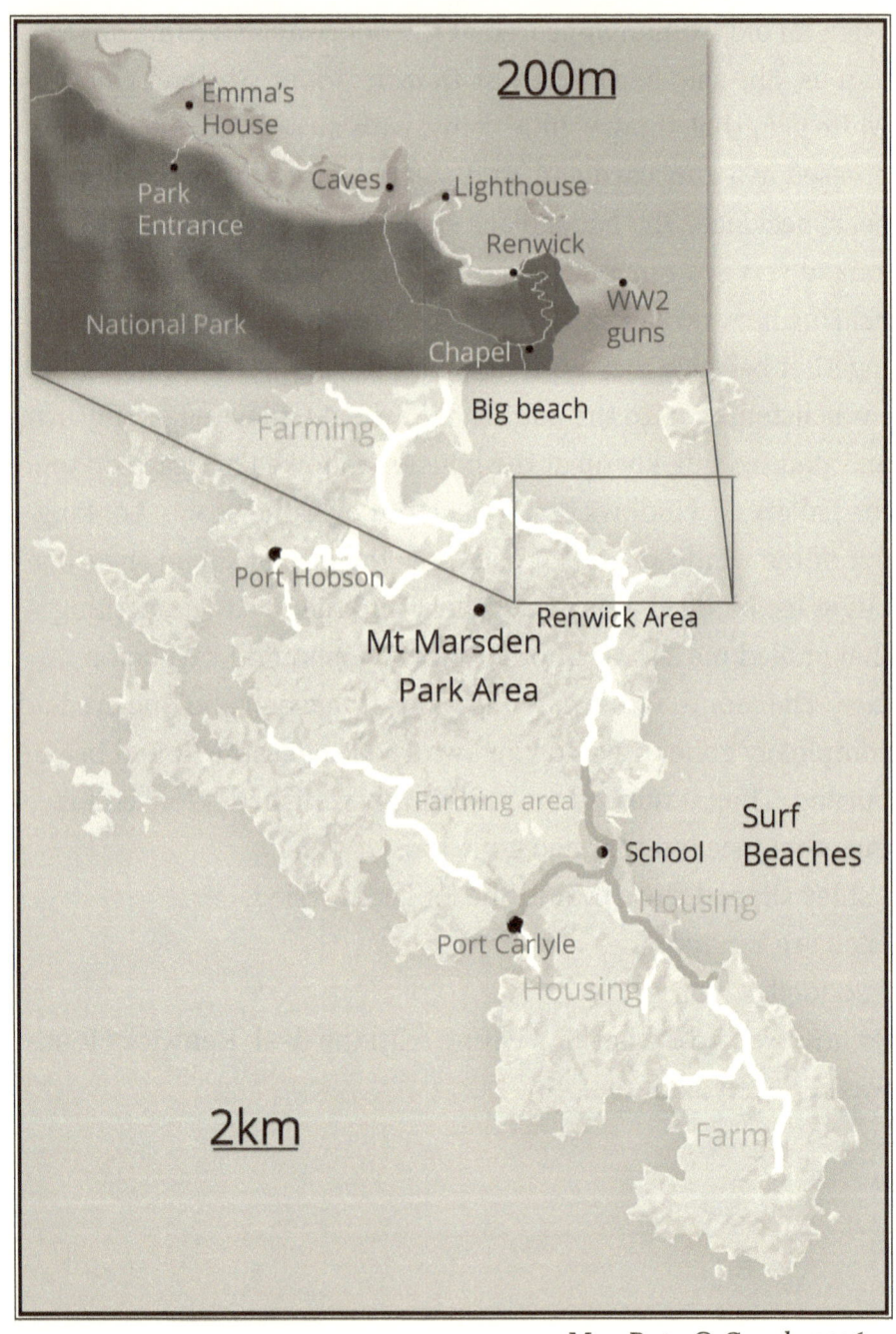

200m

Emma's
House

Caves

Lighthouse

Park
Entrance

Renwick

National Park

WW2
guns

Chapel

Big beach

Farming

Port Hobson

Renwick Area

Mt Marsden

Park Area

Farming area

Surf
Beaches

School

Housing

Port Carlyle

Housing

2km

Farm

Map Data © Google 2016

CHAP+ER €IGH+: A LI++LE CHA+

"Sam, why didn't you tell us everyone's names and descriptions? Kevin was right. It's *important*," Sue says with gentle disappointment.

"Because it could kill people," I reply, totally seriously.

I must have said it right because she doesn't try and tell me off.

"*How*?" she asks, thinking about it.

"Would you bet *your* parents' lives that your Police computer system could not be hacked by the best Russian crackers money can buy? Because I can tell you, they are pretty damn good."

"Umm..." her eyes flicked as she thought about it.

"Look, if the fire had *anything* to do with the Russian underworld that's what you're asking me to do. Because those guys are *way* mean. They don't just kill their *targets*, they kill *everyone*. Brothers, sisters, children, cousins. Now I *know* my family aren't dead and I *think* they're all safe somewhere. But if that information goes into your files and gets out I'm worried a lot of people somewhere else could die and it's not worth the risk to find out the hard way. So if you want me to keep telling you this stuff you have to promise me you won't write it down."

Sue pulls a face, thinking seriously. Then she sighs.

"Oh, alright."

She was thinking I didn't know that she has an excellent

memory. There's a pause as she realises I must have one too.

"How do *you* remember all this stuff so clearly, anyway?"

"I have total recall."

"*Total*?"

"Yes."

"You can remember everything that happens to you?"

"Absolutely every single thing."

"Everything you *ever* saw or heard? Even if you didn't think about it at the time. You can just summon up a memory and like, read it?"

"Uh-huh."

"How accurate is my wrist watch then?" she tests me, covering it.

I'd first seen it in the interview room. I could see it and the official clock.

"It's five minutes fast. Do you keep it that way?"

Sue's impressed.

"And you do that by memory?"

"Yeah, you had it on in the interview room."

She nods.

"So you remember absolutely *everything*? Does it go with being psychic?"

"No. I didn't always have it. I ... well ... of course just because I *can* recall everything doesn't mean I want to. If you didn't ask, I wouldn't bother. It takes a lot of concentration."

"It explains why you can remember so much detail and keep speaking with accents."

She pauses, then looks around her house and sighs.

"But I've spent so long listening to you I haven't even begun to tidy up," she tells me.

"Do you want me to help?" I offer.

"No, thanks Sam, it's OK."

I can tell she wants some privacy for that.

"Well, I suppose I'd better go back," I say.

"Yeah."

"Sue, can I come back and tell you more?"

"I was hoping you would," she says. She sounded a bit official
– even to herself.

"It helps me take my mind off things," she adds, looking around
grimly. And then she hesitates a little before adding,

"I was thinking of going out to look at Renwick myself. Seeing
as it's now my case and I haven't even been out there yet. Would
you come with me and show me around?"

"Sure. When do you want to go?"

"Monday, I need to pick up some things from the station."

"Cool."

I hesitate.

"Will you be OK for the weekend?" I ask.

I feel a bit silly asking an adult police officer that, but she doesn't
mind.

"Thanks Sam, it's sweet of you care. I'll be OK, I've got to go see
my parents, and I want to catch up with some of my friends.
Find out who knows what."

I get an impression.

"Don't you chase after her," I warn her, "It'll really hurt you."

"I won't," she sniffs, but I can tell she finds my advice annoying.

I'm fairly sure she's going to find out Rachel has left her for
someone else and I know she'll take it hard.

"Call me if you want to," I suggest.

"Or you," she says, evenly.

So I call a cab. She gets started on her tidying and I wait. When the cab arrives, to my surprise, she gives me a big hug.

"Sam, you're a great kid. It was really nice of you to take me to Rainbow's End. It was just what I needed and it reminded me how much I like kids. But don't forget you aren't an adult. You're allowed to goof off and have fun. Take it easy and I'll see you on Monday."

In the back of Alan176's cab I think about what Sue had said. It was true. When I first went to Renwick I'd played a lot more with the others but as the months had gone by we'd played less and less. Now I was on the run from aliens and was about to go out to dinner with an expensive lawyer and a P.I who I suspected of working for them. My closest ally was a woman police officer. Everyone around me just seemed a tad too official. I wished I could call Emma but if I got her parents they'd hang up on me. Her dad thinks I'm "a bad influence".

When I get back to the hotel I call Leonora to ask where she is. It turns out she's upstairs in our suite. She opens the door and leaves it open with a casual

"How was your friend?"

"Much better thanks."

"Good! Michael called, we're on for dinner at seven."

She goes back to her room and puts her laptop back on her lap.

"Oh, OK," I comment and go into mine.

By now my breakfast has worn off and I'm actually quite hungry. I wasn't sure how I could get a snack before seven. To pass the time I decide to try calling Emma. It's six o'clock on Friday, which was usually take-out night. I make the call but all I get is the answerphone and I don't think it would be a good idea to leave a message.

That left me alone with my empty stomach for an hour. What to do? I decide to try reading Leonora and see if I can catch anything but I discover she isn't thinking about me at all. She's emailing her friends about a party back in London in a week's time. As far as she's concerned her work here is done and she's going back home.

Her careless self-centredness depresses me because it makes me feel more alone than I had done until now. If she was plotting something evil at least it meant I was important. But she'd had as much fun as she expected to get out of me and she was moving on. That I still didn't know where I was going to live, and I still didn't know where the others were, wasn't her problem. The next half hour is a kind of food-less torture. I lie on the bed thinking about how nobody really cared about me, and for all the stuff I'd bought that morning, I was still alone in the world. Then I hear a cupboard in the lounge open, a tearing sound and Leonora appears at my door stuffing potato crisps in her gob. "Better get ready for dinner. If you want to use the bathroom, Sam, better do it now because I want to have a shower."

"Could I have some please?" I ask pointing at the crisps.

"Look in the minibar. Help yourself !" she shrugs simply.

I open the cupboard and there's a whole heap of junk food. I change my mind and take a Mars bar instead. It feels fantastic to get some food back in me again.

Leonora disappears into the bathroom and turns the shower on. I suddenly realise her laptop and phone are unprotected. Then I realise this actually isn't *my* thought. Leonora didn't interest me at all because she wasn't in on anything important. But thoughts are catching and sometimes when someone thinks them hard enough their thoughts carry outside their own mind into the minds of others. Sometimes you can find yourself saying or doing something which you wouldn't normally do, just because the thought is there. I'd fallen into that trap before. It was something Dr Prosperov had warned us about.

Then I think, "I could have some fun with this," so I sneak out of the lounge and into my own room to get changed as quietly as I can. I've decided that if Leonora suspects me, I may as well dress the part and be a gangsta. So I change into my trousers first, then pull on my new black hoodie, the black basketball shoes, take the shades out of the case and put them on. It's fun to wear this sort of stuff again, even though it can't actually *do* anything. There's no mirror in my room so I go back to the lounge to find Leonora, wrapped in a towel, sneaking up purposefully on her room's doorway, the sound of the shower in the distance.

"What d'ya think," I yell.

My sudden appearance where she hadn't expected me, made her jump, with a little squeal – a picture of girly shock. It's funny, although I notice her balance as she turns, and the speed of her hands is pretty quick. She can obviously handle herself in a fight. I make out I'm pleased with the outfit to cover my smile.

Leonora straightens up again.

"I thought you were a burglar!" she tells me clutching her chest.

"Nah," I say, pretending disappointment, "I was trying to be a gangsta."

"You need to wear the bling then, dear," she says and sweeps into her room, grabbing a bottle of something before heading back into the bathroom.

I don't like bling so I wasn't going to wear any. Tarik likes it, but me and Scotty agree it looks skeef. I like the hoodie though.

As Leonara relaxes into her shower I decide I *will* slurp her laptop's hard drive rather than her phone's Sim. Sims give you warning but hard drives give you history. There was something odd about the fact that she had got here before Sir Michael and there might be a clue in her emails.

The laptop was still switched-on lying on her bed. I pick up the remote. I can change the channel from her bedroom. I switch on the TV and slip into the bedroom, take off my watch, open it and jam it over the USB port. The gel sticks on and starts to glow. After loading the trace program the disk begins spinning fast. I change channel, then again, and again, and again, and again. I slip into the lounge to comment.

"Man this is crap."

I flip until I find the Deutsche Welle with a documentary on the Tuareg. That's different so I let it run. I guess it will take five minutes to slurp the disk. I start counting from three hundred quietly. Grandpop taught us you had to say it aloud to yourself to make sure you kept the rhythm. Then, just as I get to two hundred seconds, Leonora turns the shower off. My watch is still in her room! I force myself to keep counting and listen. My heart rate is creeping up. I get up and go to my room to get some of the bling Leonora had bought me. I put it on the couch back as if I'm trying it on and slip into her room. The watch is still running the disk hard but I have no choice. I unpeel the gel from the port and close it up, before putting the watch back on. I get to the couch just in time to lift up an ugly silver necklace in front of me as Leonora opens the bathroom door.

"I dunno, what do you think," I ask as she passes by.

"Looks fine to me," she says passing through.

The laptop has stopped running hard but I notice it has moved slightly. Luckily the watch stops anything upsetting

155

the screensaver so that's still on. I hope Leonora didn't notice anything but I know better than to freak out about it. As Dr Prosperov said, just because you can pick up others' thoughts, don't imagine your own are always that secure either.

Finally Leonora has put on her jewellery, eyeliner, lipstick, foundation, powder, blah bah blah, and got herself ready. I realise she was making a special effort for Sir Michael and she scrubs up well. By contrast my black shades, hoodie, jeans and trainers look a bit casual, but then I'm not too fussed, and as far as Leonora is concerned I'm a specimen of local teens which she thinks of as another species.

We take a cab to the restaurant. It's in the middle of a park, quite a while from anywhere. I feel a cold nervousness as we nose through the gates and along the long drive through darkened trees and lawns. Sir Michael hadn't known anything about our operations but it was always possible he too has been compromised and I'm not entirely sure what I'm getting myself into.

Sir Michael seemed a good guy. He had helped us with Ax, which was why I had messaged him. But I also knew the reason why everyone had evacuated was we had been betrayed. I had worked hard to avoid being trapped for days now, but so far there hadn't been any real challenges. If I was going to be wrong anywhere, this was it.

Despite the fact the restaurant was quite busy climbing up the back stairs to a private room made my stomach ache a bit. I wondered how far I could get if I needed to escape. The door seems a bit solid.

We go in and find Sir Michael with a wine, waiting. He gets up and gets gushy calling Leonora "darling" and kissing her cheek,

then shaking my hand in the way adults do when they want to
you to pretend you're like them. He's nervous too. He's boringly
dressed in a dark gray suit, white shirt and violet silk tie. We
settle down to drinks – wine for the adults, coke for me – and
bread with dipping oils.

It's a large room for only three. The wallpaper's yellow with
small square patterns in dark green and the lightbulbs have
a hard time not making it feel dim. It feels like a place where
people make hard decisions. Sir Michael feels that way, anyway.

"So Sam," he begins with fake cheeriness, "has Leonora been
looking after you?"

You don't have to be psychic to see something's eating him.
He's just too intense. I begin to start reading him, aware that he
might be in trouble.

"Yes, thank you Sir Michael," I say with my best manners. And
then thinking that sounds a bit empty and something more's
needed add, "At least I have some clothes now."

"Well, that's better than the alternative isn't it?" he laughs,
nervously.

I shrug and grimace. That might be a joke to him but it isn't to
me. Then he goes on. He keeps talking at me to keep me out. His
mind is fixed on practicalities but I know this is a distraction.
He's been told to do it. There's a shadow of a mind over him.
One that scares him a lot. I'm really on edge and alert now.

"Anyway, it's a start. Now, I know Dr Prosperov had a lot of
respect for you children, and especially you Sam, and while he,
and your Aunt are ... well ... wherever they are ... my duty is to
take care of you in a fashion he would approve of."

He pauses to bite some bread. He's quite hungry. He goes on.

"So far the New Zealand authorities have been reasonably

cooperative. I've met with your social worker who tells me you are seeing a bit of the youth aid police officer assigned to your case?"

"Sue, yeah," I reply with my mouth full. I'm still trying to get a reading. I figure the more talking he does the easier it will be.

"Well, as far as they are concerned as long as someone is acting *in loco parentes* and you are cooperating with authorities they don't really have any need to worry about you."

That's like a warning alarm. I've been *trying* to worry the authorities for five days. I hadn't slept in the same bed once. It was the best way to make sure *they* didn't grab me.

"So the next concern is obviously your long term care ..." reading my face he corrected himself "... or at least until your Aunt returns ... and your education."

I must have made another face which Michael responded to at once

"Yes, I'm sorry young man, but you are legally obliged to go to school."

What a bore that was. Still, at least a school would want to know if I vanish.

"Fortunately, of course, we get to choose the school. We are talking about a boarding school, of course, Sam. Much as I'm sure you could enjoy living in the Highgate we all have to come back to Earth some time. So, over the next few days we'll visit some schools in the city and decide which one you like the most."

"Yes sir," I answer miserably. The idea of being alone at some snooty boarding school doesn't appeal at all.

"Well, as I say we can't have you missing out on an education. And your welfare officer says that while you seem to have excellent maths and general knowledge for your age, your grammar and writing need work. So we'll have to find a place that can help you with that. I don't suppose you've given any thought to a career yet?"

I'm lost. Trying to read him and keep up with his talk is getting too hard. "Um ... you mean like a job?" I guess.

"Yes."

"Uh ... well ... I." I had once thought of being a policeman but after they arrested Grandpop I'd kind of got over that, and never thought about it since.

"Never mind," he interrupts, "you're still young; plenty of time to think about that. I wanted to be a pilot when I was a young man. I didn't become a commercial pilot but I did learn to fly in the end. The main thing Sam, is to keep your options open. Learn everything you can. Never let anyone tell you, you can't do something. There is always a way."

"Yes sir."

What a jolly bore this is. I really hope Dr P comes back before any of this has to happen. He studies me for a moment. He seems to be gathering his thoughts after his onslaught on my life.

"You know Sam, I don't know if you realise this but Gennady was a very interesting man. Some people regard him as an electrical genius to rival Nikolai Tesla. But his genius also extended to financial markets as well. He had ... has ... a fairly large fortune. He has taken some rather unusual market positions which will double it if they come off."

The oil plays. I know about those.

"And yet he came here to this (and I hope you won't mind me saying this about your homeland, Sam) fairly insignificant little country to provide a hostel for an unusual assortment of people. What was it all about Sam? Do you have any idea what he was doing and where he's gone?"

Now it's starting to show! Sir Michael *is* bugged and this question is for *them*. That means I'm in serious trouble! If he has all these legal rights over my life I could easily wind up disappearing in a bright silver disc having my brain pulled apart. That explained why they had taken their time. *They* were going to get at me through the system I had entered in order to hide from *them*.

As I've discovered with *them* before, *they* are very, very clever. Just as soon as you think you're winning, you discover they predicted your move before you even made it. Now I need to find a way to get out of here. I decide to try misleading him. I had been thinking about a better challenge sentence all afternoon.

"I don't know. For all I know he's gone off into the wild blue yonder with one of his Russian mates on some megayacht leaving me marooned," I say pretending to be depressed.

"Ah ..." Michael says recognising my challenge words. He sits back for a moment, dabbing his mouth with his serviette and smiling, then he looks at Leonora as if something has just occurred to him. "Leonora, would you be a diamond and find the waiter, they seem to be leaving us in the dark."

Leonora realises something's up, but also recognises she's been asked to leave us alone, so she gets up and slips out while Sir Michael eye-balls me. He feels pleased with himself, both for himself and his sponsors.

Unfortunately for him he hasn't passed the test as well as he thinks. "Dark" and "diamond" is the lowest security response to "blue" and "maroon". Dr Prosperov made diamond the lowest level because it seemed highest. That way anyone with the lowest response code would think they had the highest and wouldn't think to try fishing for others like "pearl" and "dawn". A spy might guess that, but judging from his clumsy response Sir Michael is no spy.

As the door closes behind Leonora Sir Michael is all ears.

"Well, it's not that hard Sir Michael, we were building a fortune using our psychic abilities to predict the future. The oil play you mentioned is an example."

Sir Michael looks at me shrewdly. I know from that he already knew more and realises his password isn't the key he'd hoped for.

"I surmised as much," he replies, covering. "So he was building on his earlier work in London. But you were from all over the world, how did he find you all?"

This was a throwaway question. He wants to keep me off guard. He's been warned about my sensitivities.

"Takes one to know one, Sir Michael. Dr Prosperov is sensitive himself," I lie.

"But why children?"

And that was a genuine question but it gave me the strong impression that Sir Michael was actually a *double* agent. He worked not only for *them* but also for the *infiltrators*. I answer his question according to the official script we practised.

"Dr Prosperov told us that most adult psychics had made their problems worse. A lot of them are drunks or performers or both. They aren't reliable and he wanted to train us before we got bad habits. Dr P brought some to Renwick and we saw they were pretty hopeless."

"Do you think any of *them* had anything to do with his

disappearance?"

That was another strange unbalancing question to keep me talking. I could see he was an expert at asking questions. Way better than I was. I decided to close it down.

"No, not really."

"What about Professor Lana Vilenskaya?"

And the sharp way he asks that makes me very worried. He's seen my eyes flicker. I have to feign disinterest.

"No, she's just Dr P's old friend from Russia."

Then acting on a guess I counter.

"Have you met her?"

"Of course I have, Sam," he says in a way that chills me to the bone, "It was I who helped her leave the Soviet Union twenty years ago. More recently she's been providing consulting services to some friends of my daughter."

I know at once when he says "friends" he's talking about the infiltrators. That means Lana's in danger and nobody can help her. I feel sick. There is something very bad lurking here but I get the feeling this is Sir Michael's idea of a kind of coded warning.

"Do you think Lana might know where Dr Prosperov is Sam?" he asks quietly.

That is a double question. If he knows her background it could mean he knows Dr Prosperov is with "our friends". If he doesn't it means he meant a Russian connection. I can't give anything away.

"I don't think she's involved in his business at all, Sir Michael. He was working on oil and gas with Gazprom. I've tried to tell the police that Dr P has powerful enemies in Russia."

Sir Michael seems to like that answer.

"So you suspect a Russian Oligarch?" he asks raising an eyebrow.

"Why stop at one?" I mutter.

Leonora reappears with a handsome Maori waiter whose company she seems to like.

"This could go all the way to the top," I continue.

"Ahh there you are, Leonora. Now, I think we are ready to order," Sir Michael smiles.

I'm not. The menu makes no sense to me at all. It may as well be written in Korean. The other two order quickly enough but I'm stumped. I ask for explanations of what things are but that doesn't help much because they seem to be making a hellava lot out of something as simple as steak, veges and mash.

Cam's dad didn't need fancy words to make delicious food, he just cooked it. In the end the waiter says he'll just ask the cook to make something special for me. I was OK with that, but I'm pretty sure I'm going to get a burger and fries with a fancy name. At least it's food.

"So has this police officer told you about any progress on Dr Prosperov's case Sam?" Sir Michael starts up again.

"No. All I know is they haven't found any bodies."

"Nor did they recover any documents as far as I can tell. I have impressed upon them my power of attorney should any show up," Sir Michael presses on.

Then he stops and looks at me carefully.

"Sam, I'm going to let you in on a little secret."

"What's that?"

"I have reason to believe that Dr Prosperov was involved in a little more than making money from psychic research," he says it in a way that suggests he wants to stop the dance and go up a level. I get the impression he is being told to move things along by *them*.

"Oh? Who told you that?" I ask quickly.

When anyone is asked a direct question they think of the true answer first. For a psychic this flash of insight is gold. It came to me at once. It wasn't one of *them* but someone I already knew. I couldn't quite get the name but it was someone close by who was hunting me using Sir Michael. The relationship was suppressed very quickly. Sir Michael seems to know what I'm doing, and they don't make people Queen's Counsels for nothing. He ignores the question and uses the same trick to put the pressure straight back on me.

"I believe that he was experimenting with extraterrestrial technology."

This is hard to respond to. The whole place was built on extraterrestrial technology but to the average person that's crazy talk.

"What does extra-ter-rest-ial mean?" I ask, playing the dumb Maori kid from the sticks, and buying time.

But Sir Michael isn't buying it. He leans forward, studying my face uncomfortably closely. He is hard to lie to.

"Not – of – this – Earth," he says slowly and clearly.

"You mean like aliens or something?" I answer, feeling rather uneasy and picking at breadcrumbs on my plate. He's still piling the pressure on.

"Yes."

The door opens and the waiter comes back in to refill glasses. The brief distraction helps. I realise Sir Michael will be able to tell if I'm lying but I might be able to put him off with a distraction. I wait until the waiter's gone again.

"I could believe it," I admit.

"Why's that?" he replies realising how I'm manoeuvring.

"Coz, he was doing so many spooky things. He did investigate UFOs for the Russian Airforce in the 1970s. He told us about that."

Sir Michael smiles, seeing how I'm dodging him. He's enjoying this hunt.

"Yes, I know about that," he says. "But what other 'spooky things' was he doing?"

"Mostly mind reading and remote hypnotism."

It was partly true. But I said it to make him think again. He isn't fooled. He sits back again.

"No, I'm talking about quite different technology," he says decisively.

"Oh," I answer dumbly, not sure what to say. He studies me some more, then says, "motive technology."

"You mean like what makes people do things?" I try.

"No. I mean technology to make things move. A motor."

"You mean like in a car?" I ask, looking around restlessly, as if this was boring, but I know exactly what he's after now.

He's studying my face like a hawk.

"A very small, very powerful engine," he continues, eyes boring into me.

"You mean like on a jet or a rocket or something?" I shrug, avoiding his eyes. He knows I'm struggling to avoid admitting anything, and I know he's thinking about Ka-rea-rea, my speeder, the craft that had brought me home while Renwick was self-destructing. He wants it. That must have been what he had been asking Leonora about in the late night phone call. It's his prize for cooperation with both *them* and whoever else was controlling him.

The waiters suddenly appear bringing in our food. And surprise, surprise: mine's a burger with fries. Teens equal burgers, I guess. Still, it's pretty fancy with all sorts of extras, including bacon, an egg, mushrooms and avocado, as well as frilly lettuce, so I'm not going to complain. While he's dealing with the waiters he takes his eyes off me and I can have another shot at reading him. He's hunting to get Ka-rea-rea, for sure, but there's something else. Something in the background to do with a war and his daughter. It doesn't make sense.

But as soon as the waiters leave Sir Michael is back on my case. "No, not a rocket, a very different sort of engine," he says. "An engine so small it would fit in a briefcase but so powerful it can power a craft up to Mach 7 in almost no time at all. An engine that can break all the known laws of gravity and momentum. An engine powered not by fuel but by the quantum fabric of space-time itself. That sort of engine."

He's been told exactly what he's looking for. I take a bite of my burger. It's good. Being so nervous, I've forgotten how hungry I am. I take a drink of water while I think about how to answer. Mrs Jones used to tell us it's always important to tell half-truths. She was a professional clairvoyant in Wales and was always telling lies. Not because she *didn't* know things, but because she *did* know things, and some things – like death dates and times – are best not shared. But she warned us not to lie. She always told us most people can spot a lie almost at once, but if you say something that is literally true, but deceptive, they find it much harder. I shake my head and look back into his bright blue eyes. "I never saw Prosperov playing with any engines, Sir Michael, that was more Ken. Dr P did do stuff in the lighthouse but I

166

don't think he was turning it into a rocket or anything. If he was, it never went anywhere," I tell him.

"What about Kenbish then?" he asks impatiently.

"Ken worked on his van but I don't think he had any alien technology. Otherwise he wouldn't have sworn so much."

"Could Dr Prosperov have worked in secret?" he checks.

"Yeeah, easy," I pretend to admit. "He had all sorts of strange stuff in the lighthouse and there was a room in the cellar we couldn't go into."

"Couldn't go or weren't allowed?"

"Both. It had a hand print and voice print lock. He took his Russian scientist friends down there but we never knew what they were doing," I lie utterly.

"Hmm, very interesting," he says doubtfully.

Sir Michael bends down to his briefcase and pulls out a pen and paper. The paper is a plan of the house from above and the side. "Whereabouts was the cellar?" he asks handing me the map.

"Let's see, there's the staircase, so it'd be about here, I'd guess."

"Excellent. We will investigate that on Monday when I've clarified the extent of the forensic investigation."

The room I was describing was actually the treasure vault where we kept some of our gold but it was also the entry to the tunnels. It was only about ten meters square, poorly lit and cold. If the others hadn't had time to take the treasure – which was likely because it was not important – I'd go in on Monday with Sue and try and empty it out.

"Did you ever try to go in?" Sir Michael asks taking back his plan and pen.

I feel now his guard is down, so I can start making more up.

"We weren't even meant to know about it."

Total whopper.

"How *did* you find out about it?" he checks.

"It was hidden behind a wine rack. There were footprints in the dust."

"Why were you in the cellar?"

"Playing hide and seek. We often did on wet days."

"And the police haven't asked you about this door?"

"No."

"And you don't think Dr Prosperov and the others took shelter in there?"

I genuinely had never thought of that because I knew they wouldn't. Of course they *had* passed through it to the tunnels and evacuation but nobody but us knew they even existed.

"I don't know. You know that never occurred to me! I always assumed the room was too small because he only ever took a few people down at a time. Maybe they're still there!" I pretend to get excited.

"Hmmm Sam, I don't think so," he says calmly putting the map away.

"Why not?" I say trying to be dramatic.

"Because if it were *my* sister who was missing I'd have been in there *already*," he smiles, grimly. His eyes are full of experience. Damn, he had me. It had been a trap and I'd fallen for it. He'd been really trying to find out where I'd suggest which was where he would *not* bother to look.

"*I'd* have suggested *anything* with the remotest chance of finding my sister again. I would be frantic with worry."

He searches my face with a slight smile.

"Sam, it's perfectly obvious you know where your family is. I'm willing to wager you *probably* know where Dr Prosperov is too.

And I'm further willing to bet dollars to doughnuts that they aren't hiding in the cellar strongroom."

He pauses to take a bite of his meal. Then returns to his theme. "Prosperov is a genius Sam. That doesn't make you one. And it doesn't mean I'm a fool either."

My burger suddenly tastes rather plain. I hadn't managed to fool him at all and worse, now he knows how deceptive I can be. Michael sits back in his chair and studies me for a while. Then he moves back up to the table and tries again.

"Let me explain why I'm interested in this technology Sam." He pauses to eat. Leonora has been listening-in, both confused, and fascinated. He swallows and goes on.

"As you know at the moment the world runs on oil. Without oil there would be no trade and without trade there is no civilisation. Trade is how each nation contributes to our rise as a species. Without it the top scientists in America, Asia, and Europe would have to spend their days worrying about how much food they could find. Trade allows us to specialise, and specialisation allows us to develop and move forward."

"Now there's two big problems with oil. The first is that there is only so much of it. Oil mostly comes from the time when the dinosaurs were destroyed by a giant asteroid and there was only so much carbon about at that time. So we must eventually run out. Second, and more importantly we are burning it up and making carbon dioxide at a faster rate than the great volcanoes that were going to kill the dinosaurs if the asteroids hadn't got them first. That would be problem enough, if we weren't *at the same time* wiping out the rain forests that can suck up all that carbon and store it as trees and leaves, out of harms way. Put those two together and we can expect a climate catastrophe if we don't change our ways fairly soon. Weather patterns will change and the farms everyone relies on for food will fail. When food is scarce there is war and a modern war could easily destroy civilisation completely Sam."

He stopped to see if he's made an impression. So far his argument squares with everything else I'd been told so I just nod thoughtfully.

"Now the problem with people, Sam, is once they have something they don't want to give it up. Trade is good for us, it makes people richer, live longer and generally raises them out of the gutter of poverty. Not just in the developed world Sam, but everyone. Now you can't ask a Chinaman whose father broke his back working in the fields to give up his new well paid job in a factory and go back to doing what his dad did, just because of the effect it might have on the climate. He'll just think this is a new form of robbery that the West has been practicing on his father, his father's father, and his father before him, all the way back to Marco Polo. In other words Sam, he doesn't want to give up all his hard won development up. And why should he? Why not someone else? The problem with that, Sam, is that everyone says the same thing. 'Why me? Why not the other chap?' So nothing happens."

"So the best answer to these problems is not to go backwards to sail boats and horses and carts but to go forwards, and all over the world there a thousands of scientists working on new technologies that will make a small difference.

He takes another bite because his meal is getting cold. Then he resumes.

"But Sam, it's not going to be enough! The rate of progress in technology is not as fast as the rate of degradation of the life giving properties of the planet. The result will be shortages, competition and very probably wars."

"So what we need Sam is something totally new. A leap of centuries into the future. If we can do that we can prosper as a species and avoid a lot of suffering. That is why I want to find this technology Sam. With power like that the energy problem would be solved. I am certain Dr Prosperov had access to it. I know you know more than you've told me. But I'm sure if he were here Dr Prosperov would want you to help on this project towards a better future for humanity."

What pleases me is that all Sir Michael's talking had given me time to finish my burger. I also knew everything Sir Michael had said was totally, to suck me in. I don't trust him at all.

For a start he wasn't thinking about putting that engine in power stations, but in military jets. Our speeders fly rings around jet fighters. Tahira had proved that on some American F-16s once just for fun and if any air force had fighters with speeder engines it could beat any other air force in the world – even the U.S.A. I knew that for the military to control the air means to control the land and the sea as well. But I also realised something else must be going on here. Why give me this B.S line on saving the environment? Why did he even want my cooperation? Wasn't I right where he wanted me anyway? He had to be building up to something else.

"Sir Michael?"

"Yes, Sam?"

"Don't you think that *if* there were aliens they mightn't *want* us to have an engine like that?"

He's catching up with some eating.

"I mean it's a bit like Mau-i stealing the fire from Ma-hui-ka isn't it?"

Sir Michael thinks about that, chewing.

"How does Maui steal the fire?" he asks, chewing and humouring me.

"Well, he pushes his Aunty Ma-hui-ka's goodwill until she shows him how to make it himself, but she tries to burn him first."

"Well, perhaps there are ways to avoid getting burned," he says pleasantly. He seems to think he has a deal with *them* that would help him. He's finished his meal now, as has Leonora, who is following the conversation with some interest.

"Leonora, would you be a gem and fetch the waiter please," Sir Michael suggests. Leonora slips away and out the door. As I watch her go I had finally realised his plan.

The only way *they* would deal with him was to trade something of greater value for something of lesser value. And as the engine on my speeder is probably worth more than the Bank of England, Sir Michael has to be trading something other than his relatively small fortune, and the only thing he has worth that much to *them* is *me*.

But there are obvious problems. Anyone could see that Sir Michael needs a guarantee that *they* would keep their side of the bargain. If he hands me over and gets nothing back he's screwed. That means he has an interest in keeping me out of *their* reach at least until he has the speeder. So I decide to challenge his plan on its weaknesses to see what sort of reaction I get.

"Sir Michael?" I ask quietly.

"Hmm?"

"What happens if I don't give you what you want?" I ask him quietly but directly. He too lowers his voice.

"Excellent question Sam. Perhaps we'll make a lawyer of you yet.

172

Well ... for the moment you are under my protection ..."

"And if I don't. I won't be?" I shrug.

Sir Michael puts his elbows on the table, fingertips to his lips.
"Sam, you probably know my protection doesn't mean much.
The only reason they have for dealing with me is that I can get
them what they want with much less fuss than if they just send
someone to just grab you."

"That might be harder than they think," I warn, trying to sound
tough.

"You've done well Sam, I'll give you that, but speaking from
recent unpleasant personal experience I can tell you your days of
freedom are numbered. Like me you can cooperate voluntarily,
or you can cooperate involuntarily, but we will cooperate one
way or the other. We have no power and no choice. I suggest
it would be far better for you if it were voluntary. They are
civilised, after all."

"But all you've talked about is what *you* want. What do *they*
want?"

"*They* want you to be reunited with your family, wherever they
are."

It takes a moment for me to work out what he means, but then it
sinks in.

"Oh, I'll bet they do," I say grimly.

They don't give a toss about reuniting me with my family.
What they really want to do is tag me like an animal, let me get
rescued and trace me to where the others are with "our friends".
The alien's technology for tagging people on Earth is quite
simple and assisted, unwittingly, by the United States
Department of Defense. What *they* do is fold a nanowire
antenna plus an interdimensional communicator into a food

capsule smaller than a grain of pepper. A nanowire is a tiny, tiny filament of ultrathin wire to pick up the signals from the Global Positioning System satellites.

An interdimensional communicator is actually nothing more than a device for reading and changing the spin of a subatomic particle. It's called "entanglement" and works by splitting twinned streams of particles. If the spin on one particle is changed the spin on it's separated twin also changes immediately regardless of how far apart they are. Einstein apparently had a long German name for this which translated to "spooky action at a distance". It works because the informational dimension of existence links both particles even though they are physically separated.

Alien technology uses twinned radioactive masses instead of particles. Once split the two twins maintain superdimensional information links. This link creates channels for communication down which you can send codes. By changing spin directions you can send a digital signal of zeros and ones. In this way two communicators with paired masses can exchange signals over any distance without interception or interference. The beauty of it is that it is entirely passive. It emits no signal that anyone can detect because the only signal is to the superdimensional channel which cannot be jammed or even easily detected.

The tag capsule breaks down in the stomach and attaches itself to the large intestine. The antenna then unfurls following the intestine and is about two meters long – which is still way shorter than the intestine. Being fractions of a millimeter across the only human technology that can detect the antenna is a hospital Magnetic Resonance Imaging machine. But because the MRI's magnetic field induces a huge current in the antenna it

usually disappears in a flash as the aerial filament burns up.
Of course this tag only works on Earth. If *our friends* showed
up and whisked me off to their world it would be useless. The
GPS satellite signal is detectable within our solar system but
any further away it's too faint. But "the Service", *their* military
arm, has miniaturised tags which can detect the gamma rays
from pulsars. The pulsars – which are spinning neutron stars
– act like giant GPS satellites for the whole galaxy. NASA uses
them to guide spacecraft but our detectors would never work
on earth because of all the radio signals that would drown out
the pulsar's signal. But *their* technology is way better than ours.
Their tag can provide vectors to locate a tag to within a thousand
kilometers in the galaxy, a million trillion kilometers across.
The Service tag is a shiny metallic egg-sized object which
requires an operation on the stomach cavity to be installed. I
was not keen on being tagged with one. Partly because I don't
like the idea of *them* operating on me. But more importantly it
could mean I would never see my family again because if I was
rescued by "our friends" the tag would give their home planet
away and defeat thousands of years of careful hiding.

"So you get an engine, they get a tag. What do I get out of it?" I
hiss.

"Have you enjoyed the past few days Sam?" Sir Michael asks.

"You mean the spoiling rotten?" I ask.

"Exactly," he says simply.

"Well, yeah I s'pose so. But you said yourself you can't live in the
Highgate forever."

"Yes, well most people can't but someone who had an engine of
the kind I've mentioned probably could. They could probably
buy every hotel chain in the world if they wanted to. That

175

engine is worth trillions, Sam. Even a one percent share of it's future revenues would probably make you richer than your own country. You've had only the smallest taste of the wealth that could easily be yours."

I pretend to be struck by this, even though it angers me, but then I ask the clincher.

"And if I don't cooperate?"

"I'm rather afraid *they* will get what *they* want one way or another. *They* know where you are, and *they* can act at any time. I'm just trying to offer you an opportunity to help yourself and the whole human race at the same time."

So there it was. "*They know where you are and they can act at any time,*" he'd said. They *had* tagged me. Somewhere in the meal I had just eaten, was a tag. It was probably unfurling its antenna inside me right now.

It was definitely time for plan B.

"I WON'T DO IT!" I yelled loudly at him defiantly, getting up.

"Sit down. One way or another, I rather think you will," he affirmed quietly. He reminds me of a Jaden, but with nicer manners.

"YOUR FRIENDS ARE NOT GOING TO STICK ANYTHING IN ME!" I yell again. What I was yelling made sense in the context of our talk but I knew downstairs it would sound somewhat different.

"Sam, sit down," he snaps, I can tell he's under pressure from his handler now. "You cannot win against them. Your only chance is to negotiate."

"YOU CAN'T MAKE ME," I bellow, heading for the door.

Leonora suddenly appears at the door in front of me. She looks annoyed.

"Keep your voice down. The whole restaurant can hear you," she hisses.

"NO, I WON'T BE QUIET. THAT'S HOW YOU PEOPLE OPERATE!" I yell even louder, knowing exactly how that would sound downstairs.

This infuriates Leonora who grabs me and shoves me towards my chair.

"KEEP YOUR HANDS OFF ME!" I yell again, adding more fuel to the fire.

This just makes her shove me harder. She has certainly remembered her police training. I can't resist.

"You are insulting the one man who is in a position to help you. Now shut up, and show some respect," she snarls.

Leonora is a full grown woman, and I am a pretty small fourteen-year-old, so she is not only bigger than me, but more forceful. We were never trained in amazing Kung-Fu skills of the kind you see in movies. That was partly because to do it takes decades of training and in movies most of the stunts are done with a whole bunch of guys pulling the actors around on wires in front of blue or green screens. Also, real fights I'd seen around Ax's gang as a kid were far faster and more brutal than those pretty dances, and our parents and guardians would never have allowed us to fight like that.

But it's not just physical. Adult ordering can freeze a kid in his or her tracks. Fortunately I had been trained to ignore authorities. That left her with her strength and fortunately Mariko, the Okinawan, *did* teach us just enough Judo and Aikido to get out of situations where we were being grabbed or manhandled. In pushing me down into my chair Leonora was already off balance and it took barely a sudden shrug and a side-step to send her

177

flying past me to hit her head on the table.

"LEAVE ME ALONE!" I roar heading for the door.

Now Michael's getting up, and Leonora, already sore at losing her balance and hurting herself is getting up and turning around.

"SIT DOWN! YOU MANNERLESS BRAT!" she yells.

I get to the door, turn the handle, and open it, when suddenly I feel hands grab my hair and pull me back.

"HELP!" I yelp.

I hear sudden movement down below.

Plan B works in some places and not others. In some places a brown child being abused by rich, white people in a private room is just business and nobody will lift a finger to do anything. Fortunately Plan B works in most civilised places including my home country so, as I am being dragged back to my chair, I'm not surprised to see the door fly open and two of the waiters standing there.

"What's going on in here?" the head waiter asks, looking pretty angry, from me to Leonora to Michael.

"Leave us alone," Leonora spits acidly

"No!" the waiter replies, "Not til..."

"Let him go, Leonora," Sir Michael tells her quietly.

Leonora lets go. I straighten up and go over to the Maori waiter

"You OK, little bro?" he asks, with an angry glance at the other two.

"Yeah."

But Sir Michael isn't finished.

"Sam, I'll wait a week but then it will be out of my hands and *they* know where to find you. Without my help I don't think you will come out of this very well at all. You have my number."

CHAPTER NINE: A TRAGIC PAIR

I leave with the waiters. We go downstairs to the restaurant and they lead me out the back to the kitchen. It's hot and busy but much more my style of place.

"What was that all about then?" the head waiter asks me.

"They had a proposition for me which I didn't like," I say using Scotty's famous Plan B words.

"Public school nonce," spits a young red haired chef with a strong Scottish accent. "Yew sit here a bit, son. You'll be alrigh'."

I'm told Sir Michael and Leonora decided against "pudding" and left, Sir Michael being tripped "accidentally" by someone who didn't apologise. The staff gave the guy who did it a "discount" when he paid up. They're very friendly toward me and give me a free cake and coke.

"Do you need a lift home, little bro?" the Maori waiter asks me. That's awkward. Now I don't have anywhere to sleep again. I didn't want to call Kevin.

"Ahm ... well I don't ... lemmee see."

I pull out my phone. Ring Sue, or not ring Sue? Sometimes you know in advance whether it's a good idea to call someone or not. And sometimes you don't. I wasn't sure, so I ring anyway.

The phone rings for one, two, three, four rings then Sue comes on the line.

"Sue Williams?" she sounds small and sorry. Not at all the cop I'd left.

"Hi Sue, it's Sam," I say quietly.

"Sam? Hi Sam, how are you?" in a beat her voice changes from rejected girlfriend to policewoman.

"Um ... not so good."

"What's the matter?"

"You know that rich lawyer?"

"Yeah."

"Um ... I ... I ... I don't feel safe with him."

There's a pause.

"Why not Sam?" she asks, suddenly sounding even more like a cop.

"Um ... well I'm in the middle of a restaurant kitchen right now. Everyone's being very nice."

"Where are you," she asks decisively.

"I'm at 'Raleighs in the park'," I say picking up a card.

"Wait there, I'll come and get you."

"Thanks Sue."

She rings off.

I wonder how mad she'll be when she learns the truth.

"Old lady coming to get you little bro?" the head waiter asks.

"No ... no, it's my case officer. She's a cop."

"Oh!" he says loudly. "Little bro's COP is coming to get him," he calls out loudly.

"Aw what?" someone complains.

I realise they were planning to have a smoke of weed and a cop would spoil their fun.

"I'll wait out the front," I offer.

"Nah, stay here. It's OK."

The wait for Sue is quite fun. And when one of the waitresses announces that Sue has come for me I'm a bit sad to leave. Everyone pats me or shakes my hand, especially David the Maori waiter.

Sue has her cop look on – but turned down a notch because she's dressed in jeans and a jacket. We didn't say much until we were driving down the driveway.

"OK Sam, what happened?"

I try to tell her without getting too specific but she keeps interrogating me. Finally she's had enough.

"Sam, I'm sorry but I simply don't believe in flying saucers! It's crap! And frankly you're starting to make me think you're in need of professional help."

There was a bit of a silence after that. She's mad at me for playing childish games and I'm mad at her for not believing me. I toy with the idea of showing her Qi, my watch, but she might not get that the technology simply isn't available on Earth. She might think I bought it with my new clothes. Finally I have an idea.

"Would you believe in flying saucers if you saw one?"

"What do you mean?"

"Well, if one flew around you, in daylight, right in front of you, would you believe in flying saucers then?"

"I suppose I would," she says doubtfully.

"OK then, if we go back to Aotea tomorrow I'll show you a flying saucer."

"Sam I ..."

"If you wanna see a flying saucer I'll show you mine," I tell her.

"Yours!"

"Well, mine to use. It's what Sir Michael is after. It's hidden on

181

the island. That's what I was doing when Renwick House burned down. It's totally secret OK ? but I'll show it to you if that's what it takes to make you believe me."

"And it will *fly*?"

"I'll fly in it. You can watch."

"Why can't I fly in it?"

"Because it barely takes me. It's very small."

"You'll fly it in the sky?"

"Yes. Where else do you fly things?"

"How high?"

"Well low, so you can see it."

"But higher than a few feet?" she checks. Light and shadow from the streetlights slides off her face.

I get her picture.

"No, Sue, it's not a cardboard box decorated with silver paper that I play in and make stupid noises with my mouth like a six-year-old. It's a craft more sophisticated than any other on the planet. Sir Michael thinks it's worth trillions."

She still doesn't believe me, but she's willing to humour me.

"OK Sam, show me your saucer. I wanted to take you out to Renwick House to go over the scene anyway. Doing it tomorrow might be better legally anyway."

I suddenly remember I hadn't got through to Emma yet. It's ten at night, and she's probably in bed. I set an alarm to call her in the morning.

"So how are you?" I ask.

"Fine," she answers, distractedly.

I know something's bothering her but I also know that she doesn't want to talk about it. So I talk about the waiters at the restaurant instead. I don't think she was even listening.

Before we get to her place it starts raining. We dash into her house, which is beginning to feel fairly familiar now.

"I've made you a bed in the spare room."

"Thanks Sue."

"I'll have to report all this to Geraldine. I don't know strictly what your legal status is now because Sir Michael is still your guardian. Legally he could drag you to wherever he calls home whether you like it or not."

"I know."

"I'll have to tell him where you are, you know?"

His pals know anyway thanks to the tag. They know exactly where I am to the centimeter.

"I know, do you want his number?" I offer.

"I'll do it tomorrow. I can't be fagged now. Let him think you're suffering a bit. It'll help him calm down."

"I think he can find out where I am anyway."

"How?"

"I'm not sure. What do you have to do to get your stomach MRIed?"

"Probably have cancer or something. Why do you want your stomach MRIed?"

"Don't worry about it."

I wonder where I might find a powerful electromagnet. With a big enough induced electrical current I could fry any tags Leonora had slipped into my dinner. I have to do it before I show Sue my Speeder or *they* will get me.

I think through the options: power stations; high voltage lines; lift motors; but they're all difficult to get to and extremely dangerous. Electromagnetic fields fall away very quickly from their source and I have no interest in climbing a high voltage

line tower to see how close I can get to 220,000 volts. I'd
get fried. Then I remember. The lighthouse! Nobody would
have bothered to disassemble that! I could do it tomorrow at
Renwick! Seemed rather fitting really.

We sort out a bathroom routine and I get Rachel's old
toothbrush. I hope Rachel didn't have any germs or anything.
Sue loans me an old pair of shorts and a t-shirt to wear as
pyjamas. They're too big but they have ties. I get into bed, she
says good night, turns the light out and closes the door.

I sigh finding I've been holding my breath. It's been a big day
and I try to relax by getting in tune with my surroundings. The
history of the house soaks through me. It's always been a busy
place with people coming and going. Rachel isn't the first break
up it's seen. There have been young couples, and babies, people
between marriages. It's a place that expects change and lots of it.
Perhaps in some ways it even creates change by expecting it.

But I don't feel sleepy at all. I'm totally wired; too nervous to
sleep. I'm tagged. It's the worst thing that could happen to me.
Everything I've been trying to escape over the past week has
caught up with me with an awful feeling of inevitability, like I
could never really hope to escape *them*. After all they have the
whole planet under surveillance and I know how easy it is for
them to get me here. So easy, and now I'm totally defenceless.

I imagine a grab team quietly gathering in the rain outside.
Gathering in two cars. They usually wear long black coats like
drovers with wide black hats; rain dripping from the brim.
Then there will be a knock. Sue will answer, be hypnotised in an
instant and it'll be all over. Half an hour later they'll have me in
a saucer with things up my nose tapping my brain.

I feel like slipping away into the dark like a wounded animal but, of course, it won't make any difference. I can't hide. I have a tag in my stomach telling *them* exactly where I am no matter where I go. I have to hope Sue offered some tiny protection. But ironically it's probable that my safety now depends on Sir Michael convincing *them* I will come around. I push a few buttons on my watch face and unlock the dial.

"Qi?"

Qi appears instantly on my wrist. He looks like a small Sinbad.

"I want to call today's data object of about 6pm 'Leonora's computer'."

"OK, Sam."

"When does Lenora's computer first reference coming here?"

"March 7 at 9:14 p.m. in an email from Antonio Rossi, Sir Michael Hamilton-Smythe's personal secretary to Leonora Cartwright. He asks her to fly to New Zealand immediately, e-tickets attached."

"March 7th?"

"Yes."

"Hoo boy."

Leonora had been sent two days *before* Ashley was tagged. This was worse than I thought. It meant the infiltrators were on to us before *they* were. The infiltrators already knew we were based in New Zealand before Renwick was traced. But how?

"No instructions?"

"No, just fly to Auckland, New Zealand and wait."

"And she does?"

"Her next message is March 9 at 12:42 p.m. saying she's at the Highgate and will be going to bed at 6 p.m. to beat the jetlag."

"Any reply?"

"None."

"Then what happens?"

"March 10, 7 a.m. she gets instructions to investigate the Renwick House fire."

"Who from?"

"Antonio Rossi."

"OK, does he have any suggestions?"

"Quite a few. He wants to know if there were any survivors or any signs of escape. He suggests she get to know the local cops and the nearest neighbours. His last instruction is to establish who is running the case and report in with what she's found."

"Does she?"

"Yes, it includes video clips if you'd like to see them?"

"Yes, thanks."

Qi waves his arms and a small screen appeared over his head which runs the video.

It shows Renwick looking sadly like a gutted shell filled with ash and burned wood. The shot was taken from a car and it zooms in from quite a distance to glimpse people in white suits slowly working though the debris. Then there is a conversation with a fire service investigator taken from a secret camera looking up at him. He tells her very little but gives her his card. Then there's some local TV clip and a few newspaper stories.

"When did she send this?"

"March 10, 10 p.m."

"She's a fast worker. Are there any emails about me?"

"Yes, she alerts Rossi that news reports say the police have announced a survivor."

"When's that?"

"March 11 at 10 a.m."

"And the response?"

"Find out who it is. More instructions in the morning."

That would be morning UK time. Her report was sent 10 a.m. New Zealand time but would have been received about 10 p.m. UK time if they picked it up instantly. Obviously Sir Michael wasn't going to wait up all night to find out who it was.

"And when does she send in her report?"

"At 3:17 pm. She identifies you."

"So that's early morning UK time. When does he respond?"

"Sir Michael himself replies at 6 a.m. He tells her to use the attached files to gain custody, to take you to the hotel and spoil you rotten. He says he'll fly out himself immediately."

Wow! He dropped everything to get to me. That might explain why he made a mess of it. He's probably still jet-lagged.

"Are there any files about her dealings with Sir Michael?"

"There is a lot of accounting information."

"How much does she charge him?"

"Her regular fee is five hundred British pounds a day plus travel penalties and expenses. She doubled it for having to drop something else at short notice."

I was impressed. I didn't think private detectives made *that* much.

"Does she have some kind of relationship with Sir Michael?" I ask, suspicious.

"The only relationship apparent from 'Leonora's Computer' is based on her business."

"Did this secretary dude ..."

"Antonio Rossi?"

"Yeah him. Does he have anything to say about Dr Prosperov or Renwick House?"

"He includes a plan of the house from Auckland Council."

187

"Nothing else?"

"Nothing other than general background."

That was strange. Why hadn't this Antonio dude been at the restaurant? A personal secretary generally stays close to the person they are secretary for. Was he busy somewhere else? What was he doing?"

"OK, thanks Qi. Look, I need you to do some online work for me."

"OK."

"I need you to contact para.no.ID. Challenge is Blue Maroon. Message header 'Big Blue joins Central Bank'. Body 'Tiny Falcon amber on local TV, popup plus 48.' And see what you can find out about this Antonio, what was his name?"

"Rossi."

"Yeah him. OK?"

"OK."

"Bye Qi."

Qi vanishes. I then open the watch and stick the USB port of the phone into the gel. Instantly the phone lights up and the gel begins to glow. I put them carefully under the bed and lie back with my head in my hands looking at the ceiling.

People think humans are the only intelligence on the net. But it's even more useful for *them*. For *them* the net is an awesome research tool because *they* have far more powerful computers to analyse the things people do and say, than even Google. I mean if my watch can process more than the average bank, just think what one of their massive Cyberminds can do. It's just another way they watch human civilisation. But if their security service gets involved it also means they have a very powerful tool for making us do stuff if they want to. I was running a risk using Qi

188

on the net. He was good but not perfect and my phone could be traced and counter-hacked. Then they could find out even more about us.

But I have to work this out! Sir Michael is working for the infiltrators. That's clear. He's also working with *them*. That's weird. The reward he was being offered was technology he had been told we had, because he'd never seen it. He obviously didn't think Prosperov would be coming back so it looked like he was just trying to get what he could out of the disaster.

And what if para.no.ID was compromised? It was possible. They hadn't acknowledged my first message. The whole point of the network was it was secret – even from itself. That was why I challenged them in my message. If they came back with "dark" and "diamond" I'd know it wasn't para.no.ID but "Central Bank" – our codeword for the Administration.

Sir Michael was probably hoping I'd be fretting and regretting my escape. He would know where I was, and Leonora would probably tell him about Sue. He'd given me a week. It was probably the same deadline he was under. But whether I did a deal with Sir Michael or not, both paths led to me being on board a UFO with them operating on me – something I wasn't so keen on.

I lie there for about half an hour trying to get to sleep but no matter which way I lie I can't get comfortable. The imaginary men in black are still outside in the rain, watching and waiting to get me. My mind races this way and that. I feel like a rat in a cage. My brain won't shut up. Finally I decide to raid the kitchen for some milk. I get up and creep down the hallway trying not to disturb Sue, but to my surprise I find her up, and watching TV. "Is it OK to get some milk?" I ask at the doorway.

189

"Sure Sam."

Then she gets up, "actually hot milk and honey is a good idea."

I stand back and she goes into the kitchen. I follow her and sit at the table as she automatically gets out a pot, puts it on the stove, opens the fridge and tips milk from a full two litre bottle into it. Then she looks at me.

"Can't sleep?" she asks.

"No."

"Me, neither. I had those pills for a reason. Now it's worse, and they won't let me have any more."

I feel like it's my fault.

"Sorry," I say.

She smiles at me. It's a warmer smile than she'd given me all evening.

"Don't be sorry, Sam. I'm not."

She goes back to stirring the milk with a wooden spoon. Then she speaks again.

"I feel as if she's stolen half my life, though. It's like a house where half the doors lead to a sudden drop because that half of the house isn't there anymore," she sighs.

"I keep wishing she'd just come back and yet I know she won't … she was always a selfish bitch really," she sighs again.

Then she laughs and looks at me.

"You must find this strange. Listening to the ravings of a lovelorn old dyke."

"You're not old. And my Aunt is one too."

"A lovelorn old dyke?"

"Well not lovelorn – I don't think."

"Oh. Well, I suppose you *are* used to the ravings of lovelorn old dykes then."

"Well no, she never talked about it. She ... well ... Grandpop was a bit ..." I admit.

"Yeah ... my parents are a bit ... too," she says.

She sighs again.

"Fat lot of help they were today too."

The milk is ready and she pours it into two mugs and stirs in a good amount of honey. Then she comes and sits opposite me at the table.

"What a pair," she laughs. "A lonesome lesbian cop and a deranged street kid."

"I'm not deranged," I say hotly.

"Well, you sure sounded it tonight."

"Sue. I really will show you something tomorrow," I promise.

"But it is big and I do need to be careful," I add earnestly.

"OK, OK, OK. Chill, Sam. If it is what you say it is, it will all happen. Be cool."

I knew she didn't believe me but she was right. There was no point getting uptight about it. Seeing was the only way she would believe.

"Why don't you tell me more about when you came to Renwick. I think we'd got as far as you and that girl Ashley seeing ghosts in the windows just before you moved in."

"You don't believe in ghosts either do you?" I ask, grumpily.

"No, but they made the story more interesting," she smiles.

I sigh.

"What's the point of telling you my story if you won't believe any of it?" I ask sulkily.

"Well, at least I listen to it, which is more than most would. And I admit I find it interesting to know what you *think* happened."

I make a face.

"And," she goes on, "it's eleven thirty on Friday night, TV's crap, and neither of us can sleep. So hot milk and a bedtime story sounds like a good idea," she smiles.

It was a warm smile when she did it like she meant it.

"Oh alright," I say, and this is what I tell her.

•••

CHAP+ER +EN: WELC⊕me +⊕ RENWICK H⊕USE

We were welcomed into Renwick House by Mariko, the punk Japanese bus driver; Gunter, the German craftsman; and Mrs Jones, who looked like a very frumpy old housewife. No matter how I looked at us all, I could see nothing in common. There was us three Maoris; two southern black Americans; two Vietnamese; four originally from Iran but more recently France; two originally from Turkey but had been a long time in Britain; and Scotty (who was white) and Bernard (who was black) who were from Zimbabwe.

As everyone was introduced to everyone else Mariko explained that Gunter had almost single-handedly restored the old building for the past year in his "boring way". She was obviously very proud of him, and despite the fact they were chalk and cheese, they seemed to really like each other.

"OK risten up," Mariko yelled clapping her hands. "Anyone who doesn't like sushi …" and she paused as if daring someone to admit they didn't like sushi. "Will be veeeeery hungry," she laughed.

I had no idea what sushi was and I don't think Scott did either. Mrs Jones led us in through the grand front doors. There was a large hall with black and white tiles with stairs from both sides. The whole house shone with gleaming polished timber,

193

the wallpaper was olive green, the drapes cream and the floors tiled. We passed beneath the landing into "the ballroom" as it was labelled on the old tiles above the door. The ballroom was almost as big as our old school's hall. The wooden floor was a deep, rich red while the roof was full of arches made of curving wood. Through the windows in the roof light streamed in spotlights onto the floor.

Despite the name on the door it felt like this had once been a chapel, rather than a ballroom. The effect was a strange blend of friendly and holy all at once. There were folding tables and chairs put out for us at the back. The church bits were gone but in their place were tables which were full of plates of little, round, dark green, and rice things. There were also clay pots of steaming liquid. Apparently this was called saki which the adults seemed to enjoy. We got our first taste of iced tea which was surprisingly good.

We kids were given first go at the food while the adults stood around talking and drinking the saki, discussing the allocation of rooms which were marked out on a big whiteboard plan of Renwick House. I knew nothing about sushi and was a bit suspicious of it at first. But Mariko's sushi was delicious as well as pretty and I was soon coming back for more. The big discovery was wasabi. It was Scotty who discovered that the hard way. He thought it was avocado. His eyes streamed bulging in his head and then he grabbed his nose. Of course we all had to try it after that and Tarik wanted to have wasabi eating contests – but nobody else was up for that.

When we'd eaten Mariko clapped her hands loudly again.

"OK, no servants here. We the servants! Bring the plates into kitchen. Follow me!"

So we stacked up the plates and carried them through some doors at the back of the ballroom. This was where we found my favourite room. It was a sort of like a café. It had bench seats and tables but the wall had huge windows in it that looked out over the shingle dunes and down to the beach. You could look all the way out to the horizon at a bit of an angle. From here we turned right into the kitchen. And wow! What a kitchen! It had more things for cooking than I had ever seen before. The pots shone with copper, the machines were large and made little beeping noises. It looked like a chef's dream come true. Mr Trân looked like he was in heaven. The dishwasher we loaded was a huge industrial sized machine that took every dish we had and still had room for more, and there were two of them!

From the kitchen we went out the back door past the market sized food store, past the waste processing station, and instead of going through the rear doors out to the loading bay, we hung a right through an enormous laundry full of big industrial washers and dryers, then into a corridor which ran down the west side which was where the sun was at the moment. The west wing was boarded up. Apparently that was stage three. The east wing was being built still. It had Mrs Jones and Gunter and Mariko's apartments and a big studio for Mariko but it was still only half finished. There were a few store rooms which Mrs Jones (who was leading the way) wanted to show the adults, that were pretty dull. Then we headed up a staircase around a lift in the southern side, in the shade of the pine trees, behind the house up to the next level.

This was the apartment level where we were going to live. The ballroom or chapel was in the middle of the whole house – a separate building – around which the much larger house had been built. From the windows in the corridor which ran around the inside of the apartment level you could see the ballroom's tall roof angle away to the sky. This meant the inside corridor remained reasonably well lit. Mrs Jones led us up to the front of the building.

I admit I was a bit worried about this because we were heading precisely where Ashley and me had seen the presences before. I noticed Ashley was hanging back, just as I was. But when we got there we found nothing at all. There was an open lounge at the end of the corridor complete with a large pool table, fireplace and lots of sofas and armchairs. Through the double doors in the lounge you could go out into the landing which took you up to the guest level or to go to the gallery. The gallery was a windowed room as wide as the house which looked out over the sea. Across the beach the view just seemed to stretch forever with the lighthouse on the left across the Pacific horizon to the cliffs on the right. There were cane sofas, chairs and tables, radiator heaters and the whole room was painted white.

The guest level was the next one up. It was under the tiles of the steep roof. This level was a bit darker as it lacked the big windows of the lower levels. Mrs Jones said originally this had been the staff quarters and the level below had been the patient's ward but Dr Prosperov wanted this reversed.

The apartment level had impressed me as open, light and much nicer than anywhere I'd ever even heard of anyone living. I had never been into a hotel then but I suppose now I'd have to say it felt like a comfortable sort of hotel. But the guest level was something far more intriguing and it was where Gunter's best work was to be found.

The apartments in the guest level had different themes. There was a Chinese apartment which was full of gold, lacquer and silk; a French apartment which was full of silver and dark blue; a Japanese apartment with hard looking mattresses and a huge bath; an American apartment which was like an old movie set; a Persian apartment with carpets and brass jugs; a small Mongol apartment apparently for Dr Prosperov's aide – although I noticed it had two bedrooms; and a huge Russian apartment for Dr Prosperov which we didn't go into. This level also had a library about the same size as the one we had at school but with large armchairs and a bank of screens and computers on one wall that looked like a TV station. Dr Prosperov's office was in the wing above Mariko's studio. For a kid like me, used to living in a little, busted, old house by the sea it was amazing.

Now Mrs Jones led us to our own apartments. With three of us we Kahus got the second largest apartment on the floor. The Iranians got the biggest because there was four of them. Most of the other apartments had two bedrooms. There were still a couple spare even after we had all chosen ours. For the first time ever Rewa and I would have our own rooms. The apartments were decorated in gray, brown and white with a lounge, a small kitchen area and a table. Every bedroom in the whole house had a small desk with a computer screen which was also a TV. Ours was on the east and looked out toward the lighthouse. Ashley and her mum were next door, Cam and her dad next to that. The Iranians were on the west side, along with Scotty and Bernard and Tarik and his dad.

All of us kids were excited. There was no sign of the ghosts so we started running around exploring the house in groups. Rewa, me, Ashley and Scotty went downstairs again and discovered there were two lounges on the north-east and north-western sides of the house. They looked very dull with a bar full of alcohol with more big TV screens as if they were a pub and of interest only to adults. Then we went outside around the back under the pines and discovered a huge workshop where Gunter had all his tools and materials. We also found a big shed which had the big yellow school bus in it as well as a big black Range Rover (which had to be Dr Prosperov's), a small pink BMW Mini, which we guessed belonged to Mariko, an old roundish looking wagon which seemed to be half made of wood which had Morris Oxford on the side (which we imagined belonged to Mrs Jones), a real rugged looking van which had to be Ken's and a beautiful Mercedes old-timer we guessed was Gunter's.

We went out the front and joined Tarik, Tahira, Asal, and Cam who were walking along the shingle bank throwing stones into the sea which must have been at high tide because it had covered most of the beach. There was driftwood everywhere and seaweed had been thrown on the beach as well. Gulls drifted overhead and small birds with long beaks kept a wary distance from us as they walked the beach probing for things.

We walked about two hundred meters along the beach and then turned to look at Renwick House.

"Ya know what? Dis whole place seems real familiar to me, real familiar," Ashley said.

"Is like I always live here," Cam added.

We all agreed, it did feel strangely familiar. And the other thing which was strange, but which we didn't say, was that we felt strangely familiar to each other too.

"Let's go to lighthouse!" Tarik said.

The lighthouse was about a kilometer from Renwick House on a headland that jutted slightly out to sea. We had to cross a shallow stream, walk along a long shingle bank, past a marsh and back on to the dirt road that went back to Renwick.

The headland was bare except for grass and a straggly old wire fence which wouldn't stop even the dumbest sheep. We walked for longer than we expected, but finally came to the bottom of the lighthouse.

It was about four stories high and was fairly run-down. The door was nailed shut with rusty "danger, do not enter," signs on it. We could see the glass at the top was broken, probably by kids like Tarik who threw stones at it.

The headland it was on was the most easterly point on the whole island which meant you could look back along the long, long coast to the North. The sea filled the air with haze as it dashed against the lonely beaches. The land was mixed between farmland, bush and scrub. It was so lonely. You couldn't see another house or any sign we weren't the only ones left in the world.

Suddenly we heard a distant clatter and a dot appeared over the ridge in the distance and grew rapidly.

"Helicopter!" Tarik yelled.

The helicopter flew along the coast and up and around the lighthouse. We jumped up and down and waved and the pilot circled the lighthouse once before heading up the beach toward Renwick House. We all ran back along the road toward the house to see who it was. The helicopter landed on the west side of the house by the road and one figure got out and walked quickly into the house.

The run back to the helicopter had turned into a race. Tarik, was the tallest and, not surprisingly, one of the leaders, but Ashley was right behind him and Cam, despite being the smallest, was determined to keep up. I ran with Scotty, who was not really trying, while Tahira was shushing along Rewa and Asal. She looked like a mother hen with her chicks.

The blades on the helicopter had stopped turning when we got up to it and the Mongol guy who had apparently flown it was standing next to it and smiling as we ran up.

"You guys wanna sit inside?" he asked. We were all surprised by his gentle deep voice and American accent.

"What's your name?" Rewa wanted to know.

"Well, my Mongolian name is Khenbish but everyone calls me Ken."

"How long were y'all in da States?" Ashley asked.

"Long enough to make a fortune and lose it again," he said good naturedly.

"How d'you fly this then mate?" Tarik said from the pilot's seat. Ken took the headphones off his head.

"I'll show you when you're eighteen," he answered, looking at Tarik with amused suspicion.

"Is this how Dr Prosperov gets to Auckland?" I asked.

"Yeah, most times, but he doesn't go there much."

Then he seemed to get distracted and cocked his head.

"Dr Prosperov wants to see everyone in the ballroom," he announced.

We got out of the helicopter and followed Ken inside, asking him questions about a million things.

In the ballroom Dr Prosperov was still wearing a suit and was again leaning on a table with his usual half-amused look, his stick next to him. It seemed odd that he had one as he didn't seem feeble. The parents were already gathered and had tea and coffee. There were a couple of packets of biscuits open and we quietly sidled up to grab a few.

"First, welcome. Am trusting everyone finding house comfortable. Is years work by architect craftsman Mr Zimmermann. Very good work in my opinion."

Gunter seemed to already be aware of Dr Prosperov's opinion and didn't look the slightest embarrassed.

"Second, fazility is to open on first February next year and is still much to do. Between now and New Year objective is to establish operating routines. For this we will host a few special guests. These to arrive soon. Is no panic as guests helping but remembering is workplace not vacation home."

"Third, organisation here is simple. Mrs Jones is boss. Do what she says. If you have problem talk to her. If you still have problem talk to each other and her. If you still have problem go elsewhere. Mrs Jones very reasonable woman. I have no time for stupid arguments."

"Fourth, most not legal to work here. To get around legal problem I get you all Visa card. All pay go to credit card paid in Euros. Working on longer term solution with Immigration Department. For moment you are willing workers on this small organic farm."

The adults laughed at that.

"Fifth, tomorrow is party to celebrate arrival of my wife Katya from America. Party at six, on beach. Mariko in charge of arrangements. And that is all. Mrs Jones you go."

Mrs Jones strode forward almost as if she were about to sing. Her Welsh accent was nice to listen to too.

"Well, everyone seems to be settling in very well. Now I won't keep you long because I realise some of you have come quite a long way today and must be starting to get tired, so I'll just mention a few things. First of all, while everyone has their own job, we will all need to help one another. If your job isn't busy that doesn't mean you can sit around reading magazines. It's a big house and a big house means plenty of housework. This brings me to the children. This house may seem like an adventure but it isn't. You also have jobs here, helping with the cleaning. "

All us kids suddenly looked shocked.

"Yes, that's right. Your parents aren't going to be cleaning up after you, you will be cleaning after them."

Our "parents" were looking very pleased.

"I'll be making up cleaning rosters for you all and I will assign you in teams of two. And note if your cleaning is not up to scratch I will dock your pay."

Mrs Jones was a very no-nonsense woman but the news that we would be paid was still not enough to make anyone ask the obvious question. It was Bernard who asked for us.

"Excuse me Mrs Jones, but I don't believe the children know how much they can expect to earn and for what."

"Thank you Mr Khumalo for reminding me of that. Children will be expected to work an hour a day during the school term, and four hours for the whole weekend. The rate is twelve local dollars an hour which means they can expect $108 in cash a week."

"Woo hooo!" I yelled. That was more money than I'd ever had in my life. And I don't think I was alone. All the kids looked pleased except Tarik and Ashley who didn't think so much of it.

"And during the holidays they will be expected to work two hours a day and four hours for the weekend. Which will earn them $168 in cash a week."

"But no work, no pay. And I'm certain anyone messing up anyone else's cleaning will not be very popular."

"Now I'd like to pass on to Mr Zimmermann to tell you a bit about the water, waste and systems we have installed in this house."

Gunter had a strong German accent which sometimes made him hard to understand but he told us about how the house drew its water from an underground stream that flowed through the caves that were to be found all over the island. He said the island was made of limestone and full of shafts and holes, some of them very deep indeed. The waste was processed in special digesters which also emitted gas for cooking and heating. The house had a stand-by diesel generator because the power supply was not reliable. It also had an internal computer network and every screen was wired to be a video intercom. You could also get the internet and TV via the two meter satellite dish on the roof.

There was so much to explore and it was still hard to believe we were going to live in this place at all. Only that morning we'd woken up in a cheap motel with nowhere to live and no job for Aunty Liz. Tonight we would sleep in a free apartment of Aunty Liz's – and our – new employer. It had all happened so fast we couldn't believe it. So fast, in fact, we had forgotten that somewhere out there Ax had moved back to our old village and found his mad dreams of being reunited with his kids ruined. That night we had brilliant home made Pizzas in the café. Our new chef Mr Trân whizzed them out almost as fast as we could eat them. He made it look so easy. It was obvious he could cook for this small number in his sleep. When everyone pitched in, cleaning up took less than five minutes.

It was an early night. Everyone was tired. Ashley, Cam and the little girls nearly fell asleep at the tables. I got into my new bed, which was more comfortable than any I'd ever had, and before I knew it I was in this big old empty house. I knew Ax was somewhere in it too, and he had a butchers knife. I could hear him walking the corridors, his footsteps echoing around me, so I wasn't sure where he was. Rewa was with me and we ran through the corridors to a staircase only to find he was coming up. But he didn't run, he just walked after us. We ran through more corridors. Rewa wanted to hide in a box and I was about to stop her when I realised I had to lead him away from Rewa. So I dashed away from where she was hiding.

Ax was like this bear creature and he sniffed as if he could smell Rewa so I walked out and taunted him until he started following me. I led him deeper into the maze of corridors. The way started to get tighter and tighter when suddenly it opened out into a big dome like room. In the middle was a thin bright light coming up from the floor. I ran to the light, my footsteps echoing around in the big dome. The light was coming from a hole in the floor no bigger than my finger. I peeked through and found myself looking down at green grass where Rewa was standing looking up at me. She was shouting at me to get out. Then I heard more footsteps. I got up and I could see Ax standing by the entrance looking at me. I taunted him to chase me but he silently shook his head, and then pointed up. I looked up and realised the top of the dome was covered by a huge gray spider about the size of a house looking down at me. Then I woke up, my heart galloping.

It was still dark. The only light in the room was a small red LED on the screen. I began to realise the curtains were pulled, and

finding the dark too intense, I got up and opened them. The
sky was incredible. Back home the night sky was good but there
were still street lights right outside our house which dimmed the
stars. Out here there was nothing, it was black, but the sky was
packed full of stars while the sea seemed to give off a sheen of its
own as it rhythmically washed up the beach and back.

Before I had been tired, suddenly I was excited. Being awake
at night just seemed too great an opportunity. I quietly put my
clothes and shoes on, and slipped out into the living room. There
was no lock on the door ("why would there be?" I wondered to
myself) so I slipped out into the passage.

The corridor was lit – but only just – by a few bulbs at either
end. I crept along as quiet as a mouse; checked the lounge was
clear, and ducked through that, and down the stairs; past the
gallery as fast as I could (because I was sure the ghosts were
there now); and at the ground floor found myself confronted by
the big main door. For some reason I felt opening it might set
something off, so I scampered down the side corridor feeling like
a naughty mouse that's got all the cheese.

The back door opened easily, and I slipped outside. It was very
dark in the shadow of the pines, and the sheds around the back
of the house looked spooky, so I scampered back along the drive
round to the front of the house. And there I had something of a
surprise. Over on the beach a fire was burning. I wondered what
it might mean, and as quietly as I could snuck up the gravel
road.

The people by the fire seemed to be doing something with a
large object, but I couldn't tell what it was against the light of the
flames, which smelt a little of kerosene. I crept slowly forward
keeping my eye on the shadows of the people. I was about

twenty meters away poking my head over the top of a bush when...

"Glad you could make it Sam."

My heart nearly leapt out of my body. Ken was standing behind me with a guitar under his arm, smiling. He must have followed me the whole way.

"Come over and join the fun," he said.

He led me around the bush and over the shingle down to the fire.

I recognised the figures instantly. Gunter's glasses shone in the firelight and Mariko's snub nose was silhouetted looking at him. Gunter had a big telescope on a low tripod and was carefully adjusting it.

"Sam's come to join us."

Mariko looked around and grinned, "Hi Sam."

"What are you doing," I asked.

Two voices answered at the same time.

"Astronomy," Mariko said.

"Drinking Bourbon," Ken said.

"Both," Mariko corrected.

Then they both laughed.

"Ve are ... in fact ... observing the rings of Saturn," Gunter said "... und zere sey are!"

Mariko bent over the telescope.

"Coooool," she said.

She looked up at me.

"You lrook, Sam."

I crunched over and put my eye to the viewer.

I was blown away. There they were! For real!

"Wow!" was all I said.

"Pretty cool, huh Sam," said Ken.

Gunter looked at his watch.

"I'll start recording in three ... two ... Vun. Vun twenty four exactly," said Gunter.

"What's he doing?"

"He's just taping the sky for five minutes," said Ken who was now standing next to me holding his metal cup.

"Sorry I can't give you one of these kid, but that's the law," he added.

I told him I didn't mind. Gunter wanted a refill from Ken's flask though, and Mariko snuggled up to him as he watched the sky and the equipment.

"So do you guys do this every night?"

Ken laughed, "Every night? No."

"Tonight was ezpecially good for Saturn and zere'z no cloud cover," Gunter added.

"This sky is huge," I gushed, "back home it's good, but not this good."

"In most parts of the world is now almost impossible to zee the stars, because of all the light pollution," Gunter said seriously looking up.

Ken laughed.

"You mean in most parts of Europe, Gunter. The world is a lot bigger than that. Out on the Steppe in Mongolia you see skies a lot like this. And in the desert in the States too."

"We lrost our stars in Japan," Mariko said sadly.

We were all struck by her words. I thought to myself, what does it mean, "to lose your stars?"

"Didn't your May-Orie ancestors navigate by the stars, Sam?" Ken asked.

I smiled at his mispronunciation of Maori. It's Mao-ree (with a rolled 'r' and short 'ee'). It was funny coming from a Mongolian with an American accent. But I answered his question.

"Yep, they were navigating across the Pacific by the stars a thousand years ago."

"Do you know Maori stars Sam?" Mariko asked.

"No, not many," I had to answer. I remembered something from those sleepovers on the Marae but I couldn't recall it clearly enough. And it suddenly seemed sad that nobody had ever taught me about them. I had lost my stars too. Not that I'd ever been given the opportunity to learn. The old people only passed what they knew on to very few.

"I think I'd like to find out about them now," I added almost to myself.

"So what do you think of Renwick? Do you think you'll stay?" Ken asked.

"I don't know. I think so. We haven't got anywhere else to go. But it's all so strange and sudden. Just when we needed a place to stay here it was. I haven't got used to it yet."

"Why d'you need new prace to stay?" Mariko asked.

I told them my story as quickly as I could. They were surprised, and not *so* surprised.

"I'll bet every family that he picked up tonight has a similar story," Ken said.

I was too surprised by that to react. I thought my story was pretty unusual.

"We were all in trouble when Dr Prosperov took us under his wing," he smiled nodding at the others. He sat down and picked up his guitar, beginning to pick a classical tune.

"I'd made some pretty atrocious banking decisions on behalf

of the Government of Mongolia. I fled to the States and went into banking there, but I met him through my father back in Mongolia, strangely enough," he admitted.

"I piss off Yakuza. Never know when to shut mouth," Mariko smiled.

"What's yakuza," I asked.

"Bunch of nasty rittle men with ..." Mariko began,

"The Japanese mob," Ken interrupted her.

"I vuz involved wit development in Poland. I vuz unaware my partners were fraudsters. Zey left me to take za rap," Gunter smiled.

"Dr Prosperov is very mysterious," Gunter said. "Even vee don't know much about him and vee haf verked wit him for three years."

"Four," said Mariko.

"Seven," said Ken, "and all I really know about him is that ten years ago he started the project to find a place and now it's nearly ready."

"Why here?" I asked.

"Well, he was kicked out of the States," Ken said.

"Kicked out?" I repeated, wondering what you had to do to be kicked out of a country.

"Well not kicked out, but the SEC made his life so tough he had to leave."

"SEC? What's the SEC?" I asked feeling very ignorant.

"Security and Exchange Commission. It's the police of banks and finance in the States. Very powerful."

"So is he very rich?" I asked feeling like a little kid.

"Well, he's no Warren Buffett, but he's rich enough to pay us more than we deserve and not notice it."

"But why did he want to come here," I asked a bit timidly.

"I was with him when he toured the world looking for places," said Ken.

"There were a bunch of countries he liked. Switzerland and Brunei were high on his list. So was Australia, Chile, Singapore and Norway. But he speaks no Spanish, doesn't like the heat and wanted to get away from Europe because it's too close to Russia for his comfort. Besides New Zealand is a friendly place where newcomers can fit in without too many questions. More importantly it's easily forgotten about by the rest of the world – which is something that suited him just fine. So four years ago he picks up this place for relatively little money from the Government with the help of a special May-ori lady who was interested in his project. The government didn't want to pay for it but don't want it knocked down either. Then he goes looking for an architect and a designer and finds these two," Ken smiled at the couple.

The telescope issued a couple of beeps.

"Za pictures are finished now," Gunter remarked to the woman in his arms.

"So's the bourbon," Ken commented shaking his flask.

"Bedtime," said Mariko looking at Gunter.

"Ken vould you help again vis de telescope?" Gunter asked.

"Sure, no problem."

"Can I do anything?"

"No thanks Sam, but you better get back to bed in case your Aunt misses you and freaks out," Ken said.

"OK. Night everyone."

They all said goodnight and I walked back down the road to the backdoor. I felt relaxed. It had been nice to talk to these adults.

They hadn't treated me like a little kid and tried to tell me off for being up. They'd just accepted me as being awake early in the morning and talked to me normally. I liked that.

The inside of Renwick seemed incredibly dark and I had no idea where the light switches were. I padded along the corridor not quite looking where I was going – just as Grandpop had taught me to use sideways vision in the dark. I got around to the front staircase OK, but I began to feel a bit nervous. There were presences in the house. I could feel them aware of me. It was if they were whispering all around me. They weren't friendly, but they weren't angry either. I just wanted to go bed. I put my head down and climbed the stairs.

When I got to the top of the stairs the sense of the presences was stronger. I realised this had been the wards where they'd lived, and more importantly died, and we were sleeping there. It was cold, my skin pricked. I knew they were there and I turned around. A wave of electric terror ran through me. I hadn't expected to see it as clearly. It wasn't transparent, or glowing or any cartoon story ghost, but looked real, as real as if he was still alive. The half-faced man I'd seen in the window was staring at me from the gallery entrance. His mouth a twisted hole, noseless with a single eye, the rest a mess of raw flesh dressed in a hospital gown that did not hide the metal leg and hooked hand. He started to walk toward me.

I think I barked a sort of terrified, "No!" and ran down the dark corridor. He kept walking. He seemed to be making this weird rasping noise which sounded insane. It was incredibly dark. I tripped over my own feet and leapt up again. I couldn't tell which number room I was up to. The ghost was still coming. I felt each door for numbers as I ran past them. Finally I found

211

our door. I looked up and the ghost was gone. I was covered in cold sweat and my heart was pounding.

It was still very dark inside our apartment. I could still feel the presences around me, whispering. I felt cold with fear and wanted to wake up Aunty Liz but I knew she got impatient when I talked about ghosts. I just ran into my room, kicked off my shoes and jumped into bed, lying there shivering and hoping that it wouldn't come through the walls.

Gradually the whispering seemed to reduce and I noticed a slight graying of the sky toward the East. I must have fallen asleep then because the next thing I knew my Aunt was waking me the next morning.

...

I stopped talking.

Sue's head had just slumped onto her chest.

"Sue?"

"Hmmm?"

"Sue!"

"Yeah, yeah ... what?"

"You're falling asleep."

"Yeah ... what time is it?"

"It's ... um ... well it's two oh five."

"Hmmm ... I think Sam it's bedtime."

"OK."

She got up drowsily, and started turning things off.

In the passage as I turned to my door she put a hand on my shoulder.

"Great story Sam ... really liked the ghost bit at the end."

Then she guided me to my room and shuffled off to hers.

I threw myself onto the bed, highly pissed off. She obviously didn't believe me. She thought I was just telling her stupid stories for some reason. I really was determined to show *her* in the morning. I looked under my bed. The watch had stopped glowing and the phone was dark too.

I lifted them up and unstuck the phone, lowered the watch face and dialed up Qi. He appeared on the face.

"How did it go with para.no.ID?"

"They responded."

"Which code?"

"Gray elephant."

That meant that they suspected I was compromised and wanted a new code challenge. More time lost but it was a high level challenge and it meant I could probably rely on them now. At least they were in the clear.

"Did you find anything out about Antonio Rossi?"

"He has an unverifiable cyber-shadow. I have his social networking site addresses if that would help?"

"Don't bother."

People get very jumpy about the idea of net shadows or cyber shadows. You know, telling the world about themselves on Facebook or Twitter or whatever. But most of it can't be checked. It's just a bunch of crap people write. So the fact that Antonio Rossi had a shadow meant nothing. Antonio Rossi could be a real person or a cyber-phantom – an artificial personality. It proved nothing.

"Qi I want you to use strict protocol with para.no.ID. If they break it – and I think they will – break off. Then try again in 48 minutes time. That has to be exact. Forty eight minutes exactly. The code word is 'Alice says hi'. Their response to the challenge is 'Cheshire' and a smiley. After that tell them that Michael is dealing with *them* and some of the infiltrators. Not sure who. Ask about Antonio Rossi and see if they can find anything going to him from here which might suggest who it was."

"OK Sam."

I wonder why they *aren't* coming to get me. I'm tagged. They've tracked me all the way here. But then the more I think about it, the more I realise I have actually made it quite hard for them. I'm in a policewoman's house. People know I'm here. Really, they should have struck when Leonora had me, but loyal as she had shown herself to be to Sir Michael, she isn't part of this. She knows nothing and Michael had got himself between *them* and me.

Now, as I think about it, I realise, in a way, Sir Michael is trying to *protect* me by convincing them to do everything legally. I'd seen an infiltrator murder a man as casually as putting out a cigarette because he wanted a dead body. Maybe I have more help than I think. If only I knew what had started the whole thing.

I lie there half-asleep recalling the last moments I talked to anyone from Renwick, almost a week ago. I was flying twenty five kilometers up over the Pacific, east of the Solomon Islands. The evacuation order had been given ten minutes ago. I had to get back, but I knew I wasn't going to make it. I looked up and about ninety kilometers above me and ninety kilometers ahead in the dark boundaries of space a colossal triangular craft a kilometer in length surrounded by five smaller triangles descending directly overhead doing about ten klicks a second. I could beat them home but only by minutes – and then they'd get me.

I call it in.

"Better move it guys! Service carrier and five escorts on its way. ETA ten minus."

"Sam! Hide! We can't wait for you! We're going now!" Mariko called desperately.

"Catch you later guys," was all I could think to say.

There was no acknowledgement. They'd started the self-destruction process. Renwick was burning.

The carrier didn't spot me because they were on a mission and I was so tiny, so I dived for the sea, through the cloud layer, slowing rapidly as only inertialess flight allows. I decided to swim home. The sea is so blue and pretty. I slip into it gently and begin the slow journey home underwater. And everything turns into a lovely dream about mermaids, dolphins and tropical islands with Emma on them.

CHAPTER ELEVEN: BENEATH THE ASHES

We sleep in the next morning. When I wake I'm pleasantly surprised to still to be in Sue's house. It isn't until ten o'clock on Saturday morning that I finally get out of bed, and only because Sue insists.

"C'mon Sam, it's a gorgeous day," she enthuses. Obviously she's slept well too.

And it is a great day for autumn. Blue sky, no wind and a warm eighteen degrees Celsius. It's one of those autumn days when you think winter might not come at all.

Sue rings the ferry and books us in for the twelve o'clock and six o'clock return. That means about five hours on the island.

"So what's the plan?" I ask her over breakfast.

"Well, the forensic guys still have the house roped off but they've finished gathering their evidence and we haven't yet turned it over to the owner's lawyer – the one you ran away from. So if there's anything you want to show me, now would be a good time," she explains.

"OK. But I doubt if there's anything left of Renwick House," I say remembering Leonora's video. Then I think, "Did they find radiation?"

"They weren't looking for radiation," Sue says doubtfully.

"Well, they'll be OK in those suits they wear. Dr P would have had to crash the fusion reactors so there might be residual."

"Radiation from the *fusion* reactors," Sue says, nodding.

"Yeah. Could be," I say tucking into cornflakes.

"But you think it's safe?" she checks over the lip of her coffee cup.

"Oh yeah, for short periods, under four or five hours no problem."

She smiles at me knowingly, putting down her cup.

"What?" I ask, pausing, spoon in hand.

"Sam, you're not getting cold feet about showing me your flying saucer are you?"

"No, just a bit nervous," I say playing with my food. I can't help remembering that I have a tag. They know *exactly* where I am. They could show up at any moment and I couldn't stop them. My only hope normally is to hide, but right now that was impossible.

"Oh yes. Why's that. Not so sure it will fly?" she asks directly.

"No, I only want you to see *one* flying saucer. Two flying saucers would not be so good."

"Two for the price of one, what's wrong with that?" Sue laughs. She has no idea how much shit we could be in.

"Because if you do it means they've bounced me, so you won't see me again – not that you'll remember it."

"*They* being ..." she says crunching into her toast.

"The other guy's flying saucers, yeah," I resume eating. She's still smiling. I am nervous.

"So how radioactive did you say Renwick House is?"

"I didn't. I don't know, but it's a possibility."

"And you aren't trying to put me off going there?" she smiles.

"No," I say honestly.

217

"Not a teensy bit?" she grins, inclining her head slightly.

Her smiling is making me smile. She is very cute.

"No! it's okay … really."

"And there's no monsters in the lagoon?" she asks.

"No, although I guess the ghosts will be pissed off the house is gone," I say collecting my last cornflakes.

She laughs.

"Oh yeah! I'd forgotten about *them*. So apart from the radiation *and* the other flying saucers *and* the ghosts, I'll be fine then?" she asks almost laughing.

I think of adding possible infiltrator hitmen on her doorstep but I decide not too.

"Uh-huh."

"Sam you're a crazy nut job but at least you make me feel better," she sighs, getting up and going into the kitchen,

I smile at her. I'm glad she likes me. If she knew the crap she is really in, she might not be so cheerful.

"Can I ask one favour?"

"Hmm what?" she asks with amused suspicion.

"Can I bring my flying saucer home?" I ask.

"Home?" she asks, her smile dropping.

"Sorry, to your place," I admit.

She looks at me a little sorrowfully.

"Sam, I like you and everything but … well … you can't live here. Not permanently. You will have to find a foster family, at least until you're old enough to look after yourself."

I was hurt by that. Stunned in fact. Leonora had been right. Sue really is my plan B. The idea that she's willing to ditch me to some foster family hits me hard. Where the hell would I go? Not the Moore's again. That was for sure!

I look at my empty bowl. It's mostly the rejection, but there's
also extra pain in realising she still doesn't believe a damn
thing I've told her. As far as she's concerned it's just so much
raving from a funny little Maori orphan kid with an overactive
imagination. I take a deep breath and get up to go back for my
watch. She knows she's hit me hard.

"Sam? Sam? Don't be silly now," she follows me down the
passage to my room. Then she grabs my shoulders and turns me
around.

"Sam, I am not your Aunt or your mother. I'm not a substitute
for them," she says firmly looking into my eyes while I avoid
hers.

"I can barely keep my own life together. I couldn't … and they
wouldn't let me … It's just not real Sam," she says gently.

The word "real" sets me off. Her idea of what was real was just
so simple.

"That's the problem!" I blurt out bitterly. "Your stupid reality!
You don't even realise how small and f_____d it is!" I swear.

That did it. Now she's angry! Her eyes flash and jaw hardens.

"Don't you swear at me, young man, not as a guest in my house!"
she roars.

She is actually quite frightening. She's up there with Aunty
Liz, and Grandpop. I'm impressed. We're staring each other
down but she's winning. I look away. I have to swallow a lot of
bitterness. Not all of it was towards her either – some of it is
about being left alone like this – but it's rising up and if I let it
out now at her everything I've achieved with her so far will be
lost. With as much control as I have left I face her again.

"Look, I'm sorry for swearing at you. OK? I'm sorry. But Sue,
I'm not a nutjob. I'm not a sad puppy orphan who's wigged out

because I've lost my family. They *will* come back for me."

"Sam ..." she begins sympathetically.

I have to fight down the frustration as she starts feeling sorry for me again.

"Look," I interrupt, trying not to yell at her again. "Can we go to the island now? At least we can agree on that. OK?"

"OK," she says slowly, "but we are going to have to sort this out before Monday, OK? Because *I* have to front up to your lawyer and explain why you were such a little shit ..."

I begin to object but she continues.

"Uh, uh, uh. Why you were such an ungrateful little *shit* to someone who was just trying to help you."

"OK," I agree wanting this lecture over with.

"Can we just go to the island now?"

It seems to take an age to get in the car with too much shagging around and forgetting things. We are both ratty with each other and the traffic, which is very heavy, doesn't help. We have to drive west to east across Auckland and get to the ferry on time on a day when it seems everyone in the city has suddenly decided to go out driving.

I decide to risk ringing Emma to pass the time. To my delight her brother Andrew answers. Andrew had been in the same class as Rewa. Like most kids that age he isn't great on the phone but at least he hands it to Emma rather than his dad or mum.

"Emma?" I begin

"Oh hi ... ah ... *Charli* ... hang on," she replies.

I hear her walking through the house and close the door.

"Sam! What's happening? Why haven't you called?"

"I tried a few times but it's been real complicated. First they put me in a foster home with this knife boy ..."

"What!? Are you OK?" she sounds worried.

"Yeah I got out of that. Then I stayed the night on the couch of a detective. Then I got rescued by this rich lawyer dude and his private investigator but it turned out they were ... uhh sus..."

"*Shit*! Are you OK? Where are you now?"

"Yeah, I'm OK for now. Tell you more later. Look, I've got a mobile so take this number down ..."

"Hang on ... hang on ... oh, why is there never a pen? ... I'll use eyebrow pencil, OK?"

"0251 6929211."

"0251 692... ?"

"...9211"

"0251 6929211?"

"That's it. But I'm on my way out to the island right now!"

"Now!"

"Yeah! ... I've got this cop with me. She's in charge of the case ... but I think she's OK. Anyway she's driving me back over there."

"Great! So you want to meet up?"

"Course. We're arriving at one and we'll be at Renwick at one thirty. Meet me in the usual place at two."

"OK, I'll try. I might have to bring Charli."

"Poor old Charli," I smile.

She giggles.

"See ya at two."

"OK."

Sue's curious.

"Who was that?"

"Emma Reeves."

"Who's she?"

"A friend."

"Your girlfriend?"

"Well, she's my best friend not from Renwick, and she's a girl, so I guess *you* would say that."

"Is that who you were with on Sunday night?" she asks sounding like Kevin.

I decide to make her squirm.

"You mean like having sex?" I ask, looking at her directly as she drives.

"Well ... ah if you say so," she admits uncomfortably, looking at the road.

"No," I say firmly and rather grumpily, looking forward, in a way that suggests she is way out of line.

And to my surprise she doesn't keep questioning me about it. I wonder if she'll ask Emma. I hope she won't pretend I'd said "yes" just to see what Emma says. That's a trick I'd expect of Kevin but I hope Sue is a bit more responsible.

In fact I *had* spent that night at Emma's place. In the barn. We liked each other a lot, and we're not above snogging, but we were simply too busy hiding my speeder, erasing the school records and avoiding *their* increasingly scary efforts to find me, for much more than a quick kiss. She'd been the first person I'd turned to because she had been brought into our secret a year before. That, and because she was borrowing my wetsuit at the time and I needed it. The wetsuit allowed me to get into the hiding place for the speeder which only we knew about.

We drive across town on a sunny Saturday morning. There is a lot of traffic. I could see kids out playing sports or with their parents enjoying themselves. I can't help wondering what it would be like to have a normal life. One where you didn't have to wheedle cops into driving you around or whether aliens were tracking you via stomach tags so they could abduct you later. It seemed so relaxing.

For me everything about this trip depends on the lighthouse. If I can get some power out of its supercapacitors and get the powerful electromagnets cranked up I'd soon know for sure whether Leonora had tagged me or not.

To pick up the signals from the GPS satellites the tag has to have an aerial finer than the finest old, wire, lightbulb filament. The electromagnetic field in the lighthouse lab would start a current running through any conductor anywhere near it. If I got close enough to the field the induced current would overload the aerial, like blowing an old lightbulb, and blast the tag to bits – probably burning me internally at the same time. I really hoped that it wouldn't hurt too much.

As we drive I get the feeling that Sue has started to think that if she cracks my case the embarrassing incident with the pills could be quietly forgotten by her bosses. It explains why she looks every bit the cop at the moment. She seems to think she'd let her guard down too much by letting me get involved in her personal life. She has a phrase "professional detachment" going through her head. I think it's bullshit but I can see it's attached to a bunch of memories which are not much fun, so I guess that is how cops cope. Not being a cop I can't say whether it works or not.

We get to the ferry terminal without talking much. We're both lost in our own worlds. The terminal isn't busy. It might have been a nice day but autumn isn't the tourist season on Aotea. Not like summer anyway.

We drive onto the ferry and get ourselves up on deck quickly. This process seems to change Sue's mood and she's quite

223

interested in everything going on around her. It turns out she's never been to the island before so it's nice to have work pay for something she finds interesting anyway.

On board we buy lunch. I pig out on juice, pies and cakes trying to line my stomach hoping it helps prevent burning when I overload the tag, but I know the crossing and don't see any risk of getting seasick. Sue's more careful. She doesn't trust her stomach.

Still, after we've eaten, it's nice to sit up top and watch Auckland fall away behind us. For some reason today some dolphins are playing around the boat and their presence and the sea breeze put a smile on Sue's face again.

"So ... so far you've told me about how you came to be at Renwick, and a little about the people there but there's still a lot of unanswered questions. Why did Dr Prosperov lease the place? Why did he hire foreigners? What was all this stuff about a clinic and did you ever get over being haunted? " she asks conversationally.

"I won't tell you that until you've seen me fly. There's no point. You won't believe me and I'll get mad with you again," I say looking out to sea.

"Well, what about the other kids? How did you get on?"

"We got on fine," I say.

She looks at me sharply.

"OK, Sam what are you in a snoot about?"

"I'm not in a snoot. It's just pointless telling you stuff if you won't believe what I say. I told you three days ago when I met you if you don't believe I'm psychic you won't understand anything and nothing has changed. So you'll have to see it for yourself."

Sue chews on that for a while.

"OK, have it your way," she snaps. But I can tell she isn't happy. The trip to the island brings back a lot of memories for me. Memories that seemed almost too large. As the harbour comes into view I feel as if I'm coming home and I can't wait to be off the ferry again.

It seems to take forever to berth the ferry, and for us to get in the car and get off onto the road. As we drive through town I catch glimpses of school friends and people I know. It just seems so unfair that I'm being jerked around by all these adults.

Along the ridge Sue drives the gravel road with determination and skill. I can't help sneaking a peak at her now and again wondering how she will cope with what I am going to show her. Will she simply ignore what's right in front of her? Over the past two years I've learned that adults are frighteningly good at ignoring things that don't suit them.

Finally we take the turn off towards Renwick. It's coming up to one o'clock. The sun's high in the sky and warm, but the breeze is fresh now, hinting at the winter to come. I find the familiar landmarks make me excited. Even if it all turns to crap at least I will be in my element doing what I like.

At last we're driving down the pine road that zigzags down the hill. I catch glimpses of the ruin but it isn't until we get out onto the flat that the full extent of the fire is obvious.

The whole area is marked with orange cones and police tape, hanging in the breeze. Sue drives around the drive in front of the old front doors. It's the only part of the structure still standing although the once strong looking doors now hang off their hinges, burned to crispy slabs.

The fire had obviously been at its most intense at the back by the kitchen and waste processing station where the gas from the waste and the gas cylinders were. That was where the powergel charges had been. Having seen the video I was not surprised by the sight, but the reality of it all being over, hit me again. This was it. That was my home: burned, wrecked and completely empty. I couldn't help sighing. Sue notices and gives my hand a squeeze, which is nice of her really. I find it hard to stay mad at her.

We get out of the car. The crash of the waves and the salt hits us first but the smell of ash is also strong. I notice that the walls and old door are labelled with "hazard" tape and guess they're probably unstable. I walk around the side with Sue following me. The whole place is just a tip of burnt wood and stuff. It's surprising how small it seems now that it's flattened.

"Did they find the gold?" I ask Sue.

"What gold?" she frowns.

"There's about a tonne of gold down there. Do you have a torch?"

"In the car."

We go back to the car and get a lantern sized waterproof torch. Then I lead her around to the side and pick my way through the rubbish. Sue, balancing her way through the unstable heaps, follows after me. Finally I get to the place where the cellar had been. I start moving the burned wreckage. It's heavy and in some places sharp. There's also the danger that I might fall through a burned floor. Sue catches up with me.

"What are you doing?"

"Showing you the escape route everyone took," I answer.

"How do you know what route they took?" she asks, surprised.

"Because we practiced it like a fire drill every month. Now help me make a hole to the cellar and be careful. It's deep."

Sue begins to help and the work goes a bit faster, although what we really need is a small digger.

"So you know where they went," she asks as we worked.

"Of course."

"But why did you tell Kevin all that bullshit?" she puzzles.

"Because we need a cover story to come back with and if I tell him the truth he'd think the same way you do," I say, not giving her anything.

What bothers me is there isn't a hole here already. I had told Sir Michael about this place and *they* hadn't tried to open it. They must think it strange I've headed straight for the place I actually told Sir Michael about. It's sure to attract their attention, whether I wanted it or not.

But I have to beat the tag and this is the best way to do it. I couldn't fly with it still in my stomach or they'd have me in seconds. Then I'd have to give in, or kill myself, and I wasn't sure I could blow myself up yet. I don't want to die right now. After about fifteen minutes, during which we get completely covered in charcoal and ash, we make a small hole to the cellar. It's just big enough for someone to squeeze through. I get out the flashlight and shine it down into the darkness. The beam cuts through the dust to the floor below.

As I'd expected the cellar has escaped a lot of the blaze although some of the wine has been destroyed. You can smell cooked wine and there is broken glass where some bottles closer to the ceiling have shattered in the heat. Still it's only about four meters to the floor, and the broken glass is clearer directly under me. There's a risk of a twisted ankle and a cut but not huge.

"Have you got a rope?" I ask looking up at her.

"I've got my tow rope …" she suggests, bent over looking into the hole over my shoulder.

"That'll do."

She starts back to the car to get it. As she picks her way back I lower myself into the hole and end up hanging down by my fingers. Stretched out I can reach down almost two meters but I still have another two meters to fall. It looks a long way in the near blackness down there. Sue must've looked back.

"Sam!" she shouts urgently "Where are you?"

"Here!" I call.

"What are you doing! Stop it! It's dangerous! You can't go down there!" she shouts.

I think I'm still pissed off with her for not believing me. I want to teach her a lesson.

"Follow me," I call and I drop two meters onto the wreckage strewn floor.

The landing is heavier than I'd expected and when I stand up I notice I've missed a big pile of broken glass by centimeters. I shove it away with my foot. Sue's got back to the hole.

"Sam?" Sue calls down the hole.

"Are you OK?" she sounds worried.

The air is thick with fine dust, which given that it probably *is* radioactive, is not a good thing. I'd had forgotten about that and it made me cough and brings tears to my eyes.

"Yeah but … it's really dusty down here," I cough.

I explore around with the torch. I decide to slip my hoody off and tie it around my face like a mask. That way I can breathe through it and it will filter at least some of the dust.

"What can you see?" Sue asks down the hole.

"A lot of bottles and burnt stuff."

Some of the piles look like they might not hold the debris above up for long either. I look up at Sue who is a head in a column of light.

"Sue?" I ask, shielding my eyes, looking up into the bright sunlight.

"Yeah."

"This is the escape route, but in case it's blocked would you mind getting that rope?"

"You're a bloody idiot for jumping in there," she tells me off, grumpily.

I look up at her and smile.

"I know. You're right," I agree, because she was, "But now that I've done it could you see if you can find the rope?"

"OK. Don't move!"

She disappears. I'm annoyed at myself for being such a dork in front of Sue. I'd let my desire to make her follow me, make me do something dumb. Grandpop would have given me a real hard time. But I can't wait, I have to see if I'm wasting my time. I slip through the wreckage and twist under a bit of the floor to find the way to the vault and the route to the tunnels under the house that went back into the hill behind it.

This path is clear of dangerous wreckage but the air is thick making the beam from the torch shine. It's the perfect place to meet *them* – which I really don't need – but there's no sign. Just the dust dancing in the light from my torch. I have to creep carefully through, checking the way above, below and on the sides. I get to the vault door. It's a big door built to be fire resistant and I'm pretty sure it will still open.

There's a small steel combination lock dial on the front panel. I dial up Qi on my wrist who gives me the combination. This is the big moment. If I'm right the panel will open to reveal the actual door lock panel glowing with big red LEDs. If I'm wrong I'm down in a dark hole breathing radioactive dust for nothing.

"Sam? Sam? Are you there? Where the hell are you? I told you not to move!" Sue calls angrily from the hole. She's worried again.

I open the panel and a lovely red glow lights up the dark.

"First enter numeric key," the panel says with an American woman's voice.

"Sue!" I yell.

"Sam, what are you doing?" she calls distant and frustrated.

I work my way back to the hole. Sue has the rope and is tying it to some of the heftier bits of wreckage.

"Sue!" I look up shielding my eyes from the bright day outside. Her face appears above.

"Sam, I'm just tying the rope on. Do you think you can climb up?"

I grin up at her, trying to look like I always spend Saturday in the cellars of burnt out buildings.

"Sue, come down. You're going to want to see this."

"What?" she asks shortly.

"Come and see," I say and walk back into the darkness.

"Sam! Sam! get back here!" she roars.

Training has made me such a shit when I want to do my own thing. Even scary policewomen can't shake me. I go back to the door panel. There's no need to ask Qi this time. Normally this panel was left open and I knew my number better than any phone number. I punched it in.

"Please say your password at the tone," The vault demands.

"Hua Kai."

A small panel slides open revealing a glass panel.

There's a noise behind me. I guess it's Sue coming down.

"Oh, it's horrible down here. Sam! Sam! You've got the torch! Where the f____ are you?" Sue calls.

"Hang on," I yell lazily.

I place my hand on the scanner. A light slides across my hand brightly.

"What's that?" Sue calls nervously behind me.

"Entry authorised."

And the door servos whir briefly and stop. I push the door and it swings open. Yes! So far so good. Then I go back for Sue.

She's standing in the column of light from the outside world with dust flurrying around her. Occasionally it seems to glow in points of lilac and blue. She looks pretty amazing to me as I come from the darkness. Then she starts coughing and the whole effect is ruined.

"What the hell do you think you're playing at!" she asks angrily, not really wanting an answer.

"I told you not to come down here and you did it anyway. I told you to wait and you wander off. I'm not going to put up with this!"

I sit down on a broken beam and look her in the eye.

"Sue would you stop acting like a nervous mother. Even the foster home was more dangerous than this!"

She's shocked. There's no doubt about it. I've caught her maternal instincts out, and after telling me I can't stay at her place earlier, she feels off balance. So I go on before she regains it.

"I'm leading you into something way bigger than you realise. It's not a funny little story I make up to entertain you, it's my life.

Now you can either follow me into this tunnel and discover a bigger reality, or you can go back home to the reality you think you know and forget all about me, because whether you come or not I *am* going."

And with that I stand up and head to the vault leaving her. I think she realises then that I am quite prepared to vanish down here and if I do there isn't much she can do about it.

"I just don't want you to wander off where I can't find you," she calls assertively.

"If I wanted to do that I'd be gone already," I reply from the darkness.

"Now follow me, and keep low or you'll hurt your head," I warn her.

She comes into the dusty darkness, through the broken glass and the smell of ash, around the fallen supports of the floor which in places threaten her skull and up to the door. The panel's red LEDs continue to shine in the dark.

"Welcome to my sad orphan world of make-believe," I say coldly and push open the door, shining the torch inside.

If you've never seen a lot of gold glistering in the dark you probably don't know how beautiful it is. There are reasons why people have murdered for it, enslaved whole populations for it. It is bewitching. I lead Sue into the entrance of the vault and I go in and shining the torch around. The gold is arranged on shelves. The smallest ingots – just small fingers really – are by the door. Further back there are the coins in bags, and even further in are the bricks of solid gold and silver. There are also trophies: daggers, cups, lamps, all sorts of items made of solid gold or silver and encrusted precious stones. Sue's just staring at it all with her mouth open.

"Wait there a minute. I'll be back in a second," I tell her.

"Where are you going?" she demands as I leave her in the dark.

"Just making sure the escape tunnel is still open," I tell her.

I go to the back of the vault and find the hatch. It's a simple round hatchway in the floor. I turn the seal and lift the heavy, metal hatch open. I take a quick glance inside to make sure nothing's changed and go back for Sue.

"Come in," I say and hand her the torch.

She enters and walks around inspecting the treasure.

"What do you think?" I challenge her again.

"Is this real?"

"Sure it is. Pick it up," I reply.

She picks up a small finger of gold. She weighs it in her hand, finding it surprisingly heavy. She even sniffs it. Slowly she drifts around picking up things, inspecting them, and putting them down. Finally she realises this isn't a trick. It is indeed a treasure trove.

"Who does this belong to Sam?" she asks in a small voice. She's still grumpy but she's also shocked by the scale of the treasure.

"Until the others come back. I guess me, I do," I admit.

She turns the torch on me suddenly. I cover my eyes.

"Hey!" I complain.

"No, really Sam? Is it Prosperov's," she asks.

"Half of it. But a twelfth of it really is mine. We gathered it," I tell her.

"How?"

"Not til you've seen my speeder," I say shaking my head.

"Speeder?"

"My flying saucer."

"Well, this lot will have to be looked after," Sue sighs looking around. It's cold in the vault. I put my black hoodie back on.

"I know," I agree.

Sue walks towards the back swinging her torch around the treasure.

I go to the door and pull it closed. There's a loud clunk.

"What have you *done* !" Sue screams. There's a note of real panic in her voice. It's a very loud scream inside that enclosed space and the torch is in my face again.

"Stop panicking," I tell her, wincing, "come over here and look."

She comes back around and shines the torch at the back of the door. The big manual wheel which opens the door I'd just locked is obvious.

"It's a manual exit. The system was designed for panic rooms. You know like the movie? The power system is a large battery. It's in that column behind you. But even if there's no power at all you can always get out."

"Sorry I just ..." she begins.

"I know and it was dumb of me to jump down here but you've got to remember I know this place like the back of my hand. It just didn't seem like a big deal compared to what else is down here. Now turn that torch off I want to show you something else."

She hesitates.

"Go on!" I insist, looking at it.

She switches the light off.

"I can't see a thing," she complains immediately.

"Wait," I tell her gently.

"You aren't going to do something stupid are you?" she asks a little nervously. She obviously hates being underground.

"No, I'm not doing anything stupid. Just a few more seconds."

It takes a short while for our eyes to adjust to the dark.

"OK, look behind you. It's not scary."

I see her silhouette turn in the darkness.

"Where's that glow coming from?" she asks curiously.

For a pretty rippling radiant green glow is reflecting off the ceiling above the hatchway.

"Go and have a look. It's not dangerous. I'll follow you."

She carefully steps over to the hatchway. Below her a ladder goes down the narrow tube cut into the rock, but it's the lining that's so remarkable because it shimmers and glows fluro green in the dark.

"What is that?" she breathes.

"It's the way down to the entrance tunnel."

"I meant ... entrance tunnel?" she asks, suddenly realising what I'd said.

"Yeah."

"Entrance to what?"

"A fairy grotto," I laugh. She looks at me sharply.

"Well, not anymore," I add seriously, "but you should come and have a look anyway."

And I push past and swing over the hatch and taking hold of the ladders on the outside with my hands and feet slide down to the bottom, as we always did.

Sue steps down, reluctantly, after me.

It's strange entering the tunnel again. It seems so totally lifeless. A week ago it was so busy, and now, nothing. The tunnel is oval and made of bricks coated with the green shimmering glowmoss. But the floor is hard and shiny, almost slippery, made of black glass material which seems to soak up the green light like night. It's only about two meters tall and Sue, who isn't tall, still stoops. I wait for Sue to join me.

"What is this place?" she asks and the tunnel eats her voice with its eerie green darkness.

"It was originally built in World War Two as an access way to the coastal battery command post in the hill. The ghosts led us to it."

"The ghosts," Sue repeats uncertainly in the spooky green light.

"Yeah."

"So did you get over being spooked by the ghosts," she tries to kid me half-heartedly.

"No. You never do" I say, setting off.

She shudders slightly. But I have more important things to do than freak out Sue.

"Come on, it's up here."

I set off up the tunnel which leads back toward the hill. The tap of our footsteps rings a little but is absorbed into the dark tunnel ahead. I know this path in my sleep but Sue follows unhappily along behind me, muttering about how the fire might have made the tunnel unstable, her voice sounding loud and nervous in the dull green tunnel. Knowing how it was made, I rather doubt it.

"Sam?" her voice echoes in the low tunnel. I turn.

She pauses to inspect the glowmoss, touching it with her fingers and rubbing them together.

"What is this stuff making all the light?" she asks.

"Glowmoss. 'Our friends' make it. It's genetically engineered of course. It makes light and oxygen from chemical reactions. It's perfectly safe, but don't eat it. Come on."

We clatter along the tunnel into the darkness. After a while the dead silence gets to her.

"Where are we going Sam?"

"We're following the route to the base. Eventually it will lead us out," I reply.

"Oh ... that's good," she says.

She really doesn't like being underground.

We walk about a hundred meters up the shiny black path, climbing all the way. A hundred meters feels a very long way underground. Then we come to the junction. To the left the tunnel went on into the green-lit dark. To the right it did the same. But ahead of us was the gateway that had collapsed into a dark heap of dirt and rubble. I wait for Sue to catch me up.

"What's this?" she asks, realising I'm looking at it for her benefit.

"*That* is where the others went just before the fire started," I tell her.

"Were they killed by the rockfall," she says stupidly.

I look at her like she's dumber than dumb.

"Noooo. They collapsed the tunnel behind themselves so *they* couldn't pursue. Even *they* can't get in there."

"So are they still in there?" Sue asks, confused.

"Of course not, they had another way out."

"Where does it come out?" she asks simply.

I smile and shake my head at her. Her world view was so small.

"On another planet," I tell her.

"Oh really," she says. By which she means, "I don't think so."

"Uh-huh."

"But you're left behind," she points out.

"Yeah," I admit. It *did* make me sad.

I feel her stand close behind me and then she puts a hand on my shoulder. I confess I like it so I don't stop her. I don't like fighting with her either. Then she takes a deep breath.

"I'm glad you showed me all this Sam."

"It's OK."

"You remind me of the boy left behind by the Pied Piper of Hamlin. You know he could still hear his playmates even though he was left behind," she says.

"Hang on," I tense, remembering how long all this has taken.

"What?" she asks, suddenly worried.

"What's the time?"

"It's one thirtyish," she says.

"When's the next ferry from Auckland?"

"I don't know, why?"

I dial up Qi who materialises on my wrist.

"Qi what time does the next ferry arrive from the mainland?"

"In twenty nine minutes if it's on time," he says pleasantly.

"Sam! What is *that*!" Sue demands.

"It's my watch avatar Qi, Qi meet Sue, Sue meet Qi."

"Glad to meet you Sue," Qi says chattily.

"Er ... hi!" she says looking astonished.

"How long did it take us to get to Renwick, about ten ... fifteen minutes?" I ask Sue.

"Yeah, about that."

"We've got to get out of here!" I conclude.

"What? Why?" she demands.

I don't have time to explain.

"Come on! This way!" I yell, my words echoing slightly off the walls, and I start running into the right tunnel.

"Where does *this* go?" she calls, following after me.

"Out, come on. Quick!"

As I run I dial Qi out. Sue's right behind me, determined not to let me get out of sight.

The smoothness of the path and the cool, fresh air from the glowmoss makes running easier than it might have been. Our feet clatter in the dark filling the tunnel but creating the spooky impression someone is chasing us. It's easy to feel a little disorientated in the green glowing darkness on the shiny dark floor.

"Why do we have to run?" Sue calls her voice echoing after me.

"Because *they're* coming. And if I'm not quick, they'll get me."

"Who's coming?"

"*Them* and Sir Michael."

"Sam, this is crazy."

"Better crazy than dead," I yell, and keep running.

Now we're heading on a long right hand curve following the bay downhill along the luminous green path through darkness. I was getting the stitch but I ran on. Finally we come to the end of the passage. At the end is a big door. I turn the wheel lock while Sue gasps for breath behind me. The big door swings open.

White light floods in. We pass through the door and I close it with a heavy thud behind us.

"Where are we?" Sue wonders panting.

The room is large and round with the same shiny black floor as the tunnels. Around the edges are some very high voltage devices with big ceramic couplings and heavy cables that spiral upwards.

"We're under the lighthouse!" Sue realises.

It's true. The light's coming in from the top of the lighthouse from the sides, pouring down the internal walls to light the white walls of the room. Above us a spiral staircase twists down around the walls from the floor to the very top of the tower. But most interesting is the huge tube suspended above, from the top of the lighthouse all the way to the bottom, made of countless coils of gleaming copper wire. And the whole thing is aimed at a huge copper bowl set inside a single piece of granite with enormous power cables coming out of it at regular intervals.

"What is this all this stuff?" Sue asks.

"A high energy physics lab. Now, quick, up these stairs," I tell her as I lead the way.

The stairs are set in a cage and we clatter up to a control room that looks over the floor and the big copper bowl from behind thick glass windows. The control panel is still intact, as I'd expected. The only thing missing is the control computers and the power source, but if I'm right the superconducting capacitors will still be holding a whopping charge. I don't know anything much about the set-up but I know an "on" switch when I see one. Sue's following me trying to make sense of it all. I turn to her.

"Sue, you don't have any implants or anything do you?" I ask urgently.

My intensity catches her by surprise. She looks down at her modest chest.

"What does it look like to you?" she asks ironically.

"No, I mean metal. Plates in your head, or pins in your bones?"

"Uh ... no," she responds a bit defensively.

"Where's your wallet?"

"In the car."

"Keys? Phone?"

"In my pocket."

"Right, well if you want to save your phone get up to the exit level, get about twenty five, thirty meters clear of the lighthouse. Oh ... and take my phone too," I say tossing it to her and running on up the stairs.

"What are you going to do?"

"Just turn this thing on and off again."

"Why?"

"Can you just trust me?" I demand. She shrugs.

"I'll give you two minutes," I tell her.

She starts up the stairs and the pauses looking through the bars.

"What about your watch?"

"It's optronic."

She shrugs and clambers up the stairs and slams the door going out. I count off one hundred and twenty seconds and turn on the machine. The needles on the dials of the control panel are very low but I know it will be enough. I go out of the control room and up the stairs. When I get to halfway up the lighthouse I go out of the stairwell onto a grated floor and approach the huge, shining copper coils. The hum and buzz of electricity is intense. I know immediately I *have* been tagged. I feel a long hot line in my gut. I force myself closer as the vicious pain in my stomach worsens. Then the tiny wire that acts like an aerial for the GPS signal gets overloaded by the induced current and frizzles like a popped lightbulb filament. It hurts like hell! I hope I haven't ruptured anything. My idea that eating a lot for lunch might cushion me from an internal burn has proved so wrong.

I stagger back to the stairs, clamber down them, clutching my stomach and stagger outside, letting the cleverly hidden door swing shut behind me. It's a beautiful day. The sun is bright, the air still warm and the sky blue. The green of the grass, the white of the lighthouse, and the blue of the sea looked amazing together.

I run down the road, clutching my side, to Sue who's sitting with a grass stalk in her mouth, staring out to sea.

"What's up with you," she asks, concerned.

"Something I ate. We need to get moving," I grunt through gritted teeth.

I stand up straight. It hurts a lot. I bend again and try to ignore it.

"You know this must have been a great place to be a kid in," Sue says happily, looking out over the sea.

We're just walking. I want to run, but I'm not sure I can.

"It was. Can we get back to the car?" I grimace.

"Why?"

"I want you to see my flying saucer but I don't want Sir Michael to find it."

"Why not," she asked.

"Because he's a maniac," I grunt.

"Why is he a maniac?" she asks sceptically.

"Because he wants to take over the world," I gasp.

"How do you know?"

We're heading down the hill toward the ruin of Renwick.

"Because that's why I ran out on him last night. He wants my speeder so he can build an unbeatable air force."

"Why does he want an unbeatable airforce?" Sue asks, as if that was the stupidest thing anyone could want.

"Because he thinks there's going to be a humungous war."

"A war?"

"Yes. He wants to make sure his side wins."

"Why would there be a war?"

"Any number of reasons. But he thinks it will be over natural resources."

"OK, but why do you think he's coming here?"

"Because he put a tag on me. By the way could you turn your mobile off too please?"

"No, why should I?" she objects.

"Because there's no signal here anyway and you're broadcasting where we are."

"Please?" I grunt. The pain is surprisingly bad. I hope nothing has burned the stomach lining. I don't want an ulcer.

Sue checks her phone.

"You're right. No signal. Oh, OK then may as well save some battery," she says and switches it off.

"Now what is the story about that watch of yours?"

"It's a watch."

"No watch I ever saw had talking holograms come out of it."

"It's a watch from elsewhere."

"Where elsewhere?"

"I don't know. It's a cheap data watch from a place that makes cheap data watches like that."

"It doesn't look very cheap to me."

"Well, it didn't cost me anything."

"Who gave it to you?"

"Our friends."

"Sam, you keep talking about 'your friends' but who are they?" she asks, annoyed.

"Uh-uh. Not till you've see me fly."

I turn Qi on again.

"Qi how long 'til the ferry docks?"

"Nine minutes," he responds.

"And the time is?" I ask.

"Nine minutes to two."

"Bugger. We're late," I gasp.

I started jogging, hunched over.

"What are we late for now?" Sue wants to know easily keeping pace.

"Emma."

"Oh, *right*," Sue says.

We get back to Sue's car at four minutes to two.

"OK, let's go," I say, settling down.

"Let me just get my towrope," she says getting out.

"Sue, we don't have time. Please? ... I'll buy you a new one, promise," I plead, half climbing out after her.

She looks at me sceptically.

"*Really*!" I nod, really worried. She seems to pick up my mood.

"Oh, OK, where are we going?" she says, getting back in, and starting the car.

"Up."

"Up?"

"Back up the road we came down, back to the ridge. As quick as you can."

"OK."

Sue tears back up the hill in a cloud of dust. She seems to like driving fast on gravel. We get back to the ridge at 2:04 p.m and then I direct her on back up the road. We retrace our path along the ridge as the clock ticks on. Then at 2:07 p.m we come to the turn off which forms a Y intersection with the ridge road. We turn right and north and head up the road. I keep an eye out, looking at our dust cloud, hoping that it will settle in the next ten minutes so that when Michael arrives there will be no clues as to where we've gone.

CHAPTER TWELVE: DOWN THE RABBIT HOLE

We drive from steep hillside farmland surrounded by scrub to flatter land where the roadside is lined with the big clumps of flax and the three meter tall pampas grasses we call toi-toi. Behind these are open stands of Australian blue gum trees which crowd out the view of the sea.

"Take that drive on the right there," I direct Sue.

Sue slows down and we pull off onto the narrow drive that threads through the tall toitoi with their big grassy heads like flags in the breeze.

"Who owns this place?" she asks looking around.

"It's conservation land, a public park. This is the access drive." The toitoi falls behind and it's clear that we are on a bluff, covered with rocks and occasional Australian blue gums. It overlooks a bay to the left and the bay to the right. The lighthouse is on the headland of the bay to the right, standing further out to sea.

The drive curves around to the left following the line of the island north, as a level side road appears on the right heading out onto the bluff.

"The road's a circle, there's a picnic spot up ahead."

And there, sitting on the picnic table looking at her watch, is Emma.

We draw up by her and I get out, taking Sue's torch with me.
I feel so pleased to see her again but a bit shy in front of Sue.
Emma doesn't apparently.

"Sam!" she shouts happily and runs over to me, her long black
hair flying. She gives me a big hug. It hurts heaps and feels great
at the same time. I hold her tight for a moment and it feels so
good.

Emma's a bit bigger than me. Her dad, Tama, is Maori, working
for the Conservation Department, and her Mum's white so
Emma's coffee coloured with brown eyes. She's wearing a rough,
bush-jacket and jeans. She lets me go.

"I brought your wetsuit," she says.

And she has. My most treasured possession and my first
Christmas present at Renwick House.

"Thanks. Em, this is Sue. She's a cop on the Renwick case."

"Hi," Emma says shyly, brushing her hair off her face. The
breeze is stronger here.

"Hi Emma," Sue smiles a friendly greeting.

"Sue's OK. I want to give her a little demo of the speeder." I tell
her.

"What!?" Emma goggles at me, not believing what she's just
heard.

"Why?" she asks, looking at Sue like she's quite unwanted.

"I need her to help me, when they come back Em. And for that I
need her to believe me. At the moment she thinks I'm a sad little
nutjob."

Emma gives Sue a sour look but says nothing. Sue isn't quite
sure what to make of it. I reassure Em.

"She's OK Emma. Well ... more OK than the others. Anyway let's
get going, time is getting away on us," I say.

I pick up the suit and we start through the reserve.

"Where are we going?" Sue asks.

"Well, assuming nobody interrupts us, you're going to wait up here while I get my speeder out. I'll fly it around and then land and you can have a look at it. Then seeing you don't want it at your place I guess I'll hide it again," I tell her.

Sue doesn't rise to that either.

The reserve's full of bushes, big rocks, flax and the gum trees. We cut through the brush. Emma and me, we know the way well. We're almost at the top when Emma grabs my arm.

"You know how you've told me about Administration scouts," she asks anxiously.

"Yeah," I respond nervously. I had feared this might happen when we went underground and my tag signal vanished.

"Is that one?" Emma asks.

I follow her pointing hand. About eight kilometers off the coast a metallic gray disc is sitting in mid-air gleaming in the sun. It's small but quite plain against the sky. Just what we didn't need!

"Yes! Run!" I shout.

I run on with Emma close behind me. Sue jogs behind, torn between wanting to watch the disc and follow us. We run up to the top cave entrance. It's a little crevice under a rock behind a bush. We stop to look at the disc from behind the rock, under the cover of the trees.

"Sue, quick," I call urgently.

Sue's walking along squinting at the disc out over the sea.

"What *is* that?" she's saying uncertainly to herself.

"It's a f_____ flying saucer and I'm not flying it. C'mon quick," I tell her nervously.

Emma's already at my feet scurrying down into the crevice with her torch out.

"It could be a chopper," Sue suggests, refusing to be drawn into our panic.

"It's not a goddam chopper, hurry up," I yell bending to follow Emma into the hole.

"It *could* be a chopper," Sue insists.

Just as I'm about to follow Emma the disc accelerates left and then toward us in a zigzag motion so that in less than two seconds it's in the bay on our right, right over Renwick, no more than a kilometer away. It looks as big as a small truck, dull metallic gray, round with a few bumps around the outside and a central dome in the middle. It's completely silent. The speed and the eerie silence is unnatural, and unnerving.

"*Now* do you believe me?" I demand with mock patience and dive into the hole.

"Ah yeah I ..." Sue says, her face turning gray.

"They'll spot you in about two seconds. Move!" I shout from inside the hole.

Emma's gone. I can't wait for Sue anymore. I dive down the hole, and scramble down on my hands and knees through the twisting turning tunnel. I can hear Sue following quickly.

"Wait for me," she calls. There's a pleasing note of panic in her voice.

The tunnel opens into a taller slit of rock which plunges steeply down on a bed of stones.

"Hurry," I shout back as I get up and scramble down into the dark following the yellow glow of Emma's torch.

"Ow," yells Sue as she bangs her head on a rock I'd forgotten to warn her about. I keep leading her down the dusty shingle into the darkness, following Emma's light. Sue's panic is rising.

"I can't see a ..." she begins.

Then a brilliant white light fills the narrow cave. It lights up the hole like God is looking into it. It's too bright to look at and, hearts pounding and gasping for breath, we scurry for the bottom like rats in a searchlight. The pain in my gut is way mean but I'm so scared I don't care.

I get to the bottom where the cave, widens and levels out for a bit then hits a huge boulder with a hole underneath we call the U-bend. It goes down and then comes up again but you have to wriggle through it. Emma's feet are already disappearing from view. The brilliant unearthly white light makes Sue look even paler than I know she is.

"Headfirst," I yell at Sue, "follow Emma. There's a puddle at the bottom but it's not deep."

"What if I get stuck," Sue cries, terror etched on her face.

"Moooove! Go! Go! Go!" I scream at her.

She dives into the crevice.

The ground begins to shiver, the shingle starts to dance and more dust rises, I can feel an awful churning in my stomach. It's the infrasound. Sound waves with a long frequency which start things vibrating but which are so low only an elephant could hear them. It's a search technique they use. Dirt and dust start raining down from the brilliant light but everything stays eerily silent. Behind me in the tunnel the air begins to distort like a window flexing in the wind. *They* are coming.

I'm not hanging around for this bit and dive into the crevice following so close behind Sue that I shove her in front of me. We scrabble down like desperate animals burrowing into the dark, with the brilliant white light behind us. Then we hit the muddy wet bottom and begin to climb, the rock vibrating under our quivering hands, dust pouring down on us, getting in our faces and eyes.

I'm last one up. We are in a cavern lit by Emma's pocket torch. Its not large. We call it "the dining room". I turn on Sue's big lantern torch but the brilliant light is beginning to creep under the corner of the U-bend.

"Slide hole," Emma shouts.

"Go!" I shout back.

Sue just looks pale. Emma takes off, feet tapping in the dark, and Sue's on her heels. The "dining room" has a number of trails in it that we know very well. Emma heads down one cave branch that is three meters wide and about the same height. We run, stumbling as the light behind us grows like a brilliant dawn in the dark. We turn a series of bends and then come to a hole where Emma waits. She stands, balanced by the edge holding her torch. Sue runs up next to her.

"It's a long mud slide about yay steep," Em shows Sue with a steep slope with her hand, "Then it eases out and opens up. Follow me."

Then she jumps, her light zooming away from us – but without her normal "wooohooo!". Sue follows the light.

I run up to the hole. For a moment I'm tempted to see if we *are* being followed but I know that if the answer is yes, it will be too late. I jump after Sue, watching her slide down in my bouncing torch beam.

The slide isn't exactly comfortable. You go down at huge speed and you get totally soaked in mud on the way. It's a surprisingly long fall – about five seconds – before it eases out and ends in a cold, muddy, pool up to your waist when sitting. The pool feeds into a stream but the cave around it is much larger.

We gather on a big flat rock near the slide to catch our breath. The cave is a low arc with a floor of rocks and shingle. The dark is close and oppressive, and the sound of running water not comforting. It makes your chest feel tight, making it hard to breathe.

"God damn," Sue's shivering quietly, "I *hate* caves."

By Emma's torch I can see she's completely covered in mud from feet to hair. We all are. It's cold but where I'm heated by my pain and the exercise Sue is chilled by her shock and the freezing mud.

"The good news is, so do *they*," I tell her. "They won't follow us in here."

"How do you know?" Sue demands, angry at having been frightened.

"Our friends rely on it. *They* don't usually hang around for long. We've just got to wait them out." I tell her.

"Well g-great! So h-how l-long do we w-wait in the f-freezing c-cold and d-dark?" Sue wants to know.

They'll be gone in half an hour," I tell her "It's daylight. They only came when my tag died. They'll be really annoyed with Sir Michael that they can't track me anymore."

"W-why n-not?"

"That was what I was doing in the lighthouse. I burned out their tag."

"T-tag?"

"Tracking device."

"W-what t-tracking d-device?"

"The one in my stomach."

"W-what?"

"The night you came to collect me Lenora had slipped a tiny

tracking device into my food. I burned it out just now by overloading it with induced current when I switched on the lab equipment in the lighthouse. That's when they lost track of us. Up until then they knew exactly where I was."

"B-but that m-means they know w-where I l-live," Sue points out.

"Leonora could have found that out by now anyway. She's an investigator."

Sue is looking very pissed off.

"God, I'm f-freezing, and I've g-got no ch-change of c-clothes," she says clutching herself.

"At least you aren't in that saucer having them inspect your brain," I point out.

Sue's eyes are wide. She's completely freaked.

"I ... I can't c-*cope* with this," she shivers, shaking her head.

"She's freaking out," Emma, my iron-willed friend, comments.

"You're in shock Sue," I tell her. "Not surprising really. But we're safe here underground so long as we keep moving. We know these caves, they don't. They may send in a 'snake' but it'll be more likely to get lost than find us."

"W-what's a s-snake?" Sue asks, a slight pleading look in her eyes.

"It's a snake. It's a real snake but adapted to be a biobot. Real pain in the arse because they can swim too. But they aren't too bright in the cold and become stupid. So I reckon we split up. You two head for the beach exit. I'll take the water exit, draw any snakes, and get the speeder."

Sue looks overwhelmed. Emma together. I try to reassure Sue.

"Don't worry Sue, you'll be out soon. *They* won't hang around in daylight for long."

"OK. Let's go," Emma says to Sue standing up.

"I feel c-completely u-useless," she says to Emma, turning with her.

I put my hand on Sue's shoulder.

"You aren't. Here take this." I say and give her my phone.

"I can't take it where I'm going," I say.

"Where ..." Sue begin.

"Swimming," I answer waving the wetsuit, "don't worry, just follow Emma."

"You're still bigger than we are, and you're an adult so people will listen to you," Emma says reassuringly as they set off.

"You're a cop Sue," I call after her, getting my wetsuit laid out, "my Aunt wouldn't have made it through the U-bend. You're doing fine."

Emma leads Sue away into the dark following her round torch light. I can still hear them as they leave.

"C'mon Sue, Sam's got to undressed and he's funny about girls seeing his willy," Emma says.

I'm glad it's dark. My face flames with embarrassment.

"Take c-care S-Sam," Sue calls out.

"See ya up top," Emma adds leading on.

"See you two," I reply, as calmly as I could.

Quickly I peel off my sodden, muddy clothes and wriggle into the wet suit. As I zip up I hear something slip down the slide into the freezing pool. It probably *is* a snake.

I turn my torch on. With two trails to follow it will probably be confused for a while even though I'm obviously closer. I set off upstream as quickly as I can, knowing that once it's made its mind up it will probably choose to follow the only male it can smell.

Snakes have full spectrum eyesight including thermal imaging, so they can see the heat from an animal's body. They also have a delicate sense of smell, and good hearing and touch. Instead of venom a biobot snake can have drugs, tags, or bacteria. I daren't wait for it. If it's a black mamba it can move faster than I can. The saucer crew will use it like a probe because they won't enter caves. They can be ambushed far too easily. But they don't control the biobot so much as instruct it. So the flaw in their system is using a reptile which never had much brains anyway in a freezing cold environment which slows down its whole system. Just being a mammal gives me a huge advantage.

I make extra noise, kicking the rocks, and flashing the torch around under the low roof so it will follow me rather than the others. I move quickly, lighting the rocky stream bed in my torch's strong white beam, letting the raw pain of my internal wound burn me and keep me going. Knowing a snake is following somewhere certainly makes me keep my pace up. There's no time to take it easy or look over my shoulder. Finally, as I head upstream, I find what I'm looking for. It's the point where the stream splits in two. Crossing over in a short leap I go to the other branch and start following it downstream in the darkness until I reach a long pool where the roof slopes down to meet the water. It looks like a dead end because the exit is actually under water.

We call this "the three ducks" because there are three underground pools in a row. We discovered this route with "our friends" technology, otherwise we'd never have gone in. As Grandpop said diving in caves is the most dangerous thing you can ever do. But because we'd scouted the route I knew it well and we'd had to hide the speeder somewhere where *they*

couldn't get to it, so, of course, it had to be hard to reach.
To get in you have to "duck" through the first cave, come up,
breathe, swim a bit, "duck" through the next, and then the next.
Of course the water is like ice. That should also slow the snake
down. I do a bit of hyperventilating to get my blood aerated for
the swim. I drop my clothes on the bank to further confuse the
snake. Sue's torch means I don't have to swim blind because
there is no light inside "the ducks".

I step into the water, wading silently up to my thighs before
lowering myself in to swim. It's totally freezing. So cold it hurts
and tenses every muscle in my body. I swim forward gasping
and then dive.

The "ducks" are linked by two wide channels and a third narrow
one which is much faster. The cold is biting and of course makes
me tense and less buoyant but the water is clean and clear and
the underwater passage obvious. The burning pain in my gut
drives me on. I kick out strongly, find the passage and am soon
pushing for the surface in the next cave.

The distance between the water surface and the ceiling in the
next cave is only half a meter which makes you feel horribly
enclosed. I swim along the surface on my back, pushed along
by the current. It's so cold it's hard to do more than pant. My
breath mists in the dark.

The worry here is the snake is smaller and faster than me in the
water. I swim for the second passage as fast as I can, carried
by the strong current, then dive. The passage is longer than
the first. The cold is eking into my muscles, I'm worried about
cramp, but the pain and the effort is generating heat and the
wetsuit is definitely helping.

The next passage entrance is relatively wide. Once again I shoot

up for the surface. This second cave is much bigger and the
cave ceiling higher. The current is strong and I swim along the
surface preparing for the next dive. I'm getting better attuned to
the cold now, while I know the snake is losing energy through its
long, thin body. But then as I approach the last wall I swing my
torch around and look back to see a black thin shape behind me.
It's the snake and I know my torch, as the brightest thing in the
pitch blackness, is attracting it.

I swim faster than I've ever swum in my life. I've got a twenty
meter head start but it's faster than me.

Fortunately the third passage is a waterfall and the snake is still
ten meters away when I enter the suction of the narrow drain.
I kick as hard as I can and I dive down the two meter drop into
the final deep pool below. Unfortunately as I hit the torch is
wrenched out of my grasp and falls away to the bottom beneath
me.

The final cave is the largest by far. It's forty meters long and
twenty wide. But the pool only occupies twenty meters of its
length and ten meters of its width set into a bowl like surround.
The rest of it is a large flat stone ledge about half a meter above
the bowl.

This last pool is also salt water and connects via a five meter
drop and a ten meter tunnel to a sea cave so you can swim out
into the sea relatively easily. That was how Emma and I had
found this place.

Right now Sue's torch is sinking slowly to the bottom of the salt
pool. With the snake behind me I'm under pressure and in a few
short strokes I get to the pool edge, and haul myself out of the
water. I get out just in time to see a dark line shoot down the
waterfall into the pool. I freeze in the dark as the glow from the

torch gets dimmer.

By shining the torch at the snake I've dazzled it and associated the torch with its prey. With the cold slowing down its little brain, it didn't pause to check this cave but follows the torchlight to the bottom. I have gained valuable time.

Fortunately, I can see. As the torch falls, the light in this dark cave reduces and the glow worms on the roof of the cave become visible again. Like millions of tiny stars in the night sky these little creatures light the ceiling and walls of the cavern with their soft greeny-blue light. This time I don't have time to admire them.

Quickly, I sprint up the slope away from the pool to the far end of the cave to the place me and Emma call "the altar" because it has a church-like feel to it. And there, lying right where I left him, is the last remaining thing of all the things "our friends" made for us. My speeder.

What it looks like, is exactly what it isn't. It looks exactly like a large, gray roof rack capsule for a car. It even has a common brand name on the side. We had asked "our friends" for a flying craft for some missions where we needed some form of aerial observation. Normally we worked on the ground but they had made six of these things and they had come in extremely handy because they could not only fly but swim as well.

"Ka-rea-rea," I say, quietly.

Instantly it begins to grow, its base sliding , and its top growing higher. In storage mode it compacts down by squeezing into the small passenger compartment. I put my hand on the newly exposed panel.

"Sam," he says in his pleasantly toned male voice, and the top popped open.

There is almost no room at all inside a speeder. It's smooth, shaped, passenger compartment has no windows, no controls and no nothing, but a human shaped outline one and a half meters tall with two handgrips. The lid is similarly featureless except for a metallic cap in the lid where the passenger's head goes. Only someone with the interface in their skull, like I have, can make it work at all. I step in and lie down, noticing as I put pressure on my stomach that despite being freezing cold, with aching muscles, my stomach hurts the most.

The lid closes tight over me, pressing me down in the darkness, the metallic cap presses to my head. I close my eyes and hold the handgrips. There's a flash as the interface in the speeder links with the interface in my skull and suddenly I'm in the cavern. My body feels sore and wet, and my breathing heavy, but my sight, and hearing is now that of the speeder, along with its numerous other sensors. The dark energy vortex engages, with a slight hum beneath the craft's hardened shell. The motor sucks dark energy in from the fabric of the Universe to generate antimatter which in turn produces antigravity.

Antigravity doesn't cancel out ordinary gravity. Antigravity is a separate force which just pushes masses apart. So the generator silently pushes the speeder up even as ordinary gravity continues to pull it down. At a tiny fraction of its power Ka-rea-rea floats up to the ceiling of the cave. I look down into the pool. The long black snake is clearly visible crawling slowly out of the pool. But it can't see me. It can't see me because the speeder is effectively as clear as glass.

It can be transparent in two ways. Using adaptive camouflage the tiny diamond lights on the outer shell replicate the light that falls on it almost perfectly so it blends in with any background.

This takes almost no energy at all and can be hard to detect as close as two meters away.

The other way is a warp distortion field which acts like a lens to bend light (and any other radiation) around the hull. This uses way more energy and only works if the viewer (or radar station) is over two hundred meters away. Otherwise the edges show up as an increasingly bright outline around the transparent speeder. A bright halo around "nothing" kind of ruins your invisibility. Right now I'm just blending in using adaptive camouflage.

Slowly the snake sniffs around in the dark. The poor thing is cold and clearly unlikely to survive. It seems to take forever but I know I have to be patient. Even if I was down there I would not have been defenseless either. I've seen kids smaller than me kill bigger snakes with nothing but quick hands and daring. But killing the snake wasn't my aim. I could do that now, silently and invisibly by drilling it with the speeder's beam. My plan is to let it follow my trail and sneak out through the pool behind it. That way the crew in the saucer watching through the snake's eyes, looking for me, will still focus on the snake, while I slip away.

As the snake makes its painfully slow way to where the speeder had been, I turn over and nimbly drop the speeder capsule, feet-first, until I'm *just* touching the pool. Then, slowly, I lower the speeder in, and slide down into the pool being careful not to leave so much as a ripple behind as I slide under the water.

In the pool I drop down feet first, then quickly turn end-over-end and silently zip out into the bright blue sea, accelerating away under the water like a big swordfish. I zoom out from the shallows toward the deep and noisy Pacific ocean where finding me will be pretty hard.

I've escaped.

The snake has failed and I'm gone. They'll know they've lost me. If it were dark they might search but it's a sunny day and they don't like to be too obvious. My only problem is I don't know where the scout is exactly as being underwater distorts my sensors. I have to get clear so I can get into the air. Then I will be much faster and able to watch what they're doing.

As I'm over two hundred meters away from the scout I turn on the warp distortion invisibility for total transparency and turn north-east headed for the big beach. If I just burst out of the sea I would make a pretty obvious eruption of water and the scout would see me, but waves on a beach provide cover. So I turn and zoom invisibly underwater up the bay to catch the surf and break into the air through the crashing waves.

The second I break through the foamy waves into the air I pull a quick turn to the right, due north, along the beach and hurtle out towards the north of the island gaining speed rapidly.

One of the most enjoyable things about the speeder is ... well ... its speed. You see somewhere you want to go, and it goes there. Fast. You don't so much fly it as guide it. It just goes like *stink*. And like an Administration scout if you want to go really, really fast it can go inertialess as well. That allows it to do impossible accelerations like stopped to 10,000km/h instantly without turning you to paste. It also means you can go from 10,000km/h to stopped instantly and or even reverse without slowing or stopping. Unfortunately the bigger you are and the faster you go the more you make a field distortion. The Administration have tiny satellites orbiting the Earth which can detect large field distortions so if we go too fast we become obvious, even if we are invisible.

I circle about in a wide arc ten kilometers away from the island
looking for the scout. With Ka-rea-rea's vision enhancement,
and because of the scout's huge inertialess field, I spot it easily,
still over Aotea. It's flying around Mt Marsden about five or
six kilometers from the beach. It's crew have lost me and they
know it. They also know that they are bound to be seen which
is not ideal for them either. Then as I watch I'm rewarded with
the sight I hoped for. The disc streaks into the sky, like a meteor
in reverse, on full inertialess. They're gone in sixty seconds.
They've had enough. It's three o'clock. Home for afternoon tea.
I stooge around for a little while checking the sky. They could
easily be hiding in low earth orbit, watching over the island for
me. I watch and wait, looking for the telltale twinkle of a craft
just above the atmosphere but I see nothing that suggests they're
waiting to bounce me. They can't see any reason for me to come
back. So I whizz over the sea at about one hundred meters
altitude and get back to Aotea island in seconds.
I slow down to drift invisibly over the park where we'd entered
the caves. Sue's car's still there. That's cool. Now the question
is, where is Sir Michael? I look around the bluff and spot Sue
and Emma coming out onto Lookout Rock and they are the only
ones there. They must have seen the scout leave too.
I zip over to Renwick, invisible and only one hundred meters
up. Below I spot a large black car parked where Sue had parked
two hours earlier. Nobody is in sight. I circle around probing
the hole in the rubble Sue and I had made but find no sign of
Sir Michael. Then I whiz over to the lighthouse – where he isn't
either; and then to the old gun emplacement. No sign there.
For a moment I wonder if the scout has taken him in, but realise
that is ridiculous. So I go back to Renwick. This time I find him.

He's climbing Sue's tow rope with a large shopping bag in his teeth.

I immediately wonder if he's got a passcode for our vault from the manufacturers and is stealing our gold. As he staggers out I can see Sir Michael's outdoors jacket is now somewhat grubby. Still, I can talk. All I have to wear is a wet suit. My only clothes are covered in mud back in the cave.

It annoys me that he's comfortable, with the gold we did all the hard work to collect. And it wasn't that it was even gold. It could have been marbles for all I cared. The point was we'd done the work collecting it, and he was nicking off with it!

The speeder has a range of tools. They are not serious weapons and they are no match for the ones on an Administration scout. The beam is a like an advanced laser. Because of movies people think of lasers as little lines of coloured light that shoot out with funny high-pitched noises. In fact beams are silent, complete rays from weapon to target, and, except in heavy rain or dense fog, they are completely invisible. The speeder's beam could drill a three millimeter hole in steel, while flying past at a kilometer a second, to an accuracy of about two millimeters, from about five kilometers away. Down the path of the beam's ionised air it can pump an electric charge strong enough to knock a man out, or more delicately act like a long range acupuncture needle.

Then at close range there are focused sound weapons which can give you a tummy ache, smash specific glass windows, creep people out or even just make them crabby. Finally there are the electromagnets which can zap computers, disrupt communications or lift five tonnes. In other words it wasn't a case of what I could do to this thieving bugger, it was what *couldn't* I do.

So I started by gently heating the handle of the plastic bag he's carrying so the whole thing tears and drops. Then I drill the valve in the driver's side front tyre so it begins to go flat. But just to be truly annoying I blast the car's engine management system with an electromagnetic pulse so it won't start. With luck he'll spend half an hour changing the tyre *before* discovering the car won't go. With no phone coverage it was going to be a *very* long walk home. Feeling happily evil I head back to find Emma and Sue. They are trudging back up the hill to the car. I fly up ahead of them, get right down low, disengage the invisibility and revert to the gray colour of a roof rack capsule. I then slide back along and above the gravel path flying about a meter off the ground. I'm now just a big gray, roof rack capsule hovering a meter above the ground on a walking track.

Emma is in the front as they come around the bend from behind a bush. She sees my speeder just hovering there silently. She stops still. Sue stands behind her, eyes wide, mouth open, and looks at Ka-rea-rea like her brain has completely given up. She simply doesn't seem to know what to do. I flash a smiley pattern on the front. Emma realises who I am, and smiles.

"It's Sam," she tells Sue happily.

I back up, turn around, and back down the track toward them, hovering a few centimeters above the track.

"He wants to give us a ride," Emma tells Sue happily. We've done this before.

Emma happily gets on top and sits on the side in the middle of the speeder. Sue takes a little coaxing but finally sits behind her. Then slowly I move forward remaining low and not going any faster than a jog. In five minutes we're at the top of the track. I ferry them to the car and stop meaningfully by the picnic table.

They get off, then stand back, looking at my small gray capsule. Just for fun I zoom up vertically about one hundred meters, fly a knot shape, zip out to sea about a kilometer, and zip back again to stop instantly and silently, then I land on Sue's car. I extend the landing gear which grips the car just like a roof rack. Then I pop the top and stick my head out.

"So whaddya think of my flying saucer Sue?" I call.

Sue just stares at me with her mouth open.

CHAPTER THIRTEEN: WILDER SKIES

I think she's still a bit shocked," Emma smiles at me. I like her smile.

"I... I ... I ..." Sue keeps saying but not really knowing what to say, shaking her head.

She sits down by the picnic table, looking at me. Emma sits down next to her, looking at her sympathetically.

"I don't believe this," Sue says finally, more to herself than anyone.

"*What*?" I ask, unbelieving. "You want me to do it *again*?"

"*No!*" she yells, panicking, "no ... just ... leave it alone."

I get up and slide off the car onto the ground. Ka-rea-rea closes his hatch and contracts into a roof rack capsule.

"How are you feeling," Emma asks her.

"Like ... like I seriously want a cigarette," she says.

"We don't smoke," I point out.

"No, and neither should I," Sue agrees.

She sits there looking at me and occasionally eyeing Ka-rea-rea.

"So there really were ghosts at Renwick?" she asks.

"Of course."

"And ... 'our friends' ... are ..." she begins questioningly.

"Not from around here, no," I confirm.

She sighs.

"And that guy ... Sir whatsit ... wants to get his hands on that thing?" she asks.

"Yeah."

"How on Earth did you get mixed up in this Sam?"

"That's a very long story. But this isn't the best place to tell it."

"And I'd better get back home," Emma adds.

Sue blinks and looks at her.

"You're amazing," she tells Emma. "You just kept cool even when there was ... when they were chasing you!"

"Me!" Emma laughs. "Sam's the amazing one! And the others! They are totally incredible. They dealt with situations like that all the time. I just didn't want him to think I couldn't."

Sue looks at me. Emma is too.

"What?" I ask.

And then I look at Emma.

"No ... I agree with Sue, Emma, you are amazing," I smile.

"You just think I'm cute," Emma jeers.

"No not 'cute'," I say searching for the right word. "More ... 'hot'! Yeah, hot and amazing."

Emma gives me a telling-off-but-pleased frown.

"Well, I'd better give you a lift home," Sue interrupts getting up.

"You better see if you can start the car first," I suggest.

Sue looks puzzled, "Why?"

"The electromagnetic pulse from the scout. In the old days it just stopped cars temporarily. These days it tends to fry their electronics."

Sue gets up, goes to her door searching in her pocket for her keys. She pulls them out, sits in the drivers seat. Nothing happens. Sue swears. Then she reaches down and pops the hood. She comes around and props it up and stares at the machinery. I come to join her.

"I'm acting like I have the first clue what I am looking at," she says. "And even if I did I would have no idea what I can do about it," she adds bitterly.

"It's the engine management system," I say, pointing to it, "but you'd need a replacement chip to fix it. The scout's electromagnetic field fried it," I tell her.

"Damn!" Sue swears putting the hood down.

"How far is it to your place?" she asks Emma.

"About two k's, don't worry, I can walk it," Emma says.

"Hey guys," I say, to get their attention. "I can drive you."

"How?" Sue asks.

"Well, the speeder can. It can drive. It flies itself, all I have to do is give it directions. It can easily drive a car. I did it before with my Aunt."

I didn't mention that Aunt Liz hadn't agreed.

"So what do I do?" Sue asks.

"Pretend to drive."

Sue thinks about this.

"OK, we'll do that to get Emma home, but I'm not so sure about driving like that through Auckland."

"Me either. But I have another plan for that," I say happily, noticing that "home" seems to include me now.

I was about to jump back up into Ka-rea-rea when Emma cleared her throat.

"Ahem! THAT, is not how we say goodbye Sam Kahu!" she tells me.

I feel a bit embarrassed.

"Yeah ... OK, sorry," I say.

"Come here," she commands.

I go over to her. She puts her muddy arms around me, and I her.
She pulls me close and looks me in the eyes. It feels very nice,
and I get a bit turned on. Then she gives me a kiss, just like in
the movies. She's all muddy but that doesn't matter. We both
get a bit passionate. I think she's showing off for Sue – not that I
don't like it, but my face flames bright red. Then she releases me
with a smile.

"That's better. Now say 'goodbye' nicely," she smiles.

"Goodbye nicely," I recite.

She punches me in the guts with sudden strength. It's hard
enough to make me bend over. The burn in my gut didn't like
that at all. It stings like mad.

"Aw," I cough.

"Nicely," she says.

"First you kiss me, then you sock me one!" I complain.

"Be nice!" she says.

"Oh alright. See you later ..."

"*Soon*. See you *soon*."

"See you *soon*," I agree.

"and ..."

"And ... I ... I um," I wonder if she wants me to tell her I love her,
but that seems wrong.

"... will *call* you," she coaches, nodding.

"... will call you," I agree.

"See! It's quite easy to be a human being. More boys should try
it," she smiles.

"Most boys don't get such good training," Sue observes.

"So ..." I interrupt looking at the speeder.

"Yes, off you go," Emma nods.

Feeling a bit like I was being treated like a little kid I clamber onto the roof. The other two get into the car. It's a bit awkward getting into Ka-rea-rea from this position. Once I'm in the speeder and ready to go there isn't any way to talk to them, so I just slowly start forward.

We drive carefully down the road, find the Reeve's drive, which is down the hill on the right, and I stop to let Emma out. As she looks back I have Ka-rea-rea flash a little smiley on his right side, which makes her smile.

Then feeling happy I drive down the road to a secluded spot and turn around, then I drive us back to the picnic spot again to discuss what to do next. I pop the speeder's top and Sue gets out.

"Why didn't you pull in to Emma's parent's place?"

"Less explaining to do. She can easily say she fell in a mud puddle but if she shows up with you it all starts to get a bit curious."

"Yeah, well I was hoping to ask her parents if I could borrow some clothes."

"Because you're a police officer who got muddy with their daughter hiding underground from a flying saucer?"

Sue even manages a smile. She looks at her watch.

"I wouldn't have said that but it doesn't matter now. It's four now and the ferry goes at six," Sue says. "Is there anywhere we can get some clothes? I'm cold, wet, filthy and I really just want to go home."

"Yeah, and I have nothing in the world to wear but my wetsuit. But my biggest problem is where am I going to hide this now?"

"Keep it on my car."

"But your car needs repairs and I'm not letting this out of my sight."

We stare at each other.

"Open the nearest clothes recycling bin?" I suggest.

"Where's that?"

"Miles away," I admit.

"What about the local cop?" she asks. "He might have some clothes. I might get some overalls anyway. How big is he?"

"About twice as tall as you."

"Is he married?"

"Gavin? No, that's probably why he's such a ..."

"*Sam*," Sue warns grumpily.

"Anyway he doesn't sound all that promising," she admits.

"Well, I have a better suggestion."

"What's that?"

"We fly home."

"How can I fit in that?"

"You can't. But it can easily carry the car, "

Sue looks very uncertain.

"I carried Aunty Liz and Rewa," I add, again hiding the fact that it wasn't their idea.

Sue still isn't convinced. I decide to spill the beans.

"OK, I'll level with you. I don't want to have to stay inside this box for three hours being the engine of your car. This thing has no toilet, no food and is no fun for long stays. I know because I've suffered in it before. If I can just fly you home it'll only take twenty minutes."

"Yeah twenty minutes flying and twenty days talking on TV about my flying car."

"We can do it at night."

"It'd have to be pretty late at night, by which time I'll have got hypothermia."

"OK, how about this. How about you visit the Reeves carrying

out your inquiries and see if Fiona lends you some clothes.
She probably will. She's very nice. I'll wait in the speeder. That
way you can pretend I'm not there and you haven't met Emma
before."
"Who's Fiona?"
"Emma's mum. And she is about your height."
Sue thinks about it.
"OK, that works for me," she shrugs.
So that's what we do.
Once again I park up on the street and Sue, covered in mud,
walks down doing her best to look official. I can hear her talking
to Tama, hear him invite her inside, she goes in, and the door
closes. I could use eavesdrop, but frankly I don't really care what
they say.
Half an hour passes, then an hour. It was getting pretty boring
sitting in a box with nothing much to do. There was nothing
on TV but car racing which I find very dull. Meanwhile the big
range along the length of Aotea is casting its long shadow over
the whole area while the sky is beginning to get a bit pink.
And I'm hungry. I direct the beam microphone to the windows
of Emma's house. There they are, chatting away, laughing about
the people who lived at Renwick House. Sue, has had a shower,
and now they've arranged to feed her dinner!
I was going to have to lie here listening to them feeding their
faces and laughing about my friends while I starved! Man, that
pisses me off!
Well to hell with them! I disengage from Sue's car and adopt
blend transparency and take off. I power up to five thousand
meters in about thirty seconds.
It feels fantastic to leave Mt Marsden far below in the pink gray

271

light. Auckland's lights are sparkling in the distance and the sea
looks calm and peaceful below. I fly high over Auckland but my
problem remains. Where can I get a shower, and some food,
while wearing a wetsuit? Where can I get some clothes now that
the shops are shut? I simply can't think of anything, so I ask Qi.
His answer makes me feel pretty dumb. The Gold Coast in
Queensland, Australia! Shops all along one big beach. It's two
hours earlier there, two thousand three hundred kilometers
away. I can be there in ten minutes.

I climb quickly up into the dark, starry sky to 60,000 feet,
drop invisibility and go inertialess; Ka-rea-rea is a blur of
acceleration. I curse myself for not having thought of this an
hour ago.

The Tasman Sea has a good base of cloud over it. But at twenty
klicks I'm miles above any normal aircraft. There's nothing
much to do but enjoy catching up with the sun again.

Ten minutes later I'm over the Gold Coast. I haven't actually
been here before but that doesn't matter. I've worked tougher
places than this. Hell! There's even plenty of Maoris there so I
won't even stand out. I drop out of inertialess so I can go warp-
invisible and descend to 5,000 meters.

My initial plan had been to hide Ka-rea-rea in the sea but as I
whiz around overhead I spot a large shopping centre just inland
from the beach on a little island with highways all around. From
above it looks like a shopping castle with its own moat. Zooming
in with the speeder's sensors I can see plenty of places to park
the speeder on the roof, leaving me a brief climb to get down.
That would be tricky. The most important thing is to find a spot
that isn't overlooked by anyone else, that's easy to get down
from, and back up to. Luckily the roof of this place isn't within

200 meters of anyone which means the distortion invisibility
will work all the way to the rooftop – if no-one comes out.
But it turns out to be even easier than that. The open-air,
rooftop "earlybird" carpark on the north-east side is almost
empty this late on Saturday. There are two cameras which I fry
with the beam before they see me. The trick to cameras is just
to overload their CCDs. When two go at once you don't even get
maintenance guys checking them because they assume the cable
has died.

There's no-one around. I put Ka-rea-rea down on a corner next
to a cooling tower on the rooftop carpark. Then I get out and
I'm immediately struck by how much warmer it is, and by the
smells: ice cream in rubbish bins, a distant nail parlour and
asphalt. I watch Ka-rea-rea fold up into a gray box enjoying the
warmth on my feet. I guess that it's easily 22 degrees C. I could
easily be a lazy surfer kid who couldn't be bothered getting out
of a wetsuit here.

I stroll over to the lift well and enter the mall which is
apparently called Pacific Fair. The place is pretty big, and,
strangely clad as I am, the crowd just swallows me up. I know
that shopkeepers suspect kids my age of shoplifting, so it's really
important not to loiter but just go into a shop, buy stuff, and
leave, like you are in a hurry.

And one of the beauties of being a solitary teen is that others
ignore you. You get far more patience than you would if you
were an adult doing the same thing. I would have to be doing
something seriously annoying before anyone would make a fuss.
People do notice me, of course. Let's face it most teens don't
go into a mall in a wetsuit. But nobody says anything and there
are plenty of other people to look at, including a family of Arabs

obviously down from Dubai who stick out way more than I do. I decide the first thing to do is get some money. This is no problem because just past the salad bar are a couple of ATMs. Here I'm not worried about using my Omnicard as a Mastercard. So I get $500 in bright Aussie bills out from three ATMs one after the other so my total doesn't trigger attention from the cameras. I tuck the money into the right sleeve opposite Qi and my Omnicard.

I find a sports store common to both New Zealand and Australia where I quickly buy a cheap pair of baggies and a t-shirt. The people in the shop are so sales focused I don't think they even notice me. All I have to do is queue up and pay. Cash has a way of making people relax about you.

My next destination is a toilet. Partly to get changed out of the wetsuit and partly because I need to go. Once again people notice a teen in a wetsuit going into the toilet but nobody says anything. It was *so* good to get out of the wetsuit too! I'd already got pretty clean in the three "ducks" but I took a chance to wash the salt out of my hair a bit more too.

When I come out I look just like a relaxed teen in a mall with a wetsuit in a plastic bag and some spending money. Life is looking much better. The next stop is to find some food. That isn't hard either. There's a food court just by the ATMs. Once again there's more choice than I know what to do with. There's Japanese, pies, burgers, healthy salads, seafood, grilled chicken, kebabs, Indian, Mediterranean and Mexican.

I'm sick of pies so I end up munching kebabs and drinking coke in the food hall, where once again, nobody notices you.

My mood is improving so I decide to buy some slightly better clothes instead. I find an outdoor chain which does the

expensive casual look and get myself some gear to replace the
stuff I'd left in the cave: a rather nice top and trou'. Then I go
back to Nike for some decent trainers and pick up some shades
at the sunglass bar. That leaves me with about $20 left over, so I
head back to the lift.

I've been away about an hour including flight-time and I'm
starting to worry Sue could be waiting outside by her car looking
like a dork. The local time in Aus is nearing five. That means
it's seven back in New Zealand. I take the lift to the car park, re-
activate Ka-rea-rea, but then have to wait a few minutes while
a family with two howling kids pack up in the last car in the lot
and finally drive off.

I dive into my speeder, activate transparency and take to the sky.
At ten kilometers off the Australian coast and ten kilometers
up, I go inertialess and plunge back into darkness about two
hundred kilometers off New Zealand ten minutes later.

The dark side of Aotea island is pretty dark. The lights are in the
south and north-east but the north-west where we used to live is
completely black at night. I didn't even need warp transparency
now because blend was enough and Ka-rea-rea is almost
invisible to air traffic radar because of the materials and shape.
I zoom back to the Reeves' place worrying that Sue is waiting,
pissed off.

But she's nowhere to be seen. I apply the beam mikes to the
Reeves' window and they're still yakking away! And here I was
worrying! I park Ka-rea-rea on Sue's car and lie back to wait.
I watch TV via the brain interface (which is odd because your
entire visual field is taken up by TV image) until Ka-rea-rea
interrupts to say someone is coming.

Tama's walking Sue to her car making friendly invitations

should she return, while Sue's smiling and trying to get rid of him. I think she's nervous about him watching her start the car so she chats for a moment before shaking his hand and finally getting in. I watch Tama go into the house before finally moving off.

It's dark now but the moon's coming up big and round. I want to get away from the Reeves' place completely before taking off. I also want to make sure Sue's ready before I fly over the water. So at the next corner I pull over and pop Ka-rea-rea's top. Sue gets out looking guilty as hell!

"Hey look I'm really sorry …" she begins and then stops. I'm wearing my new shades.

"Hey! You've changed!"

She on the other hand is wearing an outfit that looks like a sack. Fiona's the same height as Sue but she's a lot rounder.

"Yeah, and I look a helluva lot cooler than you," I grin.

"Howdya do that?" she wonders.

"Spot of shopping in Surfers. Had dinner there too," I raise my shades.

"You went to *Queensland*!" Sue asks, unbelieving.

"It was the best place to go shopping while wearing a wetsuit at this time of day."

"What did you use for money?"

"Oh, I can get money. Always could. That's how I got to your place the night …" I trail off.

"Are you *sure* you went to Queensland?" Sue asks gobsmacked.

I take an Aussie note from my pocket and hand it down to her.

"Pretty sure, yeah."

"How fast does that thing go?" Sue asks wonderingly.

"Well, that's what I wanted to talk about. You see with a car on it, not so fast. I mean still fast enough to be scary so I just wanted you to know how I was going to do this."

"OK," she says nervously.

"OK, so a car is not a huge radar target but it's still big enough to be pretty obvious. That means that we can be seen by ships or aircraft or air traffic control if we don't do this right."

"OK."

"So what we'll do is fly really low to look like a boat on radar. I'll fly at about a hundred kay which for this thing is almost standing still but is about as much as I'd expect a fast boat to be doing. When we get closer to the city I'll climb to about fifteen hundred meters to look like a chopper and get out of the light and then I'll wait for a chance to drop right in to your home. Now that will be the scary bit because it will be very fast so feel free to close your eyes. Obviously you should have your seatbelt firmly fastened ..."

"And my tray table folded away," Sue jokes.

"Sorry?" I'm stumped.

"It's what they say on airplanes."

"Oh? I don't know. I've only ever flown in a plane once, and that was Sir Michael's private jet."

"*Really*?" Sue asks, amazed.

"I'm a poor Maori boy from the sticks. When would I ever get to fly on a plane? Anyway what I was going to say is ... I've forgotten."

"Sorry," Sue says.

"It's OK."

"It's just I'm a bit nervous about this. I don't like the idea of dangling underneath a flying roof rack piloted by a fourteen-year-old. It seems a bit risky," she admits nervously.

"Remember it's not me flying. I'm as much a passenger as you are. It'll be fine. Shall we have a practice spin?"

"OK."

"I'll take you out to sea, round and then we'll do a practice drop on to the beach."

"OK," she gulps.

"Now get in, strap in. Bang once for go, twice for emergencies."

"OK."

We get into position. She gave a bang and I take off vertically and head around for a low circuit about ten kilometers in total at a hundred kay. The moon is up now, casting a pale light over the sea. It looks quite lovely. We come back over the beach south of the Reeve's place. It's a huge beach and sometimes people fish on it – especially on the full moon – but there's no-one there tonight. I soar up to about two hundred meters and then drop to one meter, before settling Sue's car gently on the sand. Then I pop the top.

Sue is still in the car. I hop down and find her clutching her seatbelt and steering wheel, staring and breathing hard in the moonlight. The sea roars as breakers roll along the beach behind us and the air is chilled and sandy.

"You OK?" I ask. She sits there rigidly.

"Sue?" I ask again.

"I'll be fine," she says in a high voice staring ahead with a glassy stare.

"Sure?"

"Yes."

I wait for a while, then she continues, turning her head to look at me but not actually letting go of anything.

"I didn't mind the flying part. Actually that was OK. But I

screamed all the way down."

"So not so keen on the drops," I summarise.

"No, not much," she admits.

"Well, I'll see what I can do. Actually I've just remembered what I wanted you to do."

"Yeah?"

"Make sure our phones are still off. The signal will look very odd if anyone is tracing them."

"Why would anyone be tracing them? They aren't allowed to without a warrant," she points out, suddenly all official.

I point up, "*They* can do what they like and we *really* don't want to meet them in the air."

Her eyes widen. Quickly she rummages in the glovebox and finds the phones. To my relief they were still off.

"It's a pity. It would be nice if we could talk," she says.

"Yeah. But we need to be careful. OK?"

"Yeah," she says taking a deep breath.

I climb back onto the car, close the lid and lift off, this time picking up the pace although it still felt to me like granny stepping a one hundred meter sprint to me.

It's a lovely night to fly. The moon is up and the sea's relatively calm. I decide that given the bright moon the best option is to stay very low so we skim the sea. Ka-rea-rea translates radar into audible sounds so I can hear the radar from a few boats out fishing but I stay as far away from them as I can.

As we round Aotea island I realise that flying directly over the city to our east is asking for trouble. It's early Saturday evening, the moon's up and there's lots of traffic moving. There's even air traffic. Sue's flying car could be spotted easily. So I change course and head north running parallel with the coast about twenty kilometers out to sea. It will make the flight longer but reduce the chance of being detected.

My plan is to completely encircle Auckland around the north and come into the western suburbs from the west. This means flying over the Waitakeres – the low range to Auckland's west. It's a long, nerve-wracking route. Apart from being seen by Aucklanders the other thing that's worrying me is how vulnerable we are if we are bounced by a UFO. They could pick us up in seconds and we would be completely doomed.

We fly an oblong around northern Auckland. As we approach land near Orewa I climb rapidly into cloud which I can tell makes Sue very nervous but gets us clear of the city lights. But once we've passed the densely settled strip by the sea I drop back down to two hundred meters to whizz silently over the dark countryside.

The Waitakere hills to the west of Sue's house are tricky because they are higher and have houses in them. People often look at the stars at night but there's no city light for Sue's white car to reflect so we are pretty hard to see. I take us even higher. Sue's not liking this.

Finally, an hour after setting off, we are in position one and a half kilometers above Sue's house. I know she's hating this, but I have to be careful because there's a lot to watch out for. Cars are moving around in the suburb below and the lights of the Henderson industrial district glow brightly. It's late, but not that late. Tucked away in the dark are people out walking dogs.

Then way, way to the North I notice a light. It could have been an Air Force P-3 coming in from patrol, or it could be *them*. I'm not taking any chances. We have to get down and fast. Ka-rea-rea drops for ten seconds.

I think Sue screams all the way down. Certainly when we touch
down there are people coming to the windows. But, of course, it
just looks like a car quietly pulling into a carport. So they soon
go back to their TV sets.

Sue sits for a moment and then gets out of the car looking pale
and shaky. She looks at me in Ka-rea-rea and realises I'm not
going to get out outside, so she goes to the door. She's shaking
so much she drops her keys, but she finally unlocks it and
staggers in.

There's no way I'm leaving Ka-rea-rea outside. *They* know all
about this place and could even be here already waiting inside.
I want firepower if I'm going in so instead I quietly release Sue's
car and float over to the door and nudge it open. Then I fly into
the house, sniff around for intruders body heat, and finally settle
on the floor to my room. Only then do I get out and tell Ka-rea-
rea to lock down. I turn on the light and go to find Sue.

She's sitting at the kitchen table wearing her old bathrobe
cuddled around her with a bottle of "Jack Daniels bourbon
whiskey" and a packet of cigarettes. Her hands shake as she
lights a cigarette.

Normally she didn't smoke inside but she's obviously too upset
to care. I say nothing. I just sit down while she pours herself
a drink and draws on the cigarette. She almost seems to be
challenging me to say something. I just sit there studying the
floor.

Finally she starts.

"You're a total pain in the arse, you know that!"

She inhales deeply and blows a stream of smoke out like a
grumpy dragon. It takes her a few puffs to calm down and
continue.

"I had this whole thing all sorted! You were just a screwed up kid with mental problems. Nice enough, but no bloody wonder considering your background. You were involved with a whacky cult that had filled your head with all kinds of crap. Then, they take off into their secret cavern and leave you behind. That's when you flipped out. At the lighthouse I had the whole thing pegged."

She pauses again recollecting her thoughts, letting the adrenaline from the fall subside.

"I even humoured you when you said you were late to meet up with your girlfriend! I had to meet *her* of course. I wondered what kind of lunatic she was!"

Then she sighs. She's still pale.

"And then ... then ... it all just fell apart. I sat there all through dinner with that family joking about you guys while I *knew*, and Emma *knew*, that you guys aren't the crazy ones. You knew that thing was coming. You hurried me along! Then there was all that light and you guys just kept going."

She pauses reliving it, and takes a deep drag on her fag.

"Even during dinner Emma gave nothing away. She'd been chased by aliens down a hole and there she was laughing with her parents like nothing had happened."

She stubs out her cigarette and lights another. She's smoking very fast. I'm not a big fan of smoking but it is calming her.

"And then you! You really do have a flying saucer! I mean *f____* me! I thought exactly what you said! I thought it was some sad toy or something you used to keep your poor little head together. But no. It's real! You flew *my f____ car* with it! You went all the way to Queensland and had dinner and came back in an hour! On the way home I kept thinking I was going to wake up, and then that *f*____ awful drop!"

It's all been a huge shock to her. The adrenaline from the drop had just got her all panicky again. Adults often find it hard to adjust to the idea that they can be powerless in the face of the unknown. Kids, of course, are used to not understanding adults so they adjust better. How else could I have survived Ax? But as a cop, as someone who represented protection and security, to find the rules and the whole world she understood was wrong, was a shock to her whole world view.

"I've never thought ... I mean ... you see movies but you know it's all ... well ... it's bullshit ... just actors in suits. I ... I ..."

She doesn't know what she wants to say.

"It's OK, Sue. It was the same for all of us," I reassure her quietly.

"Was it?"

"Well, it was a little different but it rocked our worlds too."

"What do *they* want?" she asks pointing up.

"*Them.* Um ... well most of the time they just study us."

"They don't want to invade or anything?" she asks.

"No, of course not. Look, imagine that we're like a tribe in the Amazon who live in a little valley called Earth. We never go anywhere and know nothing of the outside world except for the strange craft – helicopters and planes I mean – that we see sometimes in the sky. OK?"

"Yeah," she says seeing the connection.

"Now *they* are like scientists or David Attenborough or something. *They* watch us, but *they* don't interfere. What do *they* want from us? Well, they don't need our little Stone Age valley, or our crummy food, or anything *we* think is important. It's like scientists in a helicopter over the valley. Everything the scientists want comes from within their *own* world, not the tribesmens'."

"OK," she says, rubbing her chin, thinking about it. She's calmed by this explanation.

"The scary thing for us tribesmen though, is we don't understand *them* at all. We don't know what they want, or why they do what they do, and we can't do *anything* about it. So the solution that most of us find easiest to cope with, is to pretend they don't exist, even when they are staring us in the face. People are very good at ignoring things they can't control or don't want to see. That's why seeing them is such a huge shock. You have to face the fear of something powerful and unknown that you can't do anything about."

"But if they just want to study Earth why did they just chase *us*?" she asks.

"*Generally* they study us. *Me*, they want to catch."

Sue looks at me with a combination of fear and respect.

"They want to catch *you*?"

"Yeah. That's why the others burned down Renwick and blew the tunnels to stop them catching us."

"But what about you?"

"I was caught out. I was flying home over the Solomon's when they attacked Renwick. I saw them coming."

"And the others went without you?"

"They had to. It was that or be captured."

"But if you could fly anywhere and get money why did you come back?"

"I ... well, I didn't have too many friends anywhere else, except Emma."

"So that's where you went between the fire and when you turned yourself in."

"Sorta. I stayed in a barn they have. But they were watching and if I stayed they'd have caught Emma. So I decided to hide in the system. But that wasn't so safe either," I sigh.

"And now your legal guardian ... ?"

"Yes, Sir Michael is working for *them* too, by the look of it."

"And this is because they want... that craft of yours?"

"Only partially. Look Sue I can only expect you to believe so much at a time. I mean you believe in flying saucers now don't you?"

"Well, I guess I have to say '*yes*'. Nothing else would make me get filthy hiding in a cave. I hate caves."

"OK, well, so there's a whole bunch of stuff which if I had told you about before that, you would have simply thought I was totally crazy. So like I said, we on Earth are a little tribe in a forgotten valley, right? The local Administration keeps a low profile. Intervening is against an old treaty which has become a kind of standard. The other civilisations don't intervene until we've proved we can be trusted. They don't want us focused on them, they just want us to carry on doing what we do so they can watch our development."

"So they're like ... the Discovery Channel aliens?" Sue suggests. I laugh.

"Yeah, you could call them that. Like game wardens, but like Bernard, they don't call the shots. They have to do what they're told by their Government – The Center. The Center is huge and it's mostly run by synthetic intelligences: Cyberminds and biological robots like the Greys. But there are also some of the original species there as well. The Center doesn't care about our valley at all. They have a military we call 'the Service'. The

Service doesn't care about non-intervention. If they want to do something here, they will do it. A bit like the army in the rainforest. They aren't going to hide from a bunch of tribesmen. Most of the more blatant UFO cases reported in the media are because of them. They don't care if they scramble Belgian fighters or if the whole of Phoenix, Arizona sees them. The Administration only cooperate with the Service when they are absolutely forced to."

"OK, I get that. But this Service isn't after you, is it?"

"Oh, yes it is."

"Oh F____!" she says, looking terrified. She's gulping air in big breaths.

"But that's not as bad as it sounds because the Service has no local intelligence. They're like the US Navy dealing with Ethiopia. Heaps of firepower but no idea what to do with it. That's why that was an *Administration* scout, not a Service one. If it had been a *Service* one they would have taken the whole hill out."

"Sam, *I* don't want to be caught in that light again if I can avoid it." Sue says certainly.

"No, you won't be because we are dealing with the Administration, so if they do something it will be quiet, not a flying saucer parked over your house at three o'clock in the morning. In cities that's just not how they operate."

"So they'll send the 'Men in Black', or something" Sue guesses.

"Exactly."

"That was meant to be a *joke*," Sue cries, appalled, and starting to panic again.

"No, it's what they *will* do, They look like ordinary people."

"But they're not?"

"No, they're android biobots. Look like us, but they simply aren't. We psychics can spot them a mile off."

"What about *non*-psychics?" Sue pleads, worried.

"It's hard because they are built to be attractive. They look pretty and radiate pheromones."

"Oh, I thought they were spooky."

"No, the spooky ones are the infiltrators."

"Infiltrators?"

"They're aliens who live here among us."

"Jesus! They live *among* us?"

"Yeah. They're kind of against the Center. So rather than live by Center rules they live here. Some of them are OK. Others are very dangerous. They have serious psychic powers. Way more than us. This is probably all because we got the Administration to arrest some of the infiltrators last year."

"*Arrest* them?"

"For intervening. When they live here they aren't meant to intervene."

"How were they intervening?"

"Killing people mostly. They kill lots of us."

"*Killing* people? *Who*?" Sue wants to know.

"I'll have to tell you later. Look, the main thing is it seems that both the infiltrators and the Administration are now working *together* to catch us."

"*Us*?"

"Us at Renwick. Me."

"Sam, I don't know if I want to be part of this," she says shaking her head.

"I'm afraid you already are."

"Why?" she pleads.

"Because last night Sir Michael had a tracking device put in my food. They tracked me from the restaurant to your place. Remember how I asked what it would take to get a MRI done?"

"Yeah?"

"Well that was to burn out the tracker. That's what I did at the lighthouse after you went out. That's partly why I couldn't sleep last night. I was half expecting them to show up."

"*Here!*" she demands, shocked.

"Yeah."

"So, we *aren't* safe are we?" she says looking around.

"No, not at all."

"F___! What do we do now?" Sue asks.

"Get a cab, go to town and stay somewhere else. I just think it's safer," I admit.

"So do *I*," Sue says decisively, getting up, "Hang on I'll just make a call."

"We can stay at a hotel. I've got plenty of money," I call after her.

"No, I know a better place."

"Where?"

"It's a private secret refuge run by some people I know. Mostly for women."

"Won't it be a little late. It's almost ten?" I wonder.

"No, they take people at risk at any time."

"Sue?"

"Yeah?"

"Is your cell a work one?"

"Yeah, why?"

"Use it. Your landline will be bugged by now. Your cell was turned off on the island so they won't connect it to you. They watch a private phone by looking up the billing address but work

ones confuse them. But make it fast. They are *very* smart and
they aren't confused for long."

"OK," she agrees nervously.

She calls the friend, who's apparently named Julia. Sue spins
her a story about a young witness she needs to hide from his
dangerous dad. It's sort of true. Julia doesn't seem to mind.
Then Sue calls a cab and goes to pack. I fret about Ka-rea-rea.
Without antigravity he is damn heavy. Finally the cab appears.
The driver's a big cheerful Samoan dude named Siva. We tell
him the speeder is full of books but he swings it up on his head
as if it's made of cardboard, then stows it in the huge boot of his
Ford.

Julia's place is only twenty minutes away in Ponsonby, but we
pay Siva to drive to city hotels where anyone overhead couldn't
see who was getting out or in, just to make it hard to track us. If
they're watching the cab they will end up losing us like we are a
pea under a shell.

Finally we arrive about eleven. The refuge is a grand old Villa set
back off the road in a street full of pretty old settler houses, villas
and oak trees. It's pretty obvious that Julia and her partner Caz
are also lesbians like Sue, which doesn't surprise me at all.
They're so sweet: very friendly and welcoming; although they
make a point of saying I'm the only male over ten they've
allowed to stay in the place in five years. They keep a few rooms
aside for women in trouble with violent partners – male *or*
female. My mum likes them for that.

The house is decorated in old style wallpaper with lots of
polished wood everywhere. The ceilings are miles high. Siva,
the taxi driver, insists on carrying Ka-rea-rea inside and up the
stairs to the small room they have set aside for me. Sue has her

own room down the hall and there are two other rooms, but they aren't in use.

We're totally exhausted. It's been a real long day and we go through the bathroom and off to bed in no time at all. By 11:30 p.m I'm lying in my room which seems to be taller than it is long or wide, looking out the old sash windows at what little of the night sky I can see above the orange glow of the city's lights and through the big tree in the garden.

It's been six nights since the evacuation of Renwick and I've slept every one of them in a different place. That's good. For the moment I'm one step ahead again. As I lie on my back I stare up at the stars thinking how close, yet how far away they are. Just like my family.

Somehow the age of the house, which has always been a foundation in the lives of the families that live in it, affects me. I feel a sense of permanence which is quite odd given the reality of my situation. A ghost named Sarah who had been a domestic servant here all her life just makes me feel that, whatever my current difficulties, everything will be alright in the morning. And thinking a blessing for her, and with the stars twinkling in my eyes over the sounds of distant cars racing through the night, I let my mind sink softly into darkness.

•••

After her shock encounter with the UFO Sue wants to know what Sam is mixed up with. Starting with the stories of the other Changels, as they became refugees, Sam carefully leads Sue from the shallows of Earth's strangeness into the full weirdness of Dr Prosperov's experiments. Experiments that shocked two worlds...

To get your copy visit the website: www.changels.info

FACT OR FICTION?

As a work of fiction all characters in *Initiation* are fictional and any resemblance to any person living or dead is coincidental. There are, however, amalgalms of fact and fiction in this story.

The island named "Aotea" in the story does not strictly exist. It is modeled, somewhat, on Great Barrier Island from which the Maori name, "Aotea", has also been taken. However the ferry to Great Barrier only runs in summer and takes two and a half hours demonstrating that the imaginary "Aotea" is closer in location to Waiheke Island. It also shares Waiheke's wartime defensive structures. Given that the island is imaginary it can also be safely inferred that its inhabitant characters are also imaginary. The tides Sam refers to in chapter one are the actual tides for Waiheke Island at the time and date of the fictional fire at Renwick House.

As the island it is on is imaginary, so too is Renwick House. It is loosely modeled architecturally on Seacliff Lunatic Asylum built in Otago (over 1,000km away) which was finally demolished in 1992. A Renwick House *does* exist in New Zealand but is much smaller than the building depicted and actually part of Nelson Central School in the South Island.

Sam's putative ancestors Papahurihia and Te Wharete are genuine Nga Puhi ancestors and their legendary powers of teleportation and invisibility are in accordance with tradition.

The symptoms of meth addiction ascribed to Sam's cousin, Clive, are accurate.

Sam's psychic act of geolocating Sue is one of the most common, and as yet unexplained, phenomena in psychic research. The interesting part of the phenomena is that it is based on emotional bonding. Animals that have been left behind which don't walk hundreds of kilometers in search of human friends are much more common than those that do. Some have proposed that experiments based on this bond (e.g. Rupert Sheldrake's "Seven Experiments Which Could Change The World") could be revolutionary. There are, however, considerable problems with defining these experiments satisfactorily in such a way as to eliminate the confirmation bias which lies at the root of the phenomena itself. This example is deliberately placed at this point in the narrative to open minds to the inadequacy of the classical scientific method to study this type of phenomena.

The communications system used for the tag in Sam's stomach is based on science. Spukhafte Fernwirkung or "Spooky action at a distance" was the phrase used by Erwin Shrodinger when he wrote to Albert Einstein about quantum entanglement. It is a genuine phenomena under active investigation as a communications system by present day scientists and engineers.

Proximity to high voltage lines induces current in all adjacent conductors (including the human body) via the electromagnetic field. The filament in Sam's stomach is meant to pick up 25 watt signal at 1,575mhz 20,500km away. I have no idea whether this could be achieved with any material nor whether the temperature of that aerial would reach a dangerous temperature before it overloaded, But as a guide a tungsten light bulb filament operates at over 2,000 degrees Celsius – certainly not something you want inside you.

The description of UFO behaviour is an amalgam of numerous reports. The author does not automatically discount the hypothesis that alien craft visit this planet. This is not "unscientific" because the scientific method is not even hypothetically equipped to deal with the politics of superior intelligences that could deliberately evade study. At the same time, however, it is evident that many reports are mistaken interpretations of natural phenomena. Ultimately conclusive proof of alien visitation will only be available when the aliens furnish us with it – if they ever do.

The notion of inertialess drive was pioneered in fiction by E. E 'Doc' Smith in his classic 1950s "Lensmen" series. In this case the holographic principal has been pseudo-scienced into intertialess drive for the purposes of the story. Many eye-witness descriptions of UFOs flight suggest they are inertialess, although applying Occam's razor suggests this is because they are optical illusions.

Sam's speeder, Ka-rea-rea, is named after the New Zealand falcon (Falco Novaeseelandiae). It uses a number of technologies of varying degrees of possibility. Carbon based materials are theoretically capable of combining high tensile strength, semiconducting capability and laser generation. Meta-material cloaking (invisibility) and active camouflage are active fields of scientific research.

Anti-gravity (a repulsive force on mass) has not been observed experimentally and is not even theoretically possible under the 'standard model' of physics. However, the standard model has to postulate unseen 'dark matter' and 'dark energy' in vast quantities to account for huge discrepencies in its gravitation predictions for the rotation of galaxies and must be considered a 'work in progress'.

NOTES ON LANGUAGE

The spelling adopted in this text is an arbitrary mixture of UK and US English. The American spelling of "meter" and "kilometer" has been preferred over the French spelling. The British spelling of "centre" however predominates except for "The Center", the term for alien central government (borrowed from Soviet era parlance for Moscow).

The story is told in the first person by Sam Kahu, a New Zealand Maori, nominally of the Nga Puhi Iwi (tribe). Sam does not use authentic Northland slang or Maori elements and occasionally substitutes North American terms for New Zealand ones in the interests of wider comprehension. That said he does use some slang terms such as "sus'" for "suspicious" or "suspect".

The story is told in two tenses. The past is related in the past or perfect tense. The present in the present tense. This is a new feature of the third edition introduced to make the distiction between current and past narratives more immediately discernable.

Maori (pronounced Mao-ree) names and songs are used throughout the text. Wherever possible Maori language words have been hyphenated for ease of pronunciation. However Maori has a few peculiarities those not acquainted with it may wish to note.
"i" is normally short, but at the end of a word "i" is pronounced "ee" not "I"
"u" is pronounced "oo" so" Atua" (God) is said "Ah-too-ah".
"wh" is pronounced closer to "ph", so "when-u-a" (land) is said "phen-oo-a"
"ng" is pronounced as in "singer" so Nga Puhi is closer to "Nah Poo'ee"
While it is not usual to add an accent acute to Maori I have done so to aid pronunciation. Thus Tane, god of the forest has been rendered Tané which is a diacritical mark most English speakers recognise from the word café and is closer to Maori pronunciation.I have not incorporated the macron officially used in Māori (over the 'a') because most readers will not know how to pronounce it.

The terms "Khanum" (feminine of Khan) and "Ba", Sam pretends to think are names in Chapter one may be translated as "Lady" and "dad" from Farsi and Vietnamese respectively.

The Louisianan characters Ashley and Patricia Robinson come from the ninth ward of New Orleans which is the home of the "Yat" dialect. I have done my best to render a flavour of this dialect, but I am no native speaker and I apologise to speakers for any failings in advance.

www.ingramcontent.com/pod-product-compliance
Lightning Source LLC
Chambersburg PA
CBHW021946170626
46808CB00001B/45